Reflections of a Vampire

Cover design by

Livers Lambert Design
Paulette Livers Lambert
paulettelivers@attbi.com

Reflections of a Vampire

Damion Kirk

RahuBooks

The main text of this book
was set in 10 point Times
for greater readability

Reflections of a Vampire
Damion Kirk

RahuBooks

RahuBooks@aol.com

© December 1997

First Edition: February/2002

ISBN 0-9718550-5-6

Printed by United Graphics
in the United States of America

For

lorilong and her Lost Boys

Special thanks to

Judy Lynn, Herb,
Elaine and David

And great appreciation to

Anne Rice
without whom this book
would never have been written

BOOK ONE

"There's a divinity that shapes our ends,
Rough-hew them how we will–"

Shakespeare, Hamlet

CHAPTER 1

Thursday, June 21st 11:17 P.M.
Manhattan, New York City

Gérard Arnaud St. Laurue sniffed the sultry night air. His azure blue eyes flashed yellow-violet. "Ah," he whispered, "fresh young blood."

The attractive blond was half a block ahead on the dark SoHo street. As the vampire followed her, he psychically gathered information. Her name was Ashley Green. She lived nearby and had a boyfriend named Raphael.

Just as he was about to mentally retrieve something more, something consequential, a taxi cab with a hole in its muffler roared by, breaking his concentration. He pushed his extrasensory powers but came up with nothing more. *Qu'est-ce?* he thought. How strange. The living generally have more of a predisposed biography available.

St. Laurue anxiously eyed the waxing moon.

By ancient vampiric law, he must take his first millennium rest on the next full moon. Each one thousand years, a vampire must be entombed under the ground for eighteen months in order to release the on-going strain of eternal life, thus ensuring continued survival.

His body quaked as he dabbed the blood sweat off his brow with a red silk handkerchief. To leave go of life, he thought. To be buried. To be silenced. These were his worst fears. Yet, he knew there was no way to charm his way out of it. If only he could come up with a way to carry on and still fulfill the obligatory tradition. As it stood, he had less than a week to find a grave site and enlist minions to protect him while at rest.

His attention turned back to the blond up ahead. Would she turn out to be a minion or merely another meal? Instinctively he hungered for her, but while blood was his daily addiction– *survival* was the ultimate game.

He licked his lips as he watched Ashley hand a scrap of paper to a heavyset bag lady squatting by an alley up ahead.

The bag lady promptly tucked it into an old canvas sack.

Ashley whispered, "Fresh fish at the market tonight, Franny."

St. Laurue winced with irritation. Undoubtedly the phrase was some kind of secret code. Could the girl be trusted? Besides the beckoning blood that coursed through their pulsing veins and suffused his senses, what was the bond between these two very different looking women?

Not someone to give up or admit defeat, he attempted once more to probe Ashley's mind for more data, but only received psychic static.

"Too bad," he sighed. She was so provocative. So toothsome. But he would not make her his minion. Something was decidedly amiss and as his hopes of enlisting the blond faded, she went from consort to consommé in less than a minute.

Just then, a motorcycle gunned by. The smell of fresh blood mixed with exhaust fumes annoyed him further. He'd feel better after feeding.

Like a blood-lusting killer shark, he moved toward the two women. But before he could reach them, he was distracted by the riotous presence of a gang of Italian youths half a block behind him.

He halted abruptly in his tracks and tuned in. The smack of their intentions both insulted and thrilled him. The impertinence, he thought. These teens were stalking *him*.

Meanwhile, up ahead, Ashley and Franny had disappeared from in front of the alley.

St. Laurue was amazed, but had no time to satisfy his curiosity. The street gang was gaining on him. Knowing well how stalkers love to inspire panic in their victims, he decided to play with the boys. He shot the gang a frightened look and walked faster, while mentally retrieving a few facts.

The head hood's name was Angelo. The tough was eighteen and had a well proportioned body, not unlike the vampire's own. Angelo was with three other boys: Joey, Tony, and Fury. Joey was fat. Tony was pimply. Both were inconsequential. Angelo appeared to be a typical bully. But the last teen, Fury, impressed the blood drinker.

The handsome sixteen-year-old boy had raven hair and wore a sleeveless black tee-shirt and strategically torn jeans. He hung back a little from the rest of the ruffians. A loner, the undead one thought. A good sign.

St. Laurue fled into the alley ahead, where the two women had been.

The stench of piss saturated the air. He heard

hungry rats feeding on tossed food in open garbage bins along one side. His stomach turned. Despite his deep-seated fear of rodents, he hurried to the dead end and waited. A smile of self satisfaction crept across his face as the gang stormed into the alley, eager for confrontation.

"Well boys," Angelo said, as they closed in on St. Laurue, "looks like we caught ourselves a young punk."

Young, the vampire thought. How easily mortals are deceived.

"Come on Angelo, forget about it." Fury tried to sound nonchalant, but St. Laurue knew by his blush that the lad's blood ran hot.

"*You* forget about it," Angelo said to Fury. "You want in the gang, you damned well better go through the initiation."

"Perhaps the boy has changed his mind?" St. Laurue purred.

"Perhaps?" Angelo derided the vampire's slight French accent.

Fury turned to St. Laurue. "Run, man. These guys want to—"

"Shut up, you asshole," Angelo said, shoving Fury backwards.

Tension filled the alleyway, as Tony and Joey cornered St. Laurue. Even the mangy half-starved rats temporarily quit their midnight feasting.

Moonlight flashed on Angelo's switchblade. He held the sharp point against the vampire's neck.

"Cut the punk," Tony urged Angelo.

"Yeah," Joey harshly whispered. "Slice his

girly-ass up."

"Hey, pretty boy," Angelo sneered. "You want some of this?"

St. Laurue was delighted that Fury hadn't joined in with the jeers. The boy was not easily lead. Another good sign.

"Don't worry," Angelo scoffed as he traced the point of his blade along the side of St. Laurue's neck, "we ain't gonna hurt you… much."

It was rage, more than hunger, that made the vampire change so fast. His incisors lengthened into needle-pointed fangs. His eyes turned a kinetic yellow-violet. Tender, smooth, boyish-tight skin swelled into a gelatinized, mottled green. His hair grew sparse, as if his skull had risen to absorb it. Arms, neck and legs extended. Dry, chalky white cheek bones erupted past his skin and stood exposed. The vile creature's breath came in spasmodic fits of preternaturally loud wheezing.

Angelo's knife fell to the asphalt, a useless toy against the vampire's force. Tony and Joey gaped incredulously at St. Laurue, then at Angelo, then back at the vampire.

At a speed only the undead could execute, St. Laurue's arm reached up and turned Angelo's face one hundred and eighty degrees, like twisting the cap off a bottle of cheap wine. He pretzeled Angelo's body backwards, cramming the gang leader's feet into his own horror-widened mouth. Next, St. Laurue broke Tony's back. The crackling sound of bones snapping, like gears being stripped, resounded off the walls of the alley. The punk yelped once, then collapsed to the pavement.

Joey had almost escaped the alley, but St. Laurue materialized ahead. The boy's extended scream was abruptly cut short when the vampire caught him by the throat and hoisted him up. Joey's fat legs thrashed about in mid-air. He struggled for breath, but only managed intermittent gasps, until St. Laurue hurled him against a brick wall. The thug's cranium fragmentized and his headless body slid down into a heap, like a pile of dirty laundry.

Blood spore filled the alley and heightened the vampire's hunger. He stilled himself and listened. Angelo and Joey were dead, but Tony's heart was still beating.

He leached onto the boy's neck and fed.

In a state of blood-engorged bliss– after having absorbed Tony's blood essence– St. Laurue vomited out what was left of the now devitalized fluid in a long crimson trajectile, drenching all three cadavers.

Again, he listened. Another heartbeat.

He found Fury huddled behind a trash bin.

Could the boy be his minion? There was only one way to find out. A test had to be conducted. Pinning the lad against the brick wall, he expelled his rotten breath into Fury's face.

"And how would *you* like to die, my sweet?" he wheezed.

The hyperventilating kid stared at St. Laurue, terrified, yet clearly fascinated. It was evident to the undead one that the boy envied him– his power, his command, his eternal youth. All well and good, the vampire thought. What mortal wouldn't envy him? But could the teen be trusted? Would he have the courage to protect and serve? The test continued.

"Well?" the hideous creature growled.

"Please sir," the hero-worshiping teenager said. "Make me like you."

A bizarre thought crossed St. Laurue's mind.

He needed this handsome lad as much as the lad needed him. With this realization, the vampire's grotesque appearance returned to its former façade of youthful glamor.

"Like me?" St. Laurue questioned Fury. "But I am as dead as your former playmates. Do you wish to end up like them?" He grabbed the boy's head and made him look at the cadavers. "Do you find them attractive?"

The vampire tampered with Fury's vision. The dead bodies began to crawl with maggots. The boys came alive, writhed and reached out to Fury while chorusing over and over, "Join us, join us…" When the voices of the dead reached a crescendo, Fury held his ears, bent over and spewed his dinner out against the alley wall.

Meanwhile, the vampire's survival instincts drew his eyes to a light in an office building across the street. Ever curious, he quit the teen and sped to the street end of the alley. His attention focused on the fourth floor office and he instantly knew it was occupied by Bevan Preston, a publisher.

St. Laurue was suddenly very excited. To hell with the consequences, he thought. Before ancient tradition drove him underground, he would write his memoirs and have them published. By publishing his life story, something of himself would live on.

Through his book, he must live on.

Footsteps sounded from behind. He turned back toward the alley and faced Fury. The boy looked different. He was beatific, almost angelic. He appeared to have purged himself of all fear.

The final sign of courage for which the undead one had been hoping came.

As if the boy had read St. Laurue's mind, as if the boy *knew* he was being tested, Fury leaned forward and grazed his teeth against the vampire's icy neck. Electricity shot between them. "Teach me," the teen whispered, while tucking a piece of paper into St. Laurue's pocket.

Voilà, the vampire thought. This boy was born to be undead.

Fury would be his minion, but first, it was crucial to enlist Bevan Preston for his chronicles. What to do? An idea came. St. Laurue's azure eyes flashed yellow-violet as he touched Fury's chest.

"Go now," he said, "but henceforth, know you are mine forever."

The mesmerized kid about-faced, stuck his hands in his pockets, and sauntered off down the shadowy SoHo street.

Alone again, St. Laurue took out his red silk handkerchief and wiped the blood off his hands and face. After all, a gentleman must make a proper first impression. Particularly so, when he was about to introduce himself to his publisher.

Suddenly, he felt an invisible presence back in

the alleyway. His body stiffened. The feeling came upon him like a faint ill wind.

Then, as quickly as the presence was detected, it vanished.

Had it been a fledgling vampire tainted with this new blood disease, the one that makes them seek out and savagely destroy their own kind? Most probably not. Diseased newborns always strike first expeditiously and without warning.

Was it his powerfully evil father, the Marquis Antoine DeMalberet? No, he thought, father was off blood hunting in South India. So much the better. Both he and Brigitte, his younger sister, had been blood feuding with their father for centuries. The less they saw of him, the better. Still, St. Laurue knew whenever his sneak of a father was around, *anything* was possible.

He put his handkerchief away and concentrated. *Trés bein.* He wasn't being followed.

In an exhilarated mood, he crossed the street and entered the office building. Within seconds, he playfully leaned against the open doorway of Bevan Preston's office on the fourth floor.

At once, St. Laurue's mood soured. The office was an abomination. Untidy stacks of manuscripts were edificed high on the publisher's desk and in racks along the wall. The man slaving behind the mahogany desk was all but shrouded by the heaps of work surrounding him.

As yet undiscovered, St. Laurue assessed the bookmaker's serviceability.

Preston was thirty-eight. Respectable looking.

Dull brown hair. He wore contact lenses. He had a loving family. *That* would be very useful, the vampire thought. He appeared smart enough to know fear, yet able to hide it.

The man could keep secrets.

Okay, St. Laurue thought, a bit pensive. It was a felicitous match. But why bother? The mortal seemed as drab as a dirt filled coffin.

He was about to withdraw, when he saw a light brown mole the size of a black widow spider on the publisher's left cheek. He probed further and sensed a deep river of passion in the man; a dark and seething hunger that Press was either not aware of, or had deliberately buried.

For the undead one, that clinched the deal.

Still, one peculiarity did perturb St. Laurue. The publisher appeared to be annoyingly inelegant.

He'd had an accident.

CHAPTER 2

Thursday, 11:53 P.M.
Preston's office

Bevan Preston took another bite of his foot long mustard-slathered hot dog. A thick dollop of bright yellow splattered his pants.

"Damnation," he said, and grabbed a napkin. He wet it and tried to wipe his pant leg clean. The stain spread and he chuffed in frustration.

Press had risen from head copy editor to CEO of Beagles, a small but lucrative publishing house in Manhattan. He had a respectable income, an admirable wife, three charming daughters– they had lost Troy, their only boy, to leukemia two years ago– and a well kept colonial home in the suburbs of New Jersey. And although he had a picture perfect life, he knew there *had* to be more to life than burning the midnight oil, reading a never ending stack of manuscripts and wiping mustard off his pant leg.

Press heard a noise and looked up.

By desk light, the youth seemed to be in his late teens. Muscular hips gave way to a trim waist. Wide shoulders were brushed by slightly wavy auburn hair. Azure blue eyes... were they glowing? Preston's body tensed. He narrowed his eyes. Okay, that's better. The glow had disappeared.

Press watched as the interloper approached his desk, moving with grace, power and precision. Like an exotic and dangerous jungle animal.

He tried to put up a strong front to scare off the teen. "Who the hell do you think you are, barging into my office like–"

In a flash, the vampire hovered over him, midair. An ice-cold hand clutched Press by the throat. His face turned blood red. His eyes bulged. His breath stopped.

St. Laurue's voice was self-confident and authoritative. "You will publish my chronicles, *monsieur*, or you will die. Choose now."

Press knew he was being strangled, but strangely enough, it didn't matter. His mind was bemused by a peculiar aroma. What was it? Where had he...? He remembered. It was the sad sickly sweet fragrance of sun wilted flowers that greeted him whenever he visited his little boy's grave.

St. Laurue released his neck and backed off.

Press gulped for air. Should he try 911? Bad idea, he thought. That would just provoke the intruder. He could call out for help, but what good would that do at this hour on the fourth floor of an empty office building?

While his mind whirled, quickly reviewing and discarding escape plans, the teen glared at him. As if the lad could see into his busy mind, to Preston's amazement, the teen trumpeted, "Be still."

Press felt gripped by an invisible force. Hidden monsters from his youth crept to the surface of his mind. Things he hadn't thought about in years: Locked in a cobwebbed cellar by neighborhood boys. Terrified of the dark. Sure that blood-sucking, poisonous spiders were slowly crawling up his pant legs and into his shirt sleeves. Cruel laughter from the other side of darkness. "Scaredy-cat, Press," the bullies had called. Don't panic, he had told himself. Don't show your fear. Just play along.

"My survival is in your hands," St. Laurue announced courteously, but loud enough to spank the present back into Preston. "The world must *mind* me. You will publish the book?"

The vampire inched closer.

"Yes," Press quickly answered, "but why me?"

St. Laurue sat on the desk and picked up a golden framed picture of Preston's family. "Because you have much to lose."

Press peered deep into the vampire's eyes and saw a pack of hungry wolves racing through a moonlit forest. For a moment, he was one of the pack. He felt a rush of exhilaration– sprinting through the shadowy woods, the wind playing havoc with his hair– and felt alive again for the first time since his little boy's death.

"But what really *compelled* me," the vampire continued, placing the family photo back down on the desk, "was your untapped river of passion."

"Untapped passion?" Press muttered.

As the teen backed off, Press glanced at the wooden cuckoo clock on the office wall. The clock was his pet possession, shaped like a fine edition hardcover classic, a gift from one of his authors. It was designed to open up, whereupon a cuckoo would pop out and count off the hour. He noticed that the hands were fixed at midnight, but the cuckoo hadn't sung.

"Oui," St. Laurue said. "One might even say, un*sung* passion."

Press was caught between panic and euphoria. The panic, he could understand. But why this rush of blissful release? The feeling scared him. Feelings in general terrified him. They were as deep as an old cobwebbed cellar and as unreasoning as a blood-sucking, poisonous spider coming at him in the dark. Un*sung* passions indeed, he bristled internally, trying to get a grip. Stuff and nonsense. He was a solid family man, a well respected professional, a successful book publisher for Christ's sake!

But just possibly– the dark thought crawled along the softening edges of his mind– all those things had become impediments in his life, rather than advantages.

"But you must forgive my manners," the teenager said, extending a hand. "I am the vampire, Gérard Arnaud St. Laurue."

Preston's jaw dropped open. Had he heard right? A vampire? He hesitated to take the alabaster, blue-veined hand. The one which had, only moments before, nearly strangled the life out of him. But then, a strange power magnetized him and hands meshed. Initially, he only felt the deep freeze burn of the ancient undead. But the chill was immediately followed by a rush of heat so intense that he felt it melt away inner iron chains that held him back from...

"Listen closely!" St. Laurue stood and snapped to attention. "In six days, by next Wednesday's full moon, I will be forced underground for eighteen months. Before that time, I will write the book you will publish."

Press countered, "A *good* book can't be written in six days."

"I assure you," the vampire leered, "my book will be considerably different from 'the good book.' And it *will* be finished on schedule."

Press noticed the stains on the boy's tank top. Alarm spread through the publisher's body and he had to ask the question. "Is that *blood* on your shirt, uh, Mr. St. Laurue?"

The *nosferatu's* eyes glowed yellow-violet and his fangs flashed.

Press recoiled in fright.

"I grabbed a bite on my way over," St. Laurue said. "Fast food can be so messy, *oui?*" He indicated the mustard stain on Preston's pant leg.

"You. Killed. Someone. On your way here?"

"Three "someones" to be exact, in the alleyway across the street."

Preston's face blanched. Would he be the vampire's next victim?

Oh, Press, Press," St. Laurue laughed, "I won't kill you. I *need* you. But is killing so terrible when one's survival is at stake?"

Press remained mute. This was not happening. It was just an awful dream. With a little bit of rest, he'd be as good as...

"Enough!" The vampire said sharply. "I will return with my first several chapters after the next sun sets."

Dazed, Press nodded his head in agreement.

St. Laurue lifted his finger to his lips and gave a sly wink, "Tell no one of our meeting, *mon ami*. Trust me. For you, there is no safety in numbers. Adieu." The vampire bowed, then vanished.

Press trembled, waited for a moment to be sure he was alone, then lunged for the wastepaper bucket and threw up.

The office instantly reeked of vomit.

There's the explanation, he thought, wiping sweat off his forehead. This had all been some kind of weird hallucination, a bad reaction to that foot long hot dog.

Suddenly, the clock opened and its cuckoo shot out across the office, smashing against the opposite wall. The empty clock tolled. The sound of the cuckoo sped up and grew to a deafening pitch. Unable to bear with the unrelenting noise, Press bolted from his office and out of the building.

As he aimlessly wandered down the SoHo street, a thought surfaced. It wasn't safe to wander the city streets at night. Thinking himself mad, he suddenly burst out laughing. He had just come face to face with the undead. By comparison, a Manhattan mugger would seem like Mother Teresa.

Press quickened his pace. Was the vampire following him? Where the hell do you go to find refuge from the undead? Then, he had an idea. St. Michael's Church, just a couple of blocks away. Sanctuary. Having a plan made him feel better. He ran to the church and tried the front doors. Locked. He knocked feverishly, petitioning for entrance.

In between knocks, a hand cupped his shoulder

from behind. Instant dread. He fell to his knees. He was sure the vampire had found him at the enemy's door. "Don't kill me. I didn't mean to come here. I was walking and–" Press mustered the courage to look behind and was relieved to see an old, slightly disheveled, but kindly looking Catholic priest.

"Kill you?" the priest said, sounding confused. "Jesus save us. Give me your hand, my boy. The name is Father Monahan."

Press smelled wine on the priest's breath as Father Monahan helped him up.

"Just back from visiting a sick parishioner," the priest continued in a slur, "uptown at the Merriweather Hotel, don't you know."

Press sensed it was a lie, but didn't care. All he wanted was to get into the safety and comfort of St. Michael's Church.

"I know it's very late, Father," he whispered. "But please let me in."

"Sure, sure," Monahan said softly, fidgeting with a jangling ring of church keys. "There's a world of worry out there. Come on in."

The priest unlocked St. Michael's front door and told Press to sit in a back pew. "I'll put on the altar lights," Monahan said. "They make a body feel better, they do. Then, we'll *both* pray for the Good Lord's Mercy."

Press watched him drunkenly stagger up the center aisle, lined on both sides by a gauntlet of Catholic martyrs immortalized in marble. The priest genuflected at the front altar, then went into a chamber on the right.

Alone again, Press decided to pray. He entwined his hands, but the words wouldn't come. It was useless and he knew why. Through the years, he'd started to rely less on the Almighty and more on his reasoning mind. What good was that, he mused, now that he was losing it?

St. Michael's was dimly lit. There were tables of lighted candles set up along the walls. It was a church alive only with the flickering shadows of its dead marbleized saints. Still, the subtle fragrance of lingering incense made him feel safe, protected.

He was wondering whether the old priest had fallen into a drunken stupor in the back when the crucifix on the altar lit up. Monahan had been right, the lit altar did make him feel better.

He was in the church, in the palm of God's hand. The unexpected thought comforted him, until his pessimistic side wormed in. Now all God has to do is make a fist and squeeze.

The old clergyman reappeared, ambled back down the aisle and sat beside him, looking a little less tipsy. The smell of alcohol was gone. Good, Press thought, maybe the priest could help after all.

Monahan touched his shoulder in a comforting manner and said in a lilting Irish brogue, "Now what's troubling you, son?"

The priest's slur was gone. Somewhat relieved, Press let out a long gush of suppressed air. Things were looking up, he attempted to convince himself. He wasn't alone. He was in the company of another body... this time, a *living* body.

"Father," Press started, then fell silent. He felt

blocked, like earlier, when he had unsuccessfully tried to pray. His mind drifted back to when he was a boy kneeling in the dark confessional box, reciting a well rehearsed litany of sins. He had always resented that. Why did he have to reveal his shameful secrets to a priest? Why couldn't he just speak directly to God?

Ironically, now, when he *wanted* to talk with a priest, nothing would come out. Maybe if he concentrated on the lit crucifix up front, the words might tumble out. The ploy worked.

"Father, at my office, a boy..." Press said, while concentrating on the tortured eyes of Christ. "No... Not a boy... a *fiend* attacked me." He clenched his fists and tightened his jaw. "The thing said it was a... a..."

"A what?" Monahan gave Press an encouraging pat on the knee. "It's all right, son. You can tell me. You're on God's holy ground."

"He said he was a vampire!" Press confessed. "And God help me, I think it's true." Embarrassed, he buried his face in his hands. "I know this sounds fantastic, but the boy could fly. Father, this kid..."

Press tried desperately to communicate the horror of his experience, but felt he was failing dismally. With eyes that begged to be understood, he dropped his hands and looked at the kindly old priest by his side.

An ice-cold hand slid quickly to his groin and clamped onto him. He gasped as he stared directly into St. Laurue's face. Intense pain riveted his body. He moaned. More applied pressure on his testicles. His eyes shot up into his head. Then– as if silently commanded– he looked at St. Laurue.

The vampire morphed into Father Monahan, then back again, while expertly imitating the lilting voice of the old priest. "It's all right, son. You're on God's holy ground." His long vicious laugh echoed its evil throughout the church, and with a little more hand pressure, Press howled along, too– like a dog accompanying his master's voice.

"Press. What am I to do with you?"

"Please… let go…"

The ice-clamped grip relaxed.

Sharp pain slackened into a dull ache.

St. Laurue gave a bored sigh. "It'd be a shame if I had to destroy you and find another publisher. Still in all, I would– kill you that is. You *know* what I am. The risk of exposure is too great."

"Couldn't you wave your hand and make me–"

"Make you what?" the vampire blasted. "Make you go back to your inhibited little life?"

"Forget," Press said. "I was going to say, make me for–"

"Perhaps you've forgotten too much already."

"I'm begging you. I've got a family."

"And you'd do well to remember it. One more breach of faith and those dearest to you will pay. Except by my permission, our visits are to remain confidential. Do we understand one another?"

Press again fixed on the crucifix up front. His mind was bombarded with questions, each one louder than the next. What had he done to deserve this? How could this blasphemous creature accost him on hallowed ground? How had God let this happen? Suddenly, Preston heard himself shout out.

"Oh God, please take this cup away."

"Trust me," the vampire quietly advised, "that particular supplication never really gets *His* ear..." More hand pressure. Press yowled again with intense pain. "So," the vampire continued, "we have a bargain?"

"Yes," Press stammered. "I won't tell a soul. You have my word."

"And you, mine," St. Laurue said, releasing the mortal. "Henceforth, you will never know when or where I'll appear. But know this. I am ever near, least expected, and most inconvenient."

So rapidly that it might have been thought to be merely imagination, the vampire's eyes flashed yellow-violet and his razor-sharp tongue snaked out and slashed the left side of Preston's neck.

The mortal yelped.

As blood dripped from his wound, St. Laurue handed him an elegant red silk handkerchief.

A terrifying thought ran through Preston's head, as he quietly took it and dabbed at his neck. Was he a creature of the night now? Would he have to drink blood? Then, he remembered the old lore. No. The undead have to make you drink *their* blood for that sort of thing to happen... right?

"Blood," the vampire whispered.

Being wrenched from his internal worries, Press said, "What?"

The vampire went on. "Blood can be so untidy, yet so damned exciting, *oui?* Like life, is it not?"

Press looked down at the red silk handkerchief. It was soaked with blood. *His* blood. *His* life. Slowly ebbing away. Drop by drop. Moment by moment. He realized what the vampire was trying to tell him. Blood is life. And life is precious. It mustn't be allowed to drain away. It must be *lived.*

He handed the bloody silk handkerchief back to St. Laurue with a knowing look.

The undead one's nostrils flared as he closed Preston's hand around the wet silk cloth. "Keep it," he whispered in the hushed tone of an overly kind undertaker, "as a reminder."

The vampire faded into a wisp of purple vapor.

Like the scattered snickering of ten thousand tiny devils gone stark raving mad, St. Laurue's disembodied voice echoed throughout the church.

"There is no sanctuary from me."

Press was shaken and alone now.

But no. He heard footsteps behind his pew. He turned around and saw no one. Still, the mysterious sound of footsteps continued down the aisle heading toward the church door. The door opened and closed, as if some unseen visitor had exited.

Then, there was silence.

Finally gathering up his courage, Press exited the church.

Still trembling all over, he got half-way down St. Michael's front steps when strange hands shot out of the dark and restrained him.

CHAPTER 3

Friday, June 22nd 9:06 A.M.
Twenty-third Precinct

Detective Solomon Wiese had a sour look on his face as he read the New York Times' headline, "Fiend still stalks city streets." He took a swig of antacid right out of the bottle on his desk and read on: "Last night's was the most vicious of all the crimes committed to date. Three caucasian males were found brutalized and blanketed with blood in a SoHo alley."

Captain Trevor Eckles stomped into the office, holding a folder. "Solly, we've got three possible eyewitnesses found near the crime scene."

The phone rang.

"Homicide, Wiese speaking." The sixty-two-year-old detective held an index finger up to Eckles, indicating he'd only be a minute. "Rita, I'm swamped here. Yeah, I did. I *did*. I took the new heart medicine."

Eckles tossed the folder on the desk. "Here's last night's statements."

"Ritzy, gotta go," Wiese said, grabbing the folder. "The Holocaust Museum? Sure. I promise. Listen, I'll call you back." He hung up.

"Christ, I forgot," the captain said. "When's your vacation start?"

"Sunday. We're going to D.C.," Solomon said, with a pang of guilt.

He felt like he was abandoning Trevor.

"Holocaust Museum, huh? Still looking for your missing brother?"

"Until we know for sure that Maury's dead, we have to try."

Trevor flopped into a chair. "That's why you're the best."

Solomon couldn't hide his concern for the captain, who was usually wiry and high-strung, but lately had become a high pressure cooker about to blow. The big boys uptown really wanted this serial killer tagged.

Eckles tapped his finger against the arm rest. "Talk to me, buddy."

"The murders last night," Wiese started, "I figure it's got to be the same perp. Excessive violence, all the blood, the look of horror on each victims' face. Oh yeah, we also got another one of those cryptic messages."

He handed Eckles a postcard. It read, "To catch him, you must think beyond yourself, beyond the rational truth. The Daemonion Council."

Eckles tossed the card back on the desk. "Find out who they are yet?"

"Nobody's heard of them," Wiese said.

"All right, better get to those witnesses," Eckles sighed, and left.

Wiese gobbled down the last bite of his jelly donut, took a gulp of coffee, and another swig of antacid. He pocketed the postcard and picked up the folder. As he was leaving his office, he spied the bottle of unopened pills on the edge of his desk. It was standing there like a lonely tin soldier. He promised himself that he'd take his heart pill later and hurried out.

Sergeant John Barrows caught up with him in the corridor.

"That blond you're going to question first," Barrows said, "I think I recognize her from the after-hours club."

Wiese nodded, then entered the grilling room.

The small area felt more suffocating than intimate. It was purposely kept hot and stuffy. Its stark ambiance made a suspect feel the need to talk, if for no other reason than to fill in the emptiness.

Solomon winced. He disliked the many hours he had to spend there, asking questions, trying to get at the truth. After forty years on the force, he'd come to the conclusion that the truth wasn't so cut and dry. Everybody had a different version.

At times he had grave doubts if such a thing as "the real truth" existed at all.

Ashley was already seated on the chair called the "the sweat box."

"Miss Green. Thanks for coming in," Solomon said. "Can I get you some coffee, or maybe you'd like a cup of tea?"

"Nah," the blond said.

"Okay. So let me come right to the point. You were spotted near the crime scene in SoHo last night. Can you tell me why?"

"I live there. I was putting out the trash. Some law against that?"

"No. Not at all," he said mildly, thinking he might have been coming on too strong. "Tell you what, let's start over. And please, call me Solly. Everyone does. Now, Miss Green, did you by any chance happen to notice anything that struck you as unusual last night?"

"No." Ashley crossed her legs tightly.

"You might help save lives if you could remember anything. For the public's sake, think back. You were putting out the trash and—"

"And nothing," she said, glaring at him and defiantly leaning forward.

The girl seemed feisty and oddly aggressive. This wasn't going to be easy, he thought, rolling his eyes and taking a chair.

"What's the matter?" Ashley said. "Something in your eye?"

"Please, if you don't mind, I'll ask the questions. By the way, you always take out the trash at two in the morning?"

"No. Sometimes I wait for a decent hour, like *three* in the morning."

Solomon stifled a chuckle and thought Ashley half smiled herself.

Good. She's easing up. He continued. "Did you speak with anyone last night?"

"On my way home a few hours earlier I talked to Franny."

"The lady in the waiting area?"

"Yeah. I see you dragged her in, too. She's an old homeless lady. Where do you get the brass? Besides, Franny's not going to do you any good."

"And why is that?"

"Because she doesn't talk."

"Why not?"

"How the hell should I know? She doesn't like to, I guess. You get in hot water if you talk too much. Franny's not dumb, she's just homeless."

"So what did you say to her?"

"I said hello. Have a nice evening. *I* was being *nice* to her."

Solomon got the message.

"You're right," he said. "Look, I promise to be nice to Franny, too. But earlier last night on your way home, before or after you said hello to Franny, did you see anything peculiar?"

"Well. I did see... There was this guy. I'm not sure, but I thought he was after me, you know, chasing me."

"Chasing you?" Solomon said, perking up. "Can you describe him?"

"Why? He didn't *do* nothing. You have to bother him too?"

"It could be important, Miss Green. Please."

Solomon tried a smile. Ashley ignored him and tossed her reckless blond hair from in front of her face with an annoyed twitch.

"He had reddish brown hair," she said. "Sandy-like, I think."

"This could be substantial information. Thank you, Miss Green. You don't happen to recall what this man was wearing?"

"He wasn't a man. He was a kid, around my age. Maybe eighteen, twenty. He had on these oversized jeans and a tank top."

"What color?"

"Blue denim jeans. White tank. Oh, and a thick black belt."

"Shoes or sneakers?"

"I glanced. I didn't stare."

"What else? He had sandy-like hair and…" Wiese rotated his hand in a small circle, coaxing the girl to continue.

"A great body. If it wasn't for Raphael, I might've slowed down."

"But you were scared."

"A little… but I was only a building away from my apartment."

"Then what happened?"

"You think I'm stupid? I ran for my door."

"And then you called the station?"

"What?"

"We got a phone call," Wiese said. "A tip from a young lady."

"I'm not *that* young."

He got up and paced the room. "What else can you tell me?"

The blond gave him an exasperated sigh. "If I remember anymore, I'll let you know."

"You'll call again?" he said.

"Yeah. I mean no. I didn't call." Ashley got up from the chair. "Boy, you cops are something."

That the girl was acting strange, he had no doubt. But why? What was she hiding? "May I call you if I need to?"

"Yeah, whatever," Ashley said, and moved to the hall. "Anything for the public's welfare. And go easy on Franny. You want to do some public good, give her a few bucks for a decent meal."

"Maybe I'll just do that."

"And while you're at it, why don't you spring for some AC in here?"

Ashley left the room. Wiese sat down and unbuttoned his shirt collar. He jotted a few notes down in the folder.

"Solly," Sgt. Barrows called from the hall, "you want the bag lady or the man next?"

"Send in the lady," Solomon said, running the palm of his hand over the balding patch on his head. If his hair hadn't already been gray, this case would have done the trick. His stomach rumbled. He speculated it was from too much coffee. Of course, the many unanswered questions he had after talking to Ashley didn't help either. He loosened his belt a couple notches and wiped the sweat off his brow.

Barrows escorted Franny in, then left.

The bag lady floated into the cramped room like a majestic continent sailing on its own private ocean. Wiese stood and motioned her to the sweat box. She sat with a daintiness not typical of a vagrant, or for a woman of such size. She spilled over the arms of the chair, but settled in as if she and the seat were one unit. She seemed to become her environment, the positive center of all things around her.

Solomon couldn't help but notice that even the grilling room took on a more expansive air. Franny's cat-like poise and confidence amazed him. These qualities were not often found in a homeless person. Something was definitely out of whack.

Silently, Wiese stroked his chin. How to begin? After getting off on the wrong foot with Ashley, he figured he'd try to be gentler with Franny. Maybe he could try to break the ice with a small joke.

"My name is Solly. Mind if I call you Miss Franny, Miss Franny?"

The bag lady folded her hands on her lap and yawned. But this was not just any old yawn. This was a yawn that expressed indifference.

"May I ask you a few questions about last night?" Solomon said, as if he were conversing with a small child.

Franny shifted in the sweat box, looking as if she was being annoyed by a hungry mosquito. Then, she grumbled and gave a nod.

"You know about the murders by your... uh... where you stay?"

She snorted and gave another nod.

"I was wondering if you might help me solve this case. Your friend Ashley mentioned seeing a young white male in the area at the time of the murders. You saw him too?"

She moved again in the sweat box, signaling discomfort. Solomon was catching on to the bag lady's silent method of communicating.

"Ah. You *did* see him. He had auburn hair?"

Franny unfolded her hands and pointed a crusty finger at Wiese, who leaned in closer, as if straining to hear the last words of a dying woman.

"Yes? Me? What? I don't under–"

She shook her finger vigorously at him. Wiese took a step back. Her large body quaked as she erupted into peals of lilting laughter and spoke with a thick cockney accent.

"Some bloke has told you that I'm a bloomin' mute, hasn't he?"

"Well, we do speak then?" The detective raised an eyebrow.

Franny slowly nodded begrudgingly and made an affirmative sounding grunt.

"But only when necessary," Solomon guessed.

She hiccuped and jostled her shoulder a little. Her expression seemed to be saying, "Naturally."

"And what an unusual accent, Miss Franny. English, are we?"

Franny looked shocked and indignant, as if a new beau had asked a question far too intimate this early in the romance.

"So," Wiese continued. "You saw this young white male Miss Green mentioned? The one with auburn hair?"

She groaned. Her shoulder motion increased.

"He accosted three boys in the alley and killed them. You saw this?"

Wiese looked into Franny's eyes and saw a kind of panic come over her, like she'd seen something so terrible that just the thought of it startled her. Her body wavered in and out of focus. He rubbed his eyes. What was this? Were his eyes giving out? He squinted. Her face came back into place. Only now, the bag lady's eyes looked glossy and vacant.

"Talk to me, Miss Franny," Wiese coaxed. "I don't bite."

Sudden horror flashed across her face.

Then, she went deadpan and her eyes took on that empty shine again.

"Is there anything more you can tell me?" Wiese said, without much hope. He saw adamant refusal in her eyes. "Well, thank you, Miss Franny."

As she lifted up from the sweat box seat, Solomon stood and reached into his pocket. He brought out some dollar bills. "I want you to know this isn't a bribe. It's just my way of showing appreciation and... well here."

Franny silently refused his money and lumbered toward the door.

"Excuse me, Miss Franny, may I ask why you don't often speak? I know it's none of my business, but it's in my nature to be curious."

At the hall door, she turned to the detective. "Natural curiosity ain't going to help you 'ere, sir, 'cause this case ain't natural," Franny said, then waddled out of the room. Wiese hunched his shoulders. The woman knows something she's not telling, he thought, as he jotted more notes down in the folder. But how could he get her to spill? The Eliza Dolittle accent also had him confused. Then, there was that look of horror that had flashed across her face. The exact same expression he'd seen on all of the killer's victims.

Sgt. Barrows rounded the corner with Preston.

"Solly, here's the publisher."

"Thanks John," Wiese said.

Barrows gave a sharp nod and left.

"That's a nasty cut you have there on your neck, uh," he checked the folder, then looked up again. "Mr. Preston?"

"Press will do."

The guy seemed friendly enough. "Press, can I get you a band aid?"

"No. It's nothing. Just cut myself shaving."

"And that yellow stain on your pants?"

"Oh that. I was eating a hot dog and the mustard sort of–"

"That makes two accidents in one night."

"Two accidents? Oh, yeah. Sure. You mean the shaving one and the–"

"Well, never mind. Have a seat, Press." The detective pointed to the sweat box. "And call me Solly, everybody does." He looked over the report on his lap. "Let's see here. Last night's report says our men detained you on the steps of St. Michael's. You're a religious man, Press? It says you were upset. Here, let me read the account and see what you make of it.

" 'Mr. Bevan Giles Preston, hereafter referred to as the suspect,' oh, don't worry about that word, it should read the possible eyewitness. I'll change it after we talk. Okay? Let's see. The report goes on to say, here it is, 'was found badly shaken on the steps of St. Michael's in the vicinity of the homicides one-thirty in the morning. When questioned, the suspect,' there's that awful word again. 'When questioned the *possible eyewitness* appeared dazed and confused.' "

Solomon looked up at Press. "Dazed and confused." He continued to read, " 'physical tremors suggested possible substance abuse.' " Solomon looked at Press again. "So what's the story? You're an addict and suddenly got the urge to talk to God at one-thirty in the morning?"

Preston shifted uncomfortably in the grilling chair, then said, "I talked to a priest. I had... an inner struggle."

Wiese stood. "An inner struggle. I understand. I get a lot of that. My health isn't what it once was. Whose is? Am I right?" He lightly cuffed Preston's shoulder, hoping to loosen up the publisher. No response. "Yep, inner struggles," he continued. "They're the worst. So you'll tell me about it? Maybe there's a support group I can recommend."

Press barked out a curt laugh. "Not for my kind of trouble."

Wiese leaned closer. "And what kind of trouble would that be?"

"Oh... just... it's very personal."

"Personal. Okay. I get it."

"I can't talk about it yet."

Solomon sat down. "Understandable," he said, with a nonchalant flip of his hand. "Who's pushing?" He opened the folder and pretended to study it. During the uncomfortable silence, he was hoping Press would decide to elaborate on his inner struggle. No such luck. "So tell me," Wiese moved on, "The crime last night was committed across the street from your office building. I was wondering.

You saw or heard something?"

"Not a thing."

"But when you left the office at..." he scanned the report on his lap, "around twelve-thirty this morning. You saw someone across the street in the alley, or on your way to St. Michael's?"

"I'm sorry," Press said. "I guess I was too wrapped up in my own personal problems to pay attention. I really wish I could be of more help."

"Not to worry. We'll get this guy. God works in mysterious ways. But look who's talking? You're the religious one. Am I right?" He drew a blank stare from the publisher and sensed he was getting nowhere. "Well, that's good enough for now. You've got a business to run. You'll call me if you think of anything else, or just to talk?"

"Of course, Solly," Press said as he stood up.

"Sometimes a friendly ear clears a heavy heart," Wiese said, and stood up. "Who knows, maybe together we can figure out the mysteries of life." Press was almost out of the room when Wiese spoke again. "By the way, we took the liberty of keeping your silk handkerchief. The one you used last night to blot at that neck wound? Shaving accidents, huh? You've got to pay more attention. Am I right or am I right?"

"Right," Press said, smiling agreeably while heading for the door.

"One more thing. In your statement," Solomon said, pretending to look up something in the folder, "you mentioned a priest's name... a...?"

"Father Monahan?" Press filled in the blank.

"Right. Monahan. We'll probably have to talk with him, too."

"Can I go now?"

"Sure." Solomon said, closing the folder. But just as Press was about to exit, Wiese casually added, "By the way, did you happen to see a young man with auburn hair dressed in jeans and a white tank top last night?"

Press turned ashen and began to sweat. "…no… I… uh… No!"

"Okay. Just checking. Trying to be thorough."

After Press left, Wiese jotted more notes in the folder. Complex guy, he thought, but definitely not the killer type. What was up with that red silk handkerchief? And why was the guy so nervous?

His thoughts were interrupted when Sgt. Barrows marched in and handed him a crumpled piece of paper. "Solly, I found this in the bag lady's sack while you were questioning her."

Wiese flattened the paper out against his lap. It read, "Dear Slim, Call home. Mother wants a word. The clock is ticking backwards. TDC."

"Good work, John," Solomon said, brightly. "This maybe could be the lucky break we've been waiting for."

The captain shot into the room. "Did someone say 'lucky break?' "

"Could be," Wiese said. "All thanks to Sgt. Barrows here."

Eckles turned to the sergeant. "Earning your pay again, are you? That's my boy. Say, could you give Mr. Preston a lift back to SoHo?"

"Sure thing, Captain," Barrows said beaming with pride, and left.

"Trevor," Wiese said, "is that bag lady still here by any chance?"

"Left a couple of minutes ago. Why?"

"I need to question her again this afternoon."

"I'll have some men pick her up. So what's this 'lucky break?' "

Wiese scanned his notes. "The perpetrator might be a caucasian male between eighteen and twenty with auburn hair, wearing blue jeans and a white tank top."

"Figures. We finally get a description and you're leaving for D.C. on Sunday." Eckles grabbed the folder from Wiese. "I'll have to familiarize myself with this."

"So where's the harm if I stay?" Solomon said. "The vacation can wait. You know me. If I relax too much, I'll fall apart."

"It's okay, Solly. I didn't mean you should stay. You deserve that vacation."

"But things are heating up," Solomon said, tucking his hands in his pockets and lifting his shoulders. "I don't mind working through."

"Ritzy would have my head if I let you do that again this year."

"My wife's bark is worse than her bite."

"If it's all the same to you, I'd like to stay on her good side."

"So who's blaming you?" Solomon winked. "I feel the same way."

He handed Eckles the note found in Franny's

sack. "You might want to take a look at this."

While the captain looked at the note, Wiese reached into his pocket and brought out the postcard from earlier.

"Looks like the bag lady might be connected in some way with these homicides."

Wiese pointed to the bottom right hand corner of the postcard, then to the bottom of the note.

"Notice the signatures?"

The captain looked at the signature on the note– TDC. Then, he checked out the signature on the postcard– The Daemonion Council.

CHAPTER 4

Friday, 10:29 A.M.
Preston's office

After being driven back to his office from the police station, Press walked in expecting to find remnants of last night's debacle. Luckily, the maintenance crew had straightened up. The vomit with its sickening smell was gone. So was the smashed cuckoo. Everything had been restored to a comfortable normalcy. Then, he glanced at the wall and saw the birdless clock's hands pointing straight up, still proclaiming the witching hour.

Press felt slightly flushed and sat down at his desk. Okay, he said to himself trying to sort things out, what have we got here? A vampire wants me to publish his life story before he has to take this... What? Right. This millennium rest. He says this book will keep him alive.

Something about the world *minding* him.

Just what in hell did that mean?

He removed his contact lenses and rested his head in his arms on the desktop. Still, his mind wouldn't quit yapping at him. Should he help this... thing? What if he didn't? Would he be killed? Would his family be hurt?

Sleep began to pull him under.

And although Press was semi-aware of the morning's busy schedule, he was far too emotionally and physically exhausted to deal with the day. He let his eyes close and surrendered to the deadening deep sleep of his internal night.

Friday, 11:35 A.M.
a Manhattan street corner

Franny wobbled over to the open street phone on the corner and rooted through her canvas bag, but couldn't find the message that Ashley had given her the night before. It didn't matter, she thought.

The main point was to call the Motherhospice.

Something about time ticking backwards. So very typical of the Daemonion Council. Always communicating by way of cryptic codes.

She dialed the appropriate international code and was transferred to the operator in Nairn, Scotland. She requested a private number. After a minute, the operator rang through.

"Francine Styles here," she said in an elegant English accent.

She looked around to make sure she wasn't drawing undue attention.

Fortunately, the noisy street traffic discouraged eavesdroppers and her bag lady ploy was proving to be quite effective. People tended to go out of their way to pretend she didn't exist.

The voice at the other end in Scotland sounded Asian Indian. "Ah, Miss Francine, I must verify your identity by voice print. Speak now."

"Little Miss Muffet sat on a tuffet, eating her curds and whey."

Franny was hot and tired and didn't fancy being on a public phone, but what could she do? The message requested contact, and she *had* been interrogated by the police earlier this morning. That needed to be *reported.*

"Very good. Do you wish to speak to the Grand Counselor?"

"Yes," Francine said crisply. "Connect me with Alec, please."

"Right-o. And I might add, it's nice to hear your voice again."

"Thank you, Amrita. Lovely to hear your voice, too."

As Franny waited for Alec Priggins, a loud diesel truck roared by. She stuffed a finger in her free ear to muffle the clamor.

"Alec Priggins here." The man's diction smacked of formality. It was robotic and conjured up the image of slimy dead fish.

"I received a message to call you, Mother. Time ticking backwards? Can you be more specific than that, Alec?"

"Francine, how very nice to hear from you finally. I had anticipated you would check in on a per diem basis as in accordance with the Council's protocol, but you do have your own way and shall remain ever an enigma to the rest of our members here at the Motherhospice."

Franny was getting annoyed with the man's sophisticated sarcasm. "Come to the point, Alec, will you?"

"We've had a reversal of fortune," Priggins said, with what sounded like a world weary sigh. "The Marquis Antoine DeMalberet has escaped."

"St. Laurue's father? Do you think that he's headed for the States?"

"A very real possibility. But there is some good news. DeMalberet *isn't* infected with the virus. And we did *persuade* him to let us make a duplicate of his diaries. You must read them when you get back tomorrow."

Sweat beaded up on Franny's forehead, partly due to the noonday heat, but mostly because of anger. "You're ordering me back?"

"It was a decision made by the Council Board."

"And you let them!"

"I could hardly *appear* before them to argue the case. One must play by the traditional rules."

"It's a bloody stupid rule. Why shouldn't the Grand Counselor of the Daemonion Council be seen by anybody?"

"Why Francine, you of all people should know that the unseen hand keeps a tidy ship. Besides, the board wants you out of the field. It seems they've had a special election."

Franny couldn't believe her ears. There was a standard joke among the Council field agents. Board members never stoop to fieldwork. That's why they're so bored. In his usual roundabout way, Priggins was telling her that she'd been elected to the board.

"I'm flabbergasted," she said breathlessly into the phone.

"Your loyalty has earned you the position, though my guess is that you'll dearly miss your outside assignments."

Franny was reminded of her job at hand. "Can all this wait until I complete my mission?"

"No, it can't," he continued dismissively, "because another Council operative has been sent to lure St. Laurue to Scotland. His name's Jared Shannon. Too clever by half if you ask me."

"Then why send him?"

"The Council raised him from a tender age, much as they did you. Another orphan. Your male parallel, if you will. In short, Jared's being groomed as your replacement in the field."

She swallowed hard, then concluded, "I should stay and assist."

"No," Priggins said firmly. "He's only twenty, but so far he's proven to be quite capable. I don't much care for his cocky attitude, but at least he *does* keep in touch *regularly* while out on assignment, unlike some agents I know. Anything new to report?"

Franny was angered, even under these rewarding circumstances, at being booted off her mission so abruptly. However, she was a professional. After wiping the sweat from her eyes with a dirty sleeve, she managed to handle her exasperation and began to report the most recent findings.

"After witnessing him tear three young men to pieces last night in an alleyway, I'm certain St. Laurue is not aware that his feeding habits have gotten freakish and traceable. I also suspect he's spreading a mutant and virulent strain of HIV. I'll bring in a full report when I arrive."

"Does he suspect we're on to him?"

"No. I've been cloaking. Though I might've been a tad slipshod. I think he briefly detected my presence last night in the alley. Also, his new minion, Bevan Preston, might've heard me as I invisibly slipped out of St. Michael's Church."

"Francine, you're totally exhausted from all this night work. I want you back to Mother as soon as possible."

"It seems I no longer have a choice," she said, through gritted teeth.

"It's all for the good of the Council."

"If you say so," she said, not fully convinced. "Have three tickets for Scotland dropped off. Ashley and Raphael should probably like to jet back together. I'll finish up and follow on a later flight, so as not to betray any connection with them."

"Smart enough, Francine."

"Detective Wiese questioned Ashley and I this morning. We told him just enough to help him pigeonhole St. Laurue. By tonight, I should be able to put him on to the vampire."

"Good work as usual. Finish what you can and return within twenty-four hours. Now don't dawdle. Understand, you're officially off the case."

"Yes. You've made that abundantly–"

Rude hands abruptly ripped the receiver from Franny's grip. She found herself in the custody of two New York City police officers.

"Okay, you," one barked. "You're coming in for more questioning."

CHAPTER 5

Friday, 11:41 A.M.
St. Michael's Catholic Church

Solomon was met on the front steps of St. Michael's Catholic Church by a frantic matronly Irish woman named Agnes Hornesby.

He'd received her call about the missing priest just after questioning Press at the precinct and figured he'd better check it out personally.

"Detective Wiese?" the nervous woman said, raising her eyebrows.

She looked as if she were about to give birth to a set of dishes, Wiese thought, as he put on his most charming manner.

"Yes, and you must be Miss Hornesby?"

"It's not like him at all," Agnes rattled on. "Father Monahan's never missed a service. And this being the funeral of one of his dearest friends."

She took his arm and hurried him through the front doors and into the church. "I had to call St. Pat's uptown. They're sending a priest to fill in."

Wiese saw Mr. Sean O'Flarity, the deceased, resting peacefully in an open casket up by the altar. A fair number of mourners already filled the pews. One woman in the front pew was mumbling over a set of beads and sobbing hysterically.

Must be the poor widow O'Flarity, Solomon concluded, then turned his attention back to his overwrought host.

"When we spoke on the phone earlier, Miss

Hornesby," he said, stopping in the antechamber of the church, "you mentioned that you happened to see Father Monahan last night."

"I did," Agnes snapped. "Who else served him his dinner?"

The woman seemed so overly possessive of the missing priest, Wiese thought. Maybe Hornesby and Monahan were secret lovers and had a quarrel. Maybe old Agnes decided to serve him the last supper: poisoned potato soup.

He coughed away an oncoming chuckle and continued with the investigation. "And after dinner, he told you where he was going?"

"Said he was going to visit a sick parishioner," Miss Hornesby said. "Nothing unusual there. He's a good soul, he is."

A slim young priest walked into St. Michael's and approached them.

"You Father Fitzpatrick?" Agnes barked, all the while wringing her hands in despair.

"Yes, I've come to fill in for Monahan. Is he still missing?"

"Yes. I'm afraid he is," Solomon said. "I'm Detective Wiese."

"Well, wish me luck," the priest said. "This is my first funeral."

"Confidentially," Wiese joked. "This is my first missing priest."

Fitzpatrick roared with laughter.

Miss Hornesby didn't even try to hide her scowl, then steamed out an insistent shushing sound, as if her teapot shaped body had been brought to a sudden boil.

"You come along," she ordered Fitzpatrick. "I'll show you to the vestment room."

As they quickly moved up the aisle, Wiese quietly called out to Agnes, "Mind if I look around the church?"

"Suit yourself," she whispered back. "But don't interrupt the funeral. We've a fine reputation to uphold here at St. Michael's. Police detective or not. I'll not be standing by and having God's holy work blasphemed."

"I'll be as quiet as a church mouse," Wiese assured her.

Agnes gave him a grimace, then continued to hurry Fitzpatrick up the aisle– she, venting a torrent of non-stop whispered worry; he, lending his unseasoned but best confessional ear.

Solomon rolled his eyes. It wasn't enough that he had to take the time to try and locate a missing priest, but he also had to put up with being accused of blaspheming the entire Roman Catholic Church.

The pipe organ began to drone out a dirge that dressed the church in a depressing ceremonial atmosphere, as Wiese climbed the back stairs to the balcony. He was wheezing by the time he reached the top and saw the angel.

Must be a life-size statue of St. Michael, he assumed. Wasn't he the one who threw Satan into Hell? Something about the thought seemed like a premonition and made him feel uneasy.

As he combed the balcony for clues, he heard Fitzpatrick's eulogy, punctuated by sobs, moans, and the nose-blowing of friends and family of the deceased. It made him want to hurry. Instead, he drew in a deep breath and characteristically redoubled his efforts for thoroughness.

Ten minutes later, he had turned up nothing.

Then, while he was about to walk past St. Michael and back down the stairs, he saw a small pool of blood shadowed by the matrix supporting the statue.

As he went to get a closer look, an arm flung out from under the statue's base. "What the hell..." he muttered out loud, stumbling backwards.

His heart raced to the point where he had to take a moment to catch his breath and collect himself before pulling the rest of the bloodless body out from under St. Michael.

The corpse was clothed in a black cassock and was missing its head. An involuntary tremor shook Wiese's body. My God, he thought. What kind of monster would do something like this?

A sudden series of screams from below made him rush over to the balcony railing. Fitzpatrick was on his knees at the altar, tearing at his hair and howling. Miss Hornesby ran to the young priest's side and tried to calm him, while those who had attended the funeral sat still, in shocked silence.

Solomon hurried down the stairs and to the front altar. He noticed that the center chamber– where the holy hosts of the Body of Christ were kept– was left ajar.

He glanced at young Father Fitzpatrick, who was still shrieking and wildly pointing toward the half opened tabernacle.

The detective peered inside of the altar vault.

Monahan's decapitated head stared back at him.

Blood spilled from the severed neck onto the altar. A crucifix had been impaled in the forehead. The eyes were slightly tilted upward. The mouth was frozen in a wide "O" and had a wad of holy hosts stuffed into it.

A thick white froth oozed down the chin from around the sides of the tongue, which stuck out lewdly and curved up into the right nostril, devising a picture of profound perversity.

Wiese felt his stomach lurch.

As if invisibly pushed from behind, Monahan's head suddenly rolled forward out of the chamber and off the altar.

It smacked the marble floor with a thud and rolled into the lap of the kneeling priest. Fitzpatrick walloped it away, even as Miss Hornesby keeled over and fainted on top of him.

Father Fitzpatrick heaved Agnes' dead weight off and bolted down the aisle and out of the church, raving like a madman, his vestments flapping in the breeze behind him.

All hell broke loose among the bereaved, as they stampeded out of the pews and followed Fitzpatrick, as if he were a latter day Pied Piper.

Alone now, Solomon went over to Agnes and felt for a pulse. She was alive, but out cold.

He called for a rescue unit on his cell phone, then walked over toward Sean O'Flarity's casket.

As he came around the coffin, he stopped short and gasped.

He found himself staring at Monahan's bloody severed head. Miraculously, the head had rolled into an upright position. It looked as if the good father had been entombed under the blood splattered aisle with only his head left unburied.

Solomon peered into the priest's eyes– which were still slightly upturned and staring directly at him from the floor– and had the eeriest feeling that the old clergyman, though dead, was sending him a baleful warning.

CHAPTER 6

Friday, 1:38 P.M.
Twenty-third Precinct

Solomon was sure Monahan had been murdered by the serial killer he was after. The crime had all the markings: the beheading, the barbarous bloodletting, that final look of horror. The whole business made him think of long ago events that he'd rather forget, events that had taken place in the concentration camp when he was a kid. He shivered. Clear your head, he thought. But that was easier said than done, especially when a few stinging questions buzzed around in his brain. Why did the killer target a man of the cloth, and where did Bevan Preston fit into all this?

Franny was already seated in "the sweat box" when he loosened his tie and walked into the grilling room. Right now, he had to follow up on another line of questioning.

"Miss Franny," Solomon started. "Sorry for the inconvenience. Just a few more questions, if you don't mind."

She shrugged and Wiese knew he was back to square one with the silent bag lady.

"This morning we found a note in your possession. Must've dropped out of your bag. Here. Take a look. You recognize it?"

She ignored the slip of paper he offered and voiced a half grunt.

"We've been getting anonymous notes since

these homicides started. They're from a group called the Daemonion Council. Every week another message or telephone call and always with a mysterious drift. Kind of like the one in this note we found on you. See, it starts with, 'Dear Slim.' "

Franny shifted in the sweat box, looking like an amused cat.

"Anyhow, this note. It's signed TDC and I got to thinking– TDC, why do those initials ring a bell? All of a sudden I got it. They could stand for The Daemonion Council."

She yawned and scratched an underarm.

"The Daemonion Council– is that what these initials are referring to? And this 'Slim' person? It's you? You know her? Or is it a him?"

She coldly grunted.

Solomon began to pace the small room, hoping to stimulate answers.

"And something else," he continued. "We got a tip by phone last night after the alley murders. A woman's voice. We thought it was your friend Ashley. By the way, she's a close friend of yours?"

No reaction.

"Anyway, since my men said you were on a public phone when they found you, I thought maybe it was you who called and tipped us off about the murders, just like the clues in these notes you've been sending." Wiese stopped pacing and looked at Franny. "Am I getting warm? You've been sending these notes and called to tip us off last night, right Slim?"

Franny rubbed her nose and snorted to herself

as if privy to some private joke, but otherwise kept silent. Solomon put his hands on his hips, shook his head and visibly slumped.

"Well, maybe I'm wrong," he said. "May I keep your note?"

"It ain't my note," Franny said in a thick cockney accent.

He raised his hands toward Heaven. "Ah, she speaks," he said. Then looked squarely at her. "So, you're connected to this Daemonion Council?"

"I told you it ain't my bloody note."

Wiese let out a small sigh and leaned against the wall by the water cooler. He had an idea. "Like a glass of water, Miss Franny?"

She nodded and Solomon took it as a sign of cooperation. As he handed her a paper cup, he said, "You know a priest named Monahan? They say he helped the homeless. He ever help you out?"

Franny was about to take a sip of water, but the cup stopped halfway to her mouth. Wiese noticed a flash reaction. Her eyes seemed to register something ugly. They widened briefly and revealed a glimmer of terror. Then, her body began to blur. The same thing had happened the last time they talked. The thought crossed his mind that he might be getting too old for this kind of thing. He refocused and pushed on.

"Monahan was killed last night. You knew. Just now… I saw it in your eyes. Talk to me, Miss Franny. Can you identify the man who killed him?"

Franny seemed to make a deliberate decision, then slowly poured the water onto the floor.

"What?" Wiese said. "What are you trying to tell me?"

"Watch your step, sir. Slippery business, this. There's more here than meets the eye. Going to have to use the bloodhounds for this one."

*"Blood*hounds?" Solomon perked up. "In what way do we have to use bloodhounds? Can you tell me anything more specific in that vein?"

Franny pointed her index finger at him in a gesture one might make while playing charades, when another has guessed just the right word.

"You saw the killer, didn't you, Miss Franny?"

Her lips pursed and she stared straight ahead.

Oh God, Solomon thought. Don't let her clam up on me now.

"Can I get you some more water, Miss Franny?" he said, desperately trying to get any response. But it was no good. A curtain of silence had fallen in her glazed eyes and an odd hush had filled the room.

The frustrated detective dropped into a chair. He wondered how he could get an uncompromising transient to break the first commandment of the street– to keep silent. Especially this transient, who took the law to its extreme and rarely talked at all.

After a full forty-five seconds, Franny blurted out a curious phrase.

"They mostly come out after sunset, sir."

Wiese sat up straight. "Who, Miss Franny?" he said, beseechingly. "Who comes out at after sunset? The killer?"

"Not just *him,* sir. *Them* do. All of them."

CHAPTER 7

Friday, 9:03 P.M.
St. Laurue's lair

St. Laurue woke up in a blood sweat. "Father, is that you?"

His eyes darted around the dark bedroom of his luxurious high rise.

He was alone.

Still groggy, he strong willed himself out of the mighty grip of yet another suffocating vampiric dream. They were all the same. He was struggling with his father, the Marquis Antoine DeMalberet, and the Marquis had ended up dancing on his grave.

The vampire dragged himself out of bed and wandered over to the window. He pulled the two red velvet drapes apart and peered at the space that was once the Twin Towers.

He had always fancied the twin peaks a tribute of sorts to his kind, jutting out at the mouth of Manhattan, like two huge formidable fangs. How reassuring they had been.

And now... gone forever.

Mankind's modern heights always soothed his dark world. They cast such delicious shadows.

Turning from the window, he eyed the boxed manuscript on top of his desk. Things were going quite well, he thought. He had been able to speed write much of his life story before retiring. But aside from making progress with the book, he was also pleased to have found the boy.

"Fury," he spoke the name out loud, savoring its sound. It had been centuries since he'd been so fascinated by a dark beauty other than his own. The boy would be his protégé, his immortal son. And this time, he assured himself, he would not let his father destroy his new companion, like all the others. It was a cruel punishment– engineered and executed by DeMalberet– for having turned his little sister, Brigitte.

But enough was enough, he thought. This time he would brook no interference from his powerful magician of a dark father.

St. Laurue found the paper Fury had slipped him last night. It read, "Meet me tomorrow night at Nocturnal Rounds. Fury DeAdonis."

In the blink of an eye, he was walking along the city pier on his way to Preston's office, boxed manuscript in hand.

The nearby river filled him with its pungent smell, but even that could not dampen his spirits on this hot and humid night. Tonight, he'd present his partial manuscript to Press and then meet his Fury at Nocturnal Rounds.

Suddenly, he heard the frail voice calling for help. The whimpering sound fumed around him like a pneumatic drug.

Excitement quickly turned into hunger and early evening necessities demanded his attention. Not only the need to feed, but to satisfy an even greater addiction– the need to hunt.

He heard the anxious cry again. Breathing in its delicious trepidation, which served as his compass, he turned a corner and saw Elka.

She was a beautiful girl in her early twenties with long light brown hair and a very attractive body. She was also a young lady in trouble. A disheveled looking man with oil slicked black hair was about to attack her.

Instantly, St. Laurue dropped his boxed manuscript and lifted off the ground. He descended between the two in the guise of a Christ-like figure. After paralyzing the girl's tormentor with an icy glance, he commenced to float downward with his arms extended in a dramatic gesture of piety.

He willed Elka to see him as the Lord Jesus. An idea, he surmised, undoubtedly inspired from dining on the old priest's blood last night.

"You must not fear me," he spoke gently to her. "I am your Savior."

Elka immediately fell to her knees and began to pray to him.

Such purity and devotion, he thought. She reminded him of a former lover he'd had centuries before named Joan. As was the case then, he was so taken with this girl that, without further thought, he deemed her another worthy consort and lifted her into his arms to initiate the dark embrace.

They ascended upward. His left index fingernail centered on Elka's lower back. It transformed into a needle-like feeding organ and sucked her blood into his body. After the blood essence was absorbed, he pumped the girl's devitalized blood– now mixed with his own– through his right index finger-needle and back into her again.

As the girl's blood danced through him, he filled her mind with a powerful mental suggestion.

"I am your Sword. I am your Light. I am your Eternal Life."

He drank in the light brown haired beauty and absorbed her remembrances, her emotional life.

For a moment, St. Laurue thought he heard the growl of a wild beast, but being so fully involved, it seemed as insignificant as the distant buzzing of a fly. He wasn't prepared when the newborn vampire dealt him a swift blow and knocked him off his would-be bride.

St. Laurue seethed with a mighty rage. "Who deprives me of my pleasure!"

He turned and saw Elka's predator smirking at him. The creature's mouth widened into a vicious grin, sporting a set of sharp fangs.

Seeing the young man was a diseased newborn out to destroy him, St. Laurue– still masquerading as a latter day Christ– willed Elka to flee.

The girl took off, but he wasn't worried. His ancient blood ran through her veins. When the time was right, he'd call and she would come.

Meanwhile, Elka's stalker had transformed into a vision of terror.

St. Laurue was impressed.

The fledgling's eyes had turned magenta. His aura was thick and reddish yellow, leaving one with the impression of a bleeding pus filled wound. And although he looked as weighty as an iron coffin, he hovered above the river like a toy balloon, bubbling with green sores as he spoke.

"That comely little girl-pig was mine," the young vampire growled.

"Your name?" St. Laurue said softly, as would a gentle Christ.

"I am your mirror," the fledgling snarled.

"Then it looks like I'm going to have seven years of bad luck," St. Laurue said, willing a laser beam of silver blue light onto the newborn's face. The creature held his head and howled, then retaliated by hurling an industrial sized steel trash receptacle at St. Laurue, who sped aside just in time. The garbage bin smashed against a wooden shack. Lumber split and flew every which way. A piece of wood struck St. Laurue's face, just above his mouth. The girl's blood spilled over his lips and he became enraged. In a flash, he transformed from his Christ-like figure into a creature so vile in appearance that it was capable of inspiring instant terror in any onlooker.

The startled newborn backed off at first, then swaggered forth and laughed, mockingly. "So which are you... saint or sinner?"

St. Laurue's eyes flashed yellow-violet as he growled, "You tell me."

He raised a finger and made the steel cover of the trash bin hurl itself at the newborn, severing its head from its body.

The proud fledgling exploded into multicolored pieces, which vaporized, then disappeared into the nothingness from which it had risen.

All was quiet once more.

"That was a lark while it lasted," St. Laurue

said aloud, rubbing his hands together.

His wounded face healed, as he glanced at the river where the newborn had exploded, just to be sure the job was finished.

Oui, the vampire smiled and thought, that one would not be returning for an encore. The price of decapitation, followed by disintegration, was certain death for the undead.

And unlike the beheading of the old priest, there was no corpse to tuck away and hide afterward.

An atypical unsettled feeling came upon him as he walked over to where he had left his manuscript.

As he lifted up his partially written biography, his last thought repeated itself.

No corpse to tuck away and hide.

Then again, louder.

No corpse to tuck away and hide.

Tilting his head to one side, he tried to think why that idea gave him the queasy feeling that lately he'd been forgetting to do something.

CHAPTER 8

Friday, 10:13 P.M.
Preston's office

After having slept through most of the afternoon, Press focused on finishing up the day's work. He felt achy all over, but figured that was the price he had to pay for falling asleep in an awkward position at his desk.

"Good evening, Preston," St. Laurue said, suddenly appearing.

"My God!" Press said, practically falling out of his chair.

"You're in error again." The vampire flashed an incandescent smile.

Preston's first thought was to take flight, but then he looked into St. Laurue's eyes and, once again, felt a magnetic attraction as irresistible and seemingly inevitable as destiny itself.

It bothered him that such a calamitous chance meeting felt so exhilarating and foreordained.

Press jumped in his chair when the vampire tossed the boxed manuscript onto the desk with a loud thump, almost upsetting the publisher's half filled coffee cup.

"The book," the vampire proudly stated.

Press leaned forward. "You've been busy."

"I'd judge it to be about half finished."

Press opened the box and flipped through the loose pages. On first glance, the story seemed first rate, but Press saw that it would need editing. His face must have disclosed the critical appraisal.

"There's a problem?" St. Laurue said.

"No, certainly not," Press said quickly. "Not a big one in any case."

St. Laurue drew nearer. "Meaning?"

Preston's voice cracked. "You know, it's not at all unusual for an inexperienced author to have a…" He shifted uncomfortably in his seat.

"Oui?"

Press could feel his body temperature rising by degrees. "What I mean is, you could use a…"

"A what!" The vampire demanded.

"A ghost… *writer*, that is…"

The room went cold, then hot as the *nosferatu* approached. Press felt like a squirming guppy on a wet rug being eyed by a hungry cat. He looked at St. Laurue and was unnerved even further.

With each step, the vampire's facial features and body parts mutated into a variety of grotesque images, each one more frightening than the last.

When the morphing energy vortex reached him, Press feared he was about to be absorbed and consumed. To his great relief, St. Laurue suddenly stood by his desk, laughing so loud that it shook the walls of the office, threatening to shatter the windowpane.

"A *ghostwriter?*"

Press loosened his collar, and tried to explain, "It'd help immensely, especially with the…"

"And if I disagree?" St. Laurue interrupted.

"tightening," Press plowed on, "and… uh… maintaining the overall integrity of the…"

"Enough! Stop! It's all right," St. Laurue said with an annoyed looking imperious wave. "I agree. But only on *one* condition."

Press gripped his chair and wondered what eccentric condition the vampire would demand, and might it involve the letting of blood?

"The mortal must meet with my approval," St. Laurue said. "If I'm to protect him, he must appeal to me."

"What do you mean, 'protect him?' "

"Press, don't be naïve. In this book, I've spoken of things forbidden. The ancients of my kind may seek revenge. This so-called 'ghost' may very well be signing his own death warrant."

"Unless he has your protection."

"Naturally." St. Laurue folded his arms across his chest.

Press took a sip of his coffee, trying to appear relaxed, which was definitely not the case.

"Am *I* in jeopardy when this book comes out?"

He was feeling self conscious and didn't want to appear too worried, so he casually took another sip of coffee.

"You are, of course," St. Laurue said candidly.

Press choked on his coffee. His head began to spin. He closed his eyes and pinched the bridge of his nose.

Suddenly, he felt St. Laurue's hands cup both sides of his face and lift him off the chair. When he opened his eyes, he saw his own reflection in the vampire's glowing yellow-violet orbs.

"Do you think I'd let anyone, whether living,

dead or undead, harm you?" St. Laurue said softly, placing a frosty kiss on Preston's forehead.

Despite the sinking feeling in his stomach, Press began to feel a bit reassured. Then, all of a sudden, the vampire abruptly backed away from him, looking indignant.

What now? Press thought.

He followed St. Laurue's gaze and nearly fainted when he saw Detective Solomon Wiese standing in the doorway.

CHAPTER 9

St. Laurue smelled the stench of law and order around the older man in the doorway, as one would smell a poisoned rat, trapped inside a wall after several days.

What did this man have to do with Press?

One glance at his minion and he knew. Press had been interrogated by the detective and had disclosed nothing.

Trés bein, the vampire thought, as he watched Solomon shuffle into the office. This would be most entertaining.

One of his favorite games was sizing up the opposition, *unbeknownst* to the opposition.

"Oh boy," Solomon said to Press. "Here I go again, interrupting as usual. Look. I'll just wait in the hall until you two are…"

"No," Press said, nervously, "…uh… I mean, come on in."

Wiese thrust out his hand to St. Laurue. "I don't think I've had the pleasure of making your acquaintance."

"I assure you, the pleasure is all mine," the vampire said and bowed briskly, wondering how much the lawman had seen or heard.

Wiese dropped his hand just as Press launched into what sounded more like an explanation than an introduction. "Solomon Wiese, may I introduce you to Beagles' newest and most eccentric author, Mr. Gérard Arnaud St. Laurue."

"Call me Solly," Wiese said. "An author, huh?

And so young. If you don't mind my asking, what's your book about, Mr. St. Laurue?"

"Family ties," the vampire said quietly, with a mischievous grin.

"Family, huh?" the delighted detective repeated, looking impressed. "That's important. Have I seen any of your other books?"

"It's unlikely that you have, detective." St. Laurue said, and sat in a chair, handling the situation with his usual savoir-faire. "You see, this is my first."

"Wonderful." Wiese sat next to him. "By the way, how did you know I'm a detective?"

"Oh, that's my bad," Press interrupted, trying to cover for the vampire. "I've told him about... uh... how I was questioned after the alley murders and all."

St. Laurue calmly draped one leg over the other in amusement.

"You've heard?" Solomon said, turning toward St. Laurue.

"Oui. I was having breakfast. Naturally, after that, I was unable to stomach one bite more."

"That's understandable," Solomon said. "It *was* pretty gruesome."

"Still, Detective Wiese," St. Laurue said, with an impish sparkle in his eyes. "I'd think twice before incarcerating Preston. After all, he's *only* a publisher and not an actual *hardened* criminal."

Wiese chuckled. "Very clever. By the way, Mr. St. Laurue, that accent... Your family, they came from Europe?"

"France."

"Still living?"

"In the true sense of the word, no."

"Oh, I get you. They're alive in your memories. I can relate. My brother and I were separated during the Holocaust. I'm still trying to find out if he survived. Everyday, I remember."

"A similar occurrence happened to me. I was pried from my little sister," St. Laurue said, recalling how his father had separated them after discovering that he had turned Brigitte into a vampire. "I was distraught without her. Naturally, this was not during the Holocaust."

"Naturally. You should only thank God that you're way too young to remember it. I'm not saying we should forget mind you, but to remember in such great detail a person could live without, if you know what I mean."

"As it happens, I *am* somewhat familiar with the Holocaust period. The death camps have always fascinated me. I've made a... how would you say... 'hands-on' study of that singularly bloody period. Research, you know."

"Then you know what I mean: the violence, the bloodshed."

"Many a life drained."

"And for what?"

"Savage survival," St. Laurue offered, and lifted his forefinger.

" 'Savage survival,' " Wiese echoed. "You may've hit on something there. The survival of savages. That's what it all boils down to, doesn't it? Say, in your studies, you never ran across a guy named Maury Wiese, did you? Probably not. What's the chances, right? Wait a minute. I've got an old picture from just before World War Two."

Solomon pulled out a yellowing wallet sized photo of his brother and gave it to St. Laurue.

The vampire held it and closed his eyes.

His keen memory brought up images, circa Nineteen Forty-Three–

A German officer insulted him. He followed the mortal home and caught the nazi assaulting an innocent young Jewish boy. He drained the stormtrooper's blood, then uncharacteristically took pity on the boy and let him go, but not before he gave the lad a powerful hypnotic command– 'Your mind is totally blank. You have no name, no history, no previous memory before this moment.' The boy's name was Maury Wiese.

St. Laurue's reverie was interrupted when Wiese cleared his throat.

The vampire opened his eyes and made them flash yellow-violet for a second, playing with the detective's mind.

Wiese blinked, then gawked.

Press stood up and quickly moved to the side of his desk.

St. Laurue knew his minion was readying himself for whatever reaction Wiese had.

"Something?" the vampire questioned them with a wicked smile.

"No. Nothing," Wiese said, rubbing his eyes. "The old peepers play tricks on me now and then. I thought I saw..." Solomon turned to Press. "Did his eyes turn a different color?"

"Different color?" Press squeaked out. "Why no. I don't think…"

Wiese said, "But you jumped out of your seat like you saw…?"

"I… uh… I *always* do that," Press said, sitting on the edge on his desk. "I'm antsy. Been that way since I was a kid."

"Anyway," the detective pointed to the photograph in St. Laurue's hand, "my brother Maury was quite a guy, no?"

St. Laurue patted Wiese's arm. "I'm sure I would have enjoyed his company. Particularly, if he was half as charming as his younger brother."

"Why, thank you," Solomon said, then turned to Preston. "You're lucky to be working with such a personable young man. Maury was like that too. Instant friends with everybody. Hey, Press, take a look. You're shoelace is untied."

Press looked down. His laces were tied.

"Got ya," Solomon said and laughed. "That was Maury's favorite joke. He could always get me with that one."

Preston forced a grin and retied his shoe laces anyway– an action which made St. Laurue and the detective chuckle out loud.

"Such a good natured fellow, Maury was," Wiese continued. "But then, life happened. The greed, the lust, the violence."

Press chimed in randomly, "The world isn't what it used to be."

"How true," Solomon said. "We have to learn

to be kinder to one another. Am I right?"

St. Laurue handed the photo back to Wiese, saying, "Kindness either runs in the blood, or not. Your brother was very kind. I can tell. He had an extraordinarily delicious warmth in his eyes."

"...uh ...yeah, I guess you're right," Solomon said. "They broke the mold after Maury. Listen, if by any chance you come across my brother in your research work, you'll let me know?"

St. Laurue stood up. "It's a promise."

"I appreciate that," Solomon said, also rising.

"Gentlemen, I must excuse myself. I have a late night rendezvous."

"Ah, to be young and in love," Solomon said. "Right, Press?"

"Right. Young and..." Press started, but was cut off by the vampire.

"Well, Solly, it was a pleasure to have met you. Our paths will cross again. I'm sure of it."

"Hey. If you ever need any tips on a crime story, don't be shy. With the stories I know, believe me, I could write a book or three."

As the detective and the vampire shook hands, St. Laurue searched Solomon's eyes for a spark of recognition. Did the detective suspect the truth about him? Was he at risk of exposure?

No. There was nothing in Wiese's eyes that told him he had to worry.

This mortal, although more intelligent than he pretended to be, was not used to thinking beyond hard evidence and police lab results.

In an odd way, he and the detective were very

much alike.

They were both hunters of men, both involved in violence and bloodshed, and they both treasured their sibling.

Most amusing. Who'd have guessed that they would have so much in common? What a shame, he thought, if Wiese got on to him.

The vampire genuinely liked the man.

"Press," St. Laurue said sharply, turning to him. "I'll check in to see what progress you've made in hiring my ghost." He turned back to Wiese and said, "Publishing is an odd business, *oui?*"

"And getting odder by the minute," Press added. "By the way, I've already got someone in mind to ghost your book. His name's Kyle Riordan. An old college buddy. I'll give him a call."

"Riordan, you say? That would be splendid. I have a good feeling about the man. I want him. Now gentlemen, I must bid you adieu."

St. Laurue turned and exited the office.

❦❦❦❦❦❦❦❦❦❦

Wiese was about to sit again, but realized he hadn't given the author a way of reaching him. He rushed into the hall.

"Mr. St. Laurue, wait. Are you there? I wanted to give you my num–"

He stopped mid-sentence and looked up and down the corridor.

The vampire was nowhere to be seen.

Solomon was bewildered and let out with an exasperated sigh.

He stepped back into the office.

"Where'd he go so quick?" he asked Press. "The guy just disappeared."

"The stairwell?" Press offered.

"Oh. Maybe that explains it. Nice man. Next time you see him, you'll remember to give him my phone number just in case he digs up something about Maury?"

Press took out a white handkerchief and wiped the perspiration off of his brow.

"Consider it done, Solly."

"Where's your red handkerchief?" Wiese said.

"What red...?"

Solomon looked at Press questioningly.

"Oh, I ..."

"You ran out of the reds... You changed your color scheme... You... Well, what does it matter when you got sweat dripping from your face like that? Am I right?"

"Right," Press answered quickly.

"By the way," the detective continued, "St. Laurue disappears so fast all the time?"

"Sometimes even faster."

"*Faster?*" Wiese asked, with a raised eyebrow.

CHAPTER 10

Although it was nerve-racking, Press felt better now that Wiese had met St. Laurue.

Someone else had seen and heard and touched the vampire, he thought.

The monster was real, not just a figment of his fatigued fiction worn imagination.

That part was a relief. On the other hand, now he had to face an experienced New York police detective who probably had more questions than a inquisitive schoolboy attempting to comprehend a James Joyce novel.

"It's late," Press said. "I was just about to pack it in for the night."

"This'll only take a few minutes." Wiese assured him. "Now, about Father Monahan. Poor guy had his head cut off. You were the last to talk to him and I was wondering if the good Father might've said something last night that could give us a clue as to what happened."

"I'm not sure I can remember."

"Who can? I couldn't tell you what I had for dinner tonight. But try a little. What did Monahan say last night? Exactly."

"He said what priests usually say. Only it turned out–"

Press could feel the horror of last night flood back into his mind.

"You were saying, 'Only it turned out...' " Solomon prompted him.

"Huh?"

"You remembered something? You said, 'Only it turned out…' "

"Oh… Sorry, it's gone."

Wiese coached again. "You had a problem, and the priest said…"

"He sat beside me… and then…" Press jerked his head and began to perspire.

It all came back to him: the ghastly image of Monahan changing into St. Laurue, the torture he had suffered under the clutch of the demon, the malevolent laughter resounding through St. Michael's, the vampire's final admonition, 'There is no sanctuary from me.'

"You okay?" Solomon said.

"No, actually. I'm feeling achy all over and I'm really tired."

"Probably the summer flu. It's going around. By the way, how's that cut on your neck?"

"What? Oh, my neck? Just a scratch. One of the cats."

Wiese gave him a look. "I thought you cut yourself shaving?"

"Yeah. Right. I'm always doing that. Then, one of our cats took a swipe at me while I was playing with them."

"It looks a little infected."

"It'll heal eventually. Thanks for asking."

"Glad to hear it. Now, this Monahan thing. He mentioned where he was earlier in the evening?"

"No. We didn't talk long. He comforted me, then disappeared."

"He *comforted* you?"

"Yeah. I felt better."

"But the report said you were on the steps of St. Michael's and... how did it go? You were 'dazed and confused, with uncontrollable trembling.' "

"Right. It came and went."

Solomon raised an eyebrow and pulled his chair closer to the desk.

"You're not holding back on me, are you?"

Press squirmed uncomfortably in his chair. "Well..." he finally said. "After Monahan left, something rather strange *did* happen."

Solomon perked up. "Why don't you tell me about it?"

"It was crazy, though. You're not going to believe me."

Wiese got up from his chair. He went over and patted Press on the back.

"Try me. My wife, Rita. She's always telling me how gullible I am. I argue with her all the time about it. But maybe she's right? Who knows? So tell me. I might believe you."

"Okay. I heard these footsteps. Like somebody had gotten up and walked out of the church. Only, no one was visibly there except for me."

"Invisible people we got now?" Solomon shrugged and began to pace the publisher's office.

"It was a crazy night," Press said.

"You're *sure* you heard?"

"I heard."

"You think someone else was in the church?"

"Yes, I'm certain of it."

"I see."

"But that's just my point," Press said. "There was nothing to see."

Solomon stopped pacing and rolled his eyes. "But that *nothing* was actually *there*, only you couldn't see it."

"Solly. There were footsteps. No kidding. It was strange."

"I think I've got it. Footsteps, but no feet. Let me ask you another question, seeing as how we've cleared up so much already. You ever heard of a group called the Daemonion Council?"

"No. Should I have?"

"Not necessarily. Don't worry about it."

"Solly, trust me. I've told you all I can."

"But have you told me all you know? Listen, you're tired, not feeling too well. We should both go home and get some rest."

The detective's beeper went off.

"Mind if I use the phone?" Wiese reached for the desk phone and dialed the precinct. "Barrows there? Yeah. Where. Nocturnal Rounds? Where all the goth kids hang out? What's a bag lady doing there? All right. Be right over. You got backup? Good enough. Give me, say, twenty minutes." Solomon hung up the phone.

"I hate to question and run, but I have to go to a sex club."

"Nocturnal Rounds?" Press said.

"You've been there?"

"No. Why would a happily married man go to a place like that?"

"I'm happily married and I'm going," Wiese

said. "In the line of duty, of course. But I don't judge. Sgt. Barrows goes. Of course, he's on duty, too. Undercover narcotics unit."

"Well I don't go."

"Who knows? Maybe you should?"

"Sex in public places is not my thing."

"Naturally not," the detective continued. "By the way, is Mr. St. Laurue homosexual?"

Press heaved a sigh and threw his hands in the air. "I don't know."

"For a second, when he talked about Maury–about his *delicious* eyes and all– So I figured I'd ask to see if you knew the score. You're lovers, am I right?"

"No!"

"When I got here, it sort of looked like you two were embracing."

"I don't know what you're talking about." Press said. "Let's get out of here." He grabbed his jacket and turned off the office lights. On the way down in the elevator, Wiese delved further.

"One more question, Press. That is, if you don't mind?"

"Why not?" Press said, slowly shaking his head from side to side.

"You said Mr. St. Laurue was an eccentric author. I agree. So my question is, what do you mean? He's eccentric how? In what way?"

"What did *you* notice?"

"Well. He's young, but there's an old air about him, a kind of refined stature. You can hear it when he speaks. There's a formality. When I was a small kid in Germany before the war, there were plenty of old timers from World War One who gave off that kind of scent. Know what I'm saying?"

"I think so," Press said.

"And by the way, did you happen to notice the red silk handkerchief in his shirt pocket? Just like the bloodstained one we got from you? Again, old timer stuff, you get what I mean?"

Preston was flustered. He knew this might be his last opportunity to expose the vampire. But was that a wise thing to do? Maybe he could say something subtle, yet telling. His mind raced. It grabbed at several phrases, but none seemed right.

By the time they reached the sidewalk in front of the office building, he was just staring at the detective and saying nothing.

"Well, it's late," Wiese said, after an uneasy silence. "Can I drop you off at the train?"

"No. Thanks. I'll walk."

Press gave Wiese a brief glance, feeling like a drowning man going down for the third time.

The detective reached out for him. "How can I help if you won't talk to me?"

"Look. I... I just need to clear my head. Would that be okay?"

"Okay. Sure. By all means, clear your head all you want. But we've got to be honest with each other. Am I right or am I right?"

"I guess," Press said and pocketed his hands.

"Oh. Before I forget. Mr. St. Laurue knew I was Maury's *younger* brother. How did he know that? I didn't say, did I?"

"Solly, I don't know how he knows the things he knows, or does what he does. He just waltzed into my office last night off the streets."

"Last night?" Wiese tilted his head in surprise. "Is maybe Mr. St. Laurue the cause of those inner struggles you've been having recently?"

"Look," Press said. "I'm too tired to think right now. I need rest."

The publisher turned away from Wiese, hoping to avoid any further questions, but Solomon gently tugged him back by the crook of his elbow.

"Forgive me my friend. Before you go. You were going to mention, this Mr. St. Laurue, he's eccentric how?"

Press stared at Solomon thinking it was now or never. But what to say? How to say it? His mind began to spin. Take a couple of deep breaths. That should help. Shouldn't it?

Wiese tugged again at his elbow.

"In what particular way," the detective asked again, "is Mr. St. Laurue eccentric?"

"He only comes out after dark." The words flew out of Preston's mouth and were as much of a surprise to him as they might have been to the detective. Had he said too much? Would he be forced to confess more?

To his great relief, Wiese didn't question the statement, but silently stroked his chin as if deep in thought. "Is that so," Wiese finally said.

"Like I said… eccentric," Press said.

He turned and quickly headed for the train back to New Jersey, desperately yearning for the comfort and safety of his home and family.

Solomon got into his unmarked car and drove to Nocturnal Rounds.

"He only comes out after dark."

He repeated the statement over and over, as he maneuvered the busy city streets.

Preston's comment reminded him of something Franny, the bag lady, had said earlier that afternoon. But what was it?

Swimming in thought, he took a right and accidentally cut off a hurried taxi cab.

The night-shift cabbie leaned on the horn, screamed an obscenity and gave him the finger.

It was then that Solomon remembered what Miss Franny had said.

"They mostly come out after sunset."

The only problem was, Wiese didn't have a clue as to who *they* were.

CHAPTER 11

Friday, 10:44 P.M.
the New Jersey Turnpike

Jamie loved the thrill of having sex with strangers. Personal histories were not asked for, and hopefully not offered.

He preferred his lovers to be invisible.

That said, he was an average looking boy: not plain, not striking, slightly on the thin side, but well toned. Long chestnut hair hung in a pony tail. In his own eyes, he wasn't tall. Maybe that's why the boy was always trying to measure up.

So far as sex was concerned, at first, one partner was enough. But after a couple of years, only nameless numbers in long lines satisfied his passions. Between all the sex partners and all the drugs, the boy grew numb and lost his capacity to feel anything at all. Most recently, the twenty-two-year-old had been thinking that he wouldn't even mind death, as long as he could *feel* it coming.

It was only when two significant men in Jamie's life died that sorrow resuscitated the boy's body and he could feel again.

Smoking a joint while veering off the New Jersey Turnpike on his way into Manhattan, Jamie thought about his earlier conversation with the writer, Kyle Riordan, at *Moondoggies,* a bar on the Jersey shore.

"You don't get it, Kyle. I can *feel* again," Jamie said. "I'm released by these two deaths."

"Your lover's dead. Your father's dead. What are you doing here in Jersey? Go back to New York. Are you staying at your mom's?"

"No way. Edward booked me a room uptown at the Merriweather."

"Check out. Go comfort your mother."

"Miss Kitty? That's the last thing I need. After the funeral this morning, she's probably non-stop bead mumbling."

"Have a little bit of compassion. The woman just lost her husband."

"Yeah. An arrogant prick who spent his whole lifetime thinking he was the most important man in the world."

"Is that why you spend yours thinking you're the least?"

"Look Kyle, you can stow the philosophical crap. I'm in mourning."

"Oh, I see. That's why you're here at the bar orgy shopping."

"As a matter of fact, I came to make a drug drop. And don't knock group action unless you've tried it."

"What about AIDS? You're not thinking."

"Fuck thinking. My lover's dead, my father's dead, and someday I'll be dead, but it won't be from fucking thinking."

"Don't try so hard. Life happens."

"Only if you make it."

Jamie gripped the steering wheel, shook his head, and took another hit off his joint. He cranked up his CD player and pressed hard on the gas pedal.

While racing through the Lincoln Tunnel listening to the Stones, all he wanted was the peaceful oblivion of uninterrupted mindless sex.

Nocturnal Rounds, he thought. That's where he'd go. If he had his way, a number of nameless hot bodies were going to get real lucky in the downstairs back room tonight.

Friday, 11:05 P.M.
Brooklyn

Fury DeAdonis was half naked on his bed. Muffled sighs and groans escaped his sensuous lips, as he dreamed of skeletons dancing over a grave. Looking into the hole in the earth, he saw himself. His dead body-double was on its back, eyes closed and hands folded across the chest. The rattling bone janglers invited his dead self out of the grave and onto a dance floor. Then, Fury's doppelgänger danced with death to the strains of a haunting Romanian rhapsody.

A distant voice called him back to his sweltering bedroom. "Furio!" Gina's Italian accent had a way of grating on her son. "You asleep?"

The bedroom door flung open and Fury shielded his eyes from the assaulting shaft of light. "Shut the door, Ma. I was dreaming."

Mrs. DeAdonis' silhouette drooped in the doorway. The fifty-year-old Italian woman immigrated to and got married in the United States, but doggedly held on to the old ways. Since her husband's death, the boy had become her life. But the woman, like her speech, was broken.

"Yeah. You some big dreamer," Gina said. "You did the homework for tomorrow, eh?"

Fury put his head under the pillow and complained loudly, "Ma! Come on! It's Friday night, ya know? No school tomorrow? Besides, summer vacation's in a week so who gives a rat's ass anyway?"

"Wat'cha you mouth," said the angry silhouette, while raising a fist. "Tonight, you stay home. No more running all night long in the streets like a crazy little kid. You hear?"

"Yeah, yeah, I hear." He flung the pillow onto the floor. "I hear you everyday of my life."

"Smart mouth. I should come in there and give you a good smack."

"Just shut the door. Okay?"

"Why you no come to mass with me Sunday morning, eh?"

"To St. Michael's in Manhattan? Forget about it. Why don't you go to mass here in Brooklyn like a normal person?"

"I got married at St. Michael's. You come Sunday. What do you think, the church will fall down on your head?"

"Sure Ma, the church is gonna fall on my head. Now close the door."

"Next week we start a novena together for your dead father, eh?"

"I got a lot stuff to do next week," he said with a groan.

"You too good to pray for your father?"

"You pray... for both of us."

"This city is no good. One day, we gonna move to Italy."

"Whatever."

She mumbled something in Italian, and slammed the door.

Stay in tonight, Fury thought, as he turned on his bedside lamp. Yeah right? Not even! Especially since he might meet up with the power dude from the alley last night.

The teen shivered with anticipation, as he bounced out of bed and looked into the full length mirror, examining his body.

He flexed his well toned biceps, then strutted closer to the mirror and pulled back his top lip, exposing his upper teeth. "Grrrrrr," he roared aloud, then began to laugh so hard that he had to hold his sides. He jumped up on the bed and used it like a trampoline, trying to defy gravity.

Knowing his mother would soon be asleep in front of the TV, the sixteen-year-old got dressed. He'd have to look really exceptional tonight, he thought. He put on his white tee-shirt– the tight one that looked so cool under the black lights– and his baggy jeans, kind of like the ones his new friend from last night wore. Now for the hair! He grabbed a tube of gel and squeezed a glob of it onto his hands and worked it into his scalp. Yeah, he thought, as he looked into the mirror and admired the shine on his mane from all sides. Look, ma. You gave birth to a freakin' movie star!

When he heard Gina snoring, he tip-toed out of

the apartment and hopped the "A" train over to the club in Manhattan.

Nocturnal Rounds was his life now. There, he felt accepted. There, he was powerful. He was adored. Everyone wanted him. There, he wasn't just a crazy little kid.

Friday, 11:45 P.M.
Nocturnal Rounds

St. Laurue hoofed through the alley and into the club to find Fury.

The vampire drifted through the demimonde, drinking in life. With each brief brush, he sipped at the fountain of human emotions. Each chance chafe filled him with a passion that could, if he'd allow it, throw him into a wild feeding frenzy. But this club was not only popular with the living, the dangerous dead were there as well.

Most *nosferatu* would give their eye teeth for the young bloods that gathered at the club. Some of the less seasoned undead would accommodate their quarry and dance. Some targeted their prey, gave a wink and a nod, then quickly exited, drawing their victims along with them in their wake. Some walking corpses crouched in dark corners and spun hypnotic webs to ensnare any passerby. Several of the more hoary bloodsuckers posed like Greek statues by the bar, but their ancient eyes were frenetic with fiery focus, intent on inflaming some young mortal moth.

Numerous techniques were practiced, but it all

amounted to the same madness. One could see it in their eyes, all a little too bright, all with the same frenzied gaze– the look of hungry predators.

The undead one brushed against a young girl with cruel gray eyes and felt himself being drained dry of every human emotion he had just imbibed.

The girl's cold eyes started to glow.

Her jaw dropped. She bared her fangs. The undercurrent of a menacing growl worked its way up from her bowels.

St. Laurue saw she was a fledgling vampire and had mistaken him for a mortal. How odd a vampire's lot was, he mused. We're so eminently immortal, yet, given enough time, can become so frighteningly human.

The ancient one was about to teach the newcomer a lesson, when an older man instantly appeared by the girl's side and whispered in her ear. The girl suddenly became afraid and bowed before St. Laurue. Then, she and her friend both vanished into the throng of dancing club kids.

St. Laurue was amused. Clearly his reputation had preceded him. Deference was being paid. Fear always produced this sort of submissive ass-kissing. It was an obeisance to which, throughout the centuries, he'd become arrogantly accustomed.

Remembering his agenda, St. Laurue tuned in and sensed that Fury hadn't yet arrived at the club. Not used to being kept waiting, he restlessly moved through the crowd again.

Nocturnal Rounds was a club alive, like a racing human heart.

The patrons moved as one, blending into a solitary vital heartbeat.

Blood spore surged through the air, like rock music pumping out of the speakers.

The more he connected with the mob, the more excessive his hunger grew.

This wasn't good, he thought.

He had to be in control when he met Fury. He had to be charming, so as not to put off the boy.

With a little bit of patience and a lot of good timing, Fury could be skillfully fashioned into a most trustworthy consort and a vigilant defender.

But what about now? the hunger screamed from inside of his mind.

Unable to deny it, he made his way downstairs to the back room.

CHAPTER 12

Franny sat on her ample rump at the dead end of the crowded alley just outside Nocturnal Rounds.

Gothic club kids filled the alley, smoking, laughing, swearing, puking and hooking up. Many of the club kids were dressed in black, had white powdered faces with either maroon or black lipstick.

Loud rock music intermittently invaded the vicinity, as patrons used the club's alley entrance.

Perfect, Franny thought. Her prearranged meeting with Ashley and Raphael wouldn't attract undue attention. The bag lady rummaged through her canvas sack, found two airline tickets, and put them within easy reach. Just as she finished, she saw her co-agents enter the street end of the alley and come toward her through the crowd.

A drunken girl with a false set of bloody fangs suddenly stuck her face in front of Franny. The agent's heart skipped a beat, but she quickly realized there was no real threat. She snorted and made a hideous face. It worked. The girl giggled and moved on, just as Franny had hoped.

Meanwhile, Ashley and Raphael were drawing near. Franny signaled them to approach and said, "Fresh fish at the market tonight."

Ashley recognized the secret code. "St. Laurue's here already?"

"The piranha swam in fifteen minutes ago."

"What about Wiese?" Ashley said, nervously.

"Some undercover cops followed me here. I mentally suggested they contact Wiese. He's on his way, no doubt."

Raphael asked Franny, "But how did you know that St. Laurue would come to Nocturnal Rounds?"

"While invisible in the alleyway last night, I saw Fury scribble a note asking the vampire to meet him here tonight. I knew he'd show. Obviously, he wants the boy for a minion. If he didn't, the lad would be dead like his mates. St. Laurue is here tonight to claim his Fury."

Raphael smiled at Ashley and said, "A good man is hard to find."

"Is that so?" Ashley nudged the handsome twenty-three-year-old in the ribs with her elbow. He faded back to avoid her arm, then maneuvered behind her and pulled her body close to his.

They both laughed.

"Quiet, you'll draw attention," Franny said. "Here's two plane tickets back to Scotland for tomorrow at noon. I'll follow, after I tie a few things together properly."

"That's just peachy with me," Raphael said. "I miss the tranquility of Mother's libraries." He indicated the alley, packed with night people. The smell of marijuana saturated the place. "This is all too much for me. Guess I'm just a numbers nerd at heart. Don't much care for this fieldwork bit."

"Stay alert. You get sloppy, you get killed," Franny said to Raphael, then focused on Ashley. "The most important part of the assignment begins when the detective gets here."

"Point the vampire out to Detective Wiese," Raphael said in a monotone voice, pretending to be a programmed robot.

"And take care that St. Laurue doesn't see you do it," Franny warned them. "He's one of the most dangerous of his kind. After killing the three in the alley last night, he butchered a priest. I was invisible, but tired. I'm afraid Bevan Preston, his new minion, heard me as I exited St. Michael's."

Raphael shuddered. "All this psychic stuff weirds me out."

"St. Laurue has taken another minion?" Ashley said, alarmed.

"Yes," Franny said. "A publisher."

Ashley huffed. "Oh Lord, how many bloody minions does he need?"

"He'll take as many as he wants. The vampire will chose those he can trust, those whose minds can be manipulated."

"Ultra-weird," Raphael added.

"That could complicate things," Ashley said.

Franny corrected her. "Not particularly. I'm going to try and make Mr. Preston an ally."

A skirmish broke out halfway down the alley by the club entrance. The bouncers were tossing out a group of disorderly kids. Various insults and threats were traded. The vociferous disruption reminded Franny to pay attention to the job at hand.

"If all goes well," she continued, "Wiese will know who and *what* his killer is tonight."

"And if not," Raphael said jokingly to Ashley, "it's curtains!"

"That's not funny, Raphael," Ashley poked him again.

He grinned and gave her a peck on the cheek.

"Look sharp," Franny said, "and by tomorrow night, you'll be back at Mother safe and sound."

Raphael snuggled closer to Ashley and said, "Right. Safe and sound and *married*."

"What's this?" Franny said.

"We've set the date," Ashley said to Franny. "We're getting married a week from today." Ashley knelt down to Franny and touched her cheek. "You get back safe and sound, too. We can't have our wedding without the Maid of Honor, can we?"

"I'll be there, children," Franny said, beaming at the two. But her thoughts were telling a different story. True, she wanted to get back, but not before she had St. Laurue in tow, as originally planned. She just couldn't abort her mission so close to successful completion, no matter what Priggins and the Daemonion Council's Board had decided.

Suddenly, Franny's solar plexus tightened. She turned and scanned the front end of the alley. He was here. Her eyes widened and her body blurred as she began to cloak her presence.

"Franny?" Ashley said, urgently. "What is it?"

"Look," Franny said, nodding toward the street end of the alley.

Ashley turned and saw the older man coming through the crowd. By the time she turned back, the bag lady was invisible. Franny's disembodied voice urged, "Quickly, hide behind Raphael. Now!"

Ashley slid behind her betrothed and the three agents watched as Detective Wiese flashed his badge and walked into Nocturnal Rounds.

CHAPTER 13

Jamie slid through the crowded alley and entered Nocturnal Rounds.

"Well, if it ain't bisexual Betty," said Rocky Vanos, the doorman.

He handed Vanos the Friday night admission.

"How's the back room tonight?"

"Packed," Rocky said. "Just how you like it, punk. And another thing, the only way drugs get past this door is ingested."

"I'm clean, I swear."

"You're lucky I'm letting you back in."

"We came to an agreement, remember?"

"Kid, you're just another piece of tail to me. It's *my* butt on the line if the club gets busted."

Jamie began to plead. "Aw, come on, man…"

"Whatever," Rocky mumbled, as he rang up the cash register and took the next patron's cash.

Jamie dashed past a few club kids, purposely ignoring them. Old tricks, he thought. Ten minute quickies from other lonely nights. He hoped they wouldn't follow him downstairs.

Lighting up a joint, he began to prowl the back room and wondered what was wrong with him. Why did this hellish looking dump feel like his only salvation? When he was a kid, his parents had taken him to the Luray Caverns on his first out-of-state vacation. The caverns thrilled him much in the same way the back room did. He saw the similarities. Thick poles jutted up from the cement floor and plowed into the ceiling. Stalls with swinging saloon doors lined both sides of the six foot wide hall like little caves.

A droning dry ice machine pumped the place with fog. With all the cigarette smoke, disco fog, and wall mirrors, it was almost impossible to tell if you were cruising a real person or just a reflected image– and if you were stoned enough, you could easily wind up chasing yourself.

Drawing another lung full of marijuana, Jamie stepped into the fog.

The back room was a divine kingdom, where he could find himself, while losing himself. The congregation attended services in a baptismal naked innocent. As Jamie moved on, faces appeared and disappeared, like miracles in the mist. Hallowed hands reached out through mystical clouds. Flesh partook of flesh in open stalls, drawing voyeurs, peering, pounding, and poking. An organic moaning mass of starving sexuality celebrated in rapture, the blind leading the blind, humping its way toward the ecstasy of sexual communion.

Jamie navigated around a pole and bumped into a woman, wearing nothing but a black leather belt and thick fishnet stockings. She waved her whip and glared at him. He backed off gently. A fat man with beady eyes rushed out of the fog like a runaway locomotive and nearly knocked him over. At the locker area, Jamie took one last toke off his joint, tossed it to the floor, then stripped and stashed his clothes.

This was Jamie's church and Mass was in progress. He joined in the service, ready to worship.

Wiese appraised the goth club– It was too loud, too crowded and he was uncomfortable with the black leather muzzles, jock straps, hand cuffs, slings, whips and heavy iron chains that decorated the main floor's walls.

But none of that mattered to him right now. He had a serial killer to catch and was wondering where to begin. With all these club kids– these half naked dancing crazies dressed in black, with the dyed hair, or no hair, wearing tattoos, rings and pins all over their bodies, frantically enacting their wild tribal-like rituals– it'd be difficult if not impossible to figure which one among them was a bloodthirsty, homicidal maniac.

To Solomon, they all looked game.

Sgt. Barrows sidled up to him. "Downstairs, there's a back room where you can have sex."

"Was that a proposition?" Wiese joked.

"I'm just saying that *I'd* better be the one to stake it out."

"Knock yourself out, kid," Wiese said, but his smile betrayed a sharp undercurrent of tension. "The precinct radioed me on my way over. Got another phone tip from the same woman, whoever she is. The perp should be here tonight. A caucasian male. Around eighteen. Almost six foot tall. Good build. Longish auburn hair. Handsome. That's what the caller says, but who knows what's real? Listen up. You see any funny business, call for backup pronto. This guy's out for blood. Got it?"

"Right."

"And John, before you go downstairs, put a man on each exit."

"Done." Barrows slipped off.

Wiese stood alone in the middle of the frenzied horde, feeling about as snug as a snowman caught in a four alarm fire. He thought of Rita. He could just imagine how she'd kid him about this crazy place when he'd tell her about it later. These club kids, he thought, they only wanted to belong. So who didn't? They needed friends, a loving family. But why search in such a place? Maybe Ritzy wouldn't kid about this place so much after all, he decided. Maybe she'd feel exactly what he was feeling now. Compassion. Suddenly, he felt a warm wave of love and gratitude for his wife.

It was then, he saw the blond approaching him through the crowd.

☆⌒☆⌒☆⌒☆⌒☆⌒☆⌒☆⌒☆⌒☆

Ashley and Raphael were in the corner of the bar just off the dance floor. They'd already spotted Solomon up front by the main bar, talking with Sergeant Barrows. Neither had seen them yet.

"Tricky business, this," Raphael whispered, and nervously downed a shot of whiskey.

Ashley grimaced. She felt that she'd made a big mistake by selfishly insisting that Raphael come to the States with her and Franny. What had she been thinking? Raphael was in the financial section of Mother and not cut out for chasing vampires. What if he did something stupid and got himself killed?

The barmaid started to pour Raphael another shot, but Ashley turned his glass over.

"Bloody hell," Raphael started in on Ashley.

"Are you out of your mind? Do you realize the danger we're in? I shouldn't have let you have the first one." She tried to concentrate on the present. "Let's go over the plan again."

"I *know* the plan," he said, irritably.

"I introduce you to Wiese," she continued anyway, partially because of nerves. "You chat him up. When St. Laurue shows, I point him out."

"Right. But remember, I don't have ESP or powers like you or your Maid of Honor. Everything has to be pretty much spelled out for me."

"Tell me about it," Ashley said.

Raphael gave her a look.

She patted his arm and smiled softly. "If anything ever happened to you, I'd blame myself for the rest of my life."

Raphael kissed her gently. "I know that, babe."

Ashley wanted another playful kiss, but got worried when she saw Raphael focusing on something over her shoulder.

"There's our target." Raphael pointed toward St. Laurue, who had just appeared on the edge of the dance floor.

"Good going." She took Raphael's hand and they navigated toward Wiese, having to push past a number of club kids to get to the detective.

"Miss Green," Solomon said. "Fancy meeting you here."

"What's so fancy about it?" Ashley quipped, then pointed to Raphael. "He's my lover, Raphael."

"Pleased to make your acquaintance, Raphael."

They shook hands.

"So you're the detective looking for the man who killed all those people last night in the alley?"

"This is true," Wiese said, speaking in a loud voice. "Can you hear me through all this noise?"

"What noise?" Ashley shrugged. "Oh, you mean the music."

"This you call music?" Solomon said.

Raphael moved closer to Wiese. "I think we can help you out."

Ashley tugged on Raphael's sleeve. She looked toward the spot where they had last seen St. Laurue. He had disappeared again. She gave Raphael a worried glance and whispered, "He's gone." The *I-know-something-you-don't-know* smile faded from Raphael's face.

Solomon looked baffled for a moment, then said, "So if you can help me out, go ahead. Who's stopping you?"

"Excuse me," Ashley said. "I have to use the little girl's room. Now you two gentlemen talk nice about me while I'm gone." She gave Solomon a wink and hurried off after shooting Raphael a look that told him she was going to locate St. Laurue, and that he had better keep Wiese preoccupied.

The blond agent reluctantly headed downstairs for the back room.

CHAPTER 14

Was that auburn-haired hot young man cruising him? With all the fog and mirrors in the downstairs back room of Nocturnal Rounds, Jamie had difficulty telling what was real or just his drug-laced imagination. It was like a dream, he thought. The stranger had appeared in front of him, winked, disappeared, then reappeared again at the far end of the hall in a matter of seconds.

Impossible, Jamie decided. Nobody moved that fast. He looked again and saw the guy leaning against the wall over by the last sex stall.

Beauty. The word sprang up in his mind out of nowhere. Perfect. He'd name the stranger Beauty.

And when Beauty wet his lips and nodded– as if responding to Jamie's thought– the boy couldn't resist and followed him into the end stall.

Like Ahab to the white whale, Jamie felt irresistibly drawn into the stranger's arms. He rested his head on Beauty's chest– lost, yet found.

Who he was wasn't important anymore. Such trivial matters were consumed by the fire of his overwhelming desire for Beauty.

The need to be touched by Beauty, to be held by Beauty, to be kissed by Beauty.

Jamie lifted his head.

Eyes met.

Like warm honey dripping over his eyelids, a delicious drowsiness overcame him.

He heard a silent command.

Know me!

He was awed– Beauty's voice had come from inside his own head.

"Hey, handsome," Rocky Vanos said, giving Fury a wink.

Fury pulled out some dollar bills and offered them to the doorman.

"Like I told you before, your money's no good here. Far as I'm concerned, you're a freebie."

"Thanks, Rocky," Fury mumbled.

"If you ever need a place to crash kid, don't be shy, huh? Don't worry. I'll be gentle."

The teen smiled and was swallowed up into the glittering darkness of Nocturnal Rounds.

Once inside, many searching eyes showered the boy with adoration.

But tonight, it wasn't enough.

Tonight, he wanted St. Laurue.

The vampire was everything he longed to be– mysterious, powerful, master of his own destiny.

In all his envy, it hadn't yet fully dawned on the teen– to enjoy that kind of life, one first had to face death.

A sickening odor of decay filled the stall. Jamie helplessly watched as Beauty transformed into the beast standing before him. It wasn't human. It was a thing that drooled green sputum, had lizard-like purple slimy scales, sharp pointed teeth, and long fingernails that dug into his flesh. Two deep hollow eye pockets, each holding red-hot pilot lights, shot flames across his chest. Then, the creature's bloodteeth extended. Jamie's eyes widened. He turned and tried to escape the stall, but the thing's tongue unraveled like a party favor and surrounded his waist, whisking him back into its clutches.

Jamie cringed as two sharp fangs plunged into his neck. That wasn't so bad. It was the sucking, the sound of insatiable greed, that nearly drove him mad. Suddenly, the noise stopped and his head fell forward, knocking open the swinging stall door. He saw his reflection in a mirror across the foggy hall and was bewildered. The monster, which should have reflected behind him, didn't.

A loud echoing snicker filled the back room.

Jamie turned around and peered behind. Both Beauty and the beast were gone. He looked back at the mirror across the hall. Again, it verified there was no other– only the boy's own vacuous eyes stared back.

He staggered out of the stall, smacked up against the end wall and closed his eyes. It was just a bad trip, he told himself. Anytime now, he'd awaken with Edward, his lover, by his side back at the Merriweather hotel. Anytime now, he's realize that Sean, his dad– who he'd never gotten along with, but nevertheless missed– was still alive. Anytime now, Beauty would deliver him from evil.

Losing consciousness, he was barely aware of something liquid and warm dripping down his neck and onto his scorched chest, as he slowly slid down the wall. Somewhere deep in his mind, he was on a mad dash toward the doorknob of oblivion. At last, he thought. The final escape. But wait, something was horribly wrong. Some *thing* was chasing him.

As Jamie was about to rush through the threshold of forgetfulness, a haunting, hypnotic voice held him back and refused to let him rest in peace, as it echoed in the dimming corridors of the lad's consciousness.

It is I, St. Laurue– your invisible lover.

CHAPTER 15

Ashley was ill at ease bumbling around the downstairs sex room, but she had a job to do.

St. Laurue had to be found.

Halfway down the long, befogged hall, she felt the presence of evil coming from the end stall. It had to be the vampire, she thought. What else would feel so undeniably diabolic? Suddenly, she heard a grotesque echoing snicker and the stall door swung open. A naked young man staggered out of the booth and smacked against the end wall. Ashley refused to be sick as she watched the wounded young man slide down the wall into a crouch, blood pouring from his neck and pooling out around him.

A middle-aged man rushed to the boy's side. She recognized him. It was Sergeant Barrows. He took out a cell phone and called an ambulance.

Others began to panic and scatter.

Ashley knew the boy's neck wound was inflicted by St. Laurue, but was the vampire still in the stall? She took a deep breath and moved toward it, knowing she had to be fast so that Barrows would not see her. The fog would help.

Now, directly in front of the end stall, her heart was beating double time. She braced herself for the worse and swung open the doors.

The cubicle was empty.

St. Laurue had vanished again. Must have backtracked up the stairs, she thought. Luckily, Barrows was preoccupied with the hurt young man and hadn't noticed her. As she hastened away, a shiver electrified her body. What if St. Laurue *had* been in that booth? How could she have protected herself? She could have been killed. Her entire future, lost in an instant. No Raphael. No marriage. No children.

She moved toward the stairs, navigating around other denizens of the deep. Anxious faces materialized out of the fog, like skittish ships on pirate waters passing through the night. Ashley loathed the unnaturalness of it all. Every muscle in her body tensed and seemed to scream at her to get away from this gruesome place and the elusive blood beast while she could.

Then, her conscience called out. What about the Daemonion Council? What about those who depended on her? What about her job? Steady girl, she cautioned herself. There was a job to do, and it was almost finished.

Almost, she thought, but not *quite* finished. An optimistic smile lifted the corners of her lips. Then, it disappeared and for a brief moment, she felt as though she were watching herself from above, like a confused child kneeling over a dead puppy, wondering why it could no longer move.

No, she thought, snapping herself back in action. This was no time to freeze, and certainly, no time for death premonitions. A sobering chill took up residence within her as she determinedly took the first step on the ascending staircase and followed the vampire back to the first floor.

St. Laurue had been mid-quaff on Jamie's neck when the vampire sensed Fury's presence at the club. He snickered and shot up the back stairs.

The dance floor was a snake pit of club kids entangled in a savage frenzy of flinging arms, jutting legs and twitching contortions.

He was exhilarated to see the mortals so savagely and unabashedly rough-housing through the night. How true to form, he thought. Nothing had changed in a thousand years. Life was still the eternal dance of the damned and Nocturnal Rounds was simply a microcosm of the world at large. Here, life happened, as sudden and unpredictable as a grand mal seizure. Then, he spied Fury.

The boy was off to one side of the dance floor. Disco mist caressed the lad's legs, almost up to his thighs. He was dancing with his own image by the wall mirror, but not for lack of partners. There were many eager admirers hovering close by– hopefuls, waiting for that secret invitation, that special look, that certain smile. But the boy didn't seem to notice. He was in his own world, seductively gyrating his body and ignoring those who greedily thirsted for him.

St. Laurue worried that the boy might be a common tempter. Was he addicted to human admiration? That *would* be a pity. He psychically tuned in and was relieved. Fury was thinking only of him, wanting him. He sent the boy a potent mental command.

See me. Now!

Fury's head jerked toward him. The boy's attention sent a thousand soothing fingers fluttering over his undead flesh. Their cerebral connection allowed him to see himself through the boy's eyes. St. Laurue knew that to Fury, he was invincibility itself, but even more importantly, he knew the boy needed him. He sent Fury another bold thought.

Come to me!

They both moved across the crowded dance floor toward each other. While yet apart, the loud music weaved them into their own cocoon. The others faded away. Their eyes locked. Ice met fire. Fangs extended.

Then, it happened– St. Laurue's inner alarm bells went off. Like a startled animal aware of danger and keen enough to target its source, he focused on the blond and her boyfriend and instantly realized they were conspiring with Detective Wiese, who was standing by their side.

Ashley's outstretched arm was rigidly flung straight forward. Her accusative index finger pointed unmistakably toward him. The undead one mentally picked up her words to the detective.

"There's your killer," the blond spat out. "The vampire Gérard Arnaud St. Laurue."

I am exposed, St. Laurue thought. As his embarrassment escalated into irrational resentment, he mentally transmitted this thought to the girl's mind, *Desist or die!* But still, her offensive index finger would not drop. Finally, one indignant thought took precedence in his outraged mind– This impudent girl dares to hunt *me!*

CHAPTER 16

"Can somebody get a blanket for this kid?" Barrows called out.

By the time the sergeant got to Jamie, the young man was slumped against the wall in the downstairs back room and bleeding profusely from the neck. The kid's exposed chest was scorched with severe third degree burns and he was drifting in and out of consciousness.

Got to stop that bleeding, Barrows thought.

He did what he could.

Jamie opened his eyes.

"Thank you," the boy whispered weakly.

Barrows looked at Jamie, but didn't see him. Instead, the policeman saw Ray, his dead son.

He wanted to hold the boy in his arms. He wanted to assure him that things would be all right. He had never gotten the chance to say goodbye to Ray, or to his wife. The car crash had taken them out on impact. He winced at the painful memory and shook his head.

This wasn't Ray, he told himself as he gently wiped the blood off Jamie's naked shoulder. This wasn't personal. He was a Manhattan cop. This was his job and *professionalism* had to be maintained.

"Are you able to speak?" the sergeant asked. "Can you tell me your name?"

"Am I under arrest?"

Barrows felt Jamie's eyes penetrating his soul. He thought he saw his deceased son again in the lad's face. An unexpected rush of compassion ran through him. He knelt down and held Jamie's hand.

"It's all right, son," he said softly. "You're safe now. I'm on your side."

Someone handed him a blanket and he covered the boy's nakedness.

The boy reached for the sergeant's hand again. "My name is Jamie."

To hell with the rules, Barrows thought. This could be my own kid dying here. He cradled Jamie against himself and his usually rigid body easily rocked back and forth in an attempt to heal the broken boy.

"Who did this to you?" Barrows said. "What did he look like?"

"He was beautiful… and terrible."

"Did you get a name?"

Jamie snuggled in the sergeant's arms. "You know something? You remind me of my Edward. He was a priest, but he's dead now."

"A priest?" Barrows said. "Can you tell me his church name?"

"Monahan," the boy answered.

"And your last name, son?"

"O'Flarity, sir. Jamie O'Flarity."

***

St. Laurue glowered from the dance floor at Wiese, Raphael, and Ashley. The girl was still pointing her index finger at him.

He gave them a frigid stare, which temporarily left them paralyzed, then turned back to Fury and whispered in the lad's ear, "Can I trust you?"

The boy's doe-like eyes slowly moistened as he answered, "Forever."

St. Laurue flashed him a smile as disarming as the glare that had incapacitated the detective, the boyfriend, and the blond.

"Forgive me," the undead one said. "I must leave you now."

"No!" the boy protested. "Take me with you. Please! I'll do whatever you want."

St. Laurue smiled his approval. "I will come to you, later tonight."

The boy reached out quickly to bid him stay, but the vampire was already diffusing into a purple mist, blending into the surrounding disco fog.

❈❈❈❈❈❈❈❈❈❈

Almost instantly, Solomon was at Fury's side, but it was too late.

"Where'd he go?" the detective said.

"Who?" Fury shrugged.

Wiese could see the boy probably wasn't going to be too much help.

"You stay put," he told the boy and hurried to the front entrance, where he ordered his men to detain any Caucasian male with auburn hair.

When he turned to find Fury again, he saw Barrows ably shepherding the rescue squad carrying Jamie on a stretcher through the dance floor.

Wiese watched the club kids convulsing to the driving beat of selfish satisfaction and was amazed that they hadn't bothered to notice the rescue squad. Even the music swelled, as if to thumb its nose at him for thinking they would.

When the stretcher reached the front door where he stood, Solomon asked Barrows, "What gives?"

"This kid was attacked by our serial killer," Barrows said, racing out of the club entrance with the EMS squad.

Wiese raced along. "Did he talk?"

"His name's Jamie O'Flarity. The decapitated priest's lover. And the funeral this morning? Sean O'Flarity's? That was this kid's dad."

"Better go to the hospital," Wiese said, in-between heaving breaths. "When the kid comes to, try to get a name and description of his assailant."

"Right." Barrows got into a squad car to escort the ambulance.

Wiese called out to the moving car, "And ask him if he recognizes the name Gérard St. Laurue."

Solomon walked back into the club, trying to add things up.

Press had said the eccentric author only met with him at night.

Franny had told him, "They mostly come out after sunset."

Ashley identified St. Laurue as the killer and a *vampire*. That would explain the blood fetish and the vanishing acts.

Then, catching himself in absurdity of it all, Solomon shook his head. Vampires? What the hell kind of nonsense was he thinking? He wondered if he was losing his mind.

As Solomon brushed past people exiting the club, he decided not to say anything to anyone else just yet. Right now, he had to question Fury.

He casually walked up to the boy, who was now leaning against the main bar looking dejected. Was that a tear in the kid's eye?

"Who was that guy with you?" Wiese said.

Fury put his hands in his pockets. "You a cop or something?"

"Yeah. Who was he?"

"I don't know."

Solomon looked the kid in the eyes. "Ever seen him before?"

"Nope."

"Bet you wouldn't be such a smart ass if I carded you. Now, let's try this again. The guy you were with. His name is…?"

"He was just a guy."

"You know his phone number?"

"Yeah, right?" Fury said with mild sarcasm. "I told you. I never saw him before."

"Yeah?" Wiese said. "You two looked pretty chummy to me." Solomon felt a pat on his back and turned around.

"What's wrong, detective?" Rocky interrupted. "Don't you believe in love at first sight?" The doorman grabbed Fury by the arm. "Hey kid. You coming home with me or what?"

"Yeah sure, Rocky," Fury hurriedly said. "Let's go, huh?"

"Okay by you?" Vanos shot a defiant look at the detective.

Solomon grumbled under his breath and backed off. Sure, he could card the kid and probably close down the joint, but that wouldn't get him an inch closer to the killer. The sad fact was, it'd probably be a waste of time.

His stomach acted up as he watched the two leave the club. Something was very fouled up here.

What's become of the world? Didn't anyone care if a maniac was on the loose, killing people left and right?

It was frustrating. He had asked all the right questions, but had gotten *bubkis*– nobody knew from nothing.

CHAPTER 17

Saturday, June 23rd 3:09 A.M.
Ashley's apartment

"Jesus God," Ashley said as she and Raphael walked into the SoHo apartment. "St. Laurue saw me point him out. I'm as good as dead."

"You don't look dead," he said seductively and kissed her.

The air conditioner had been on, but the place was still too hot for his taste. He turned it up and felt the cool air going through his shoulder length jet black hair. Their hair lengths had attracted them to one another. They had met at the Motherhospice. After two dates, they had moved in together, hoping to see if marriage was the next appropriate step.

The answer was a resounding yes. Now, it was just a matter of making the whole thing legal.

"How can you be so calm?" she asked, lighting a cigarette.

"It's over. We're safe. You smoke too much."

She stabbed out the cigarette and hugged him. "You're right. I don't want our first baby coming out of the womb with a nicotine addiction."

Raphael adored everything about Ashley, except for her job. Okay. He had heard of the undead. Who hadn't? But he'd never seen a vampire in action. Not even St. Laurue. Nor had he ever come across any of the other occult creatures the agents of the Council constantly blathered about.

"Let's not worry about St. Laurue right now,"

he purred in her ear. "Tomorrow, we're off to the comfort of the Motherhospice back in Scotland."

"But you don't understand these things, Raffy, St. Laurue is a most dangerous–"

"Right. I *don't* understand," he interrupted, then kissed her again. She responded. When their lips parted, he added, "All I know is we're going to be married and live happily ever after."

He scooped her up in his arms and carried her into the bedroom, where he tossed her on the bed and quickly got up for the love-making.

"Give me a minute," she said softly with a bewitching smile and excused herself to the bathroom down the hall.

Thank God the assignment was over, Raphael thought. He'd never seen Ashley so nervous. But then again, he'd never accompanied her on a mission before. Maybe she was always that way. What did he know? He was only an accountant, hired to keep the Daemonion Council's books in order. Absentmindedly, he reached for a condom, then remembered that wasn't necessary. There'd be a marriage, a baby, and a loving family. One plus one will equal yet another one.

His happy reverie was interrupted by a sudden loud thud.

"Ashley?"

"Sorry," she called from the bathroom. "Just being clumsy. I've got a surprise for you."

A moment later, she returned to the bedroom, sporting a new pink teddy and black leather boots with spiked heels. He sat up on the bed. She was wearing the naughty outfit he had given her for a present on her last birthday, the one she had always modestly refused to wear.

"You told me you'd never be caught—"

"Well, just this once then," Ashley said. "It is a celebration of sorts."

"That's my wicked little pet. I might have to get a bit kinky."

Ashley leaned forward and her long blond hair draped down in front of her bosom. Her breasts played hide and seek with him as she fell into his arms. He wanted everything to be perfect tonight. He wanted to make love to her slowly, letting his fingers pause in all the places he knew she liked his touch to linger. Mouth's found each other. Tongues tangoed feverishly. When need would not let them dally any longer, they coupled. She, with her black boots on. He, uncapped and primed for the charge. Then, in a surge of familiar yet always surprising fullness, it was finished.

"I'll get a towel," he whispered.

Raphael went to the hall bathroom and flipped on the light switch. He was about to grab a clean towel when he heard an annoying drip coming from behind the shower curtain. He whisked the curtains back and had to steady himself. The foul odor doubled him over. His girlfriend's impaled nude body hung limp from the shower head. Fecal matter and scarlet blood dripped into the bathtub. Suddenly, the corpse fell forward and hit the hard porcelain tub with a heavy thump. The body convulsed with muscle spasms. A throaty wheeze escaped its mouth, as trapped air accordioned out of the lungs. Raphael retched. He blinked tears out of his eyes and looked again in disbelief, but the corpse was still sprawled in the tub.

Ashley's voice called out from the bedroom. "Raffy! You okay?"

"What the hell?" His mind struggled with confusion as he raced back to the bedroom and found his betrothed, inviting him into her arms.

"Ashley?" he asked, uncertain.

"Where's the towel?" she said, suggestively raising her body off the bed. Her hair cascaded backwards like a golden waterfall. "Does this mean you're to have your way with me again?"

He stared at her for a moment. "You won't believe what I thought I saw in the bathroom."

"Cockroaches? Never mind. Come on back to bed, lover."

Her soft seductive voice was like a magnet. Whatever he had thought he'd seen back in the bathroom was quickly forgotten. But as he neared the bed, he froze in his tracks. Ashley's tongue was flicking in and out of her mouth like a serpent's.

Was he going mad? He blinked. It was gone.

"Your tongue was…"

"Was what?" she asked, innocently.

He waved his hand. "Forget it. It's madness."

"Silly," she laughed, teasingly. "Come here."

He dismissed his misgivings and hurried to her arms. Kneeling on the bed, he reached for her lips with his, but was repelled by a hideous odor. Good God, he thought. Her breath. When he started to back away, Ashley's tongue shot out and lassoed his neck. He managed to break away and run down the hall toward the front door, but there she was, up ahead, standing by the exit.

He stopped short. How could it be? Had the bartender drugged him back at the club? Was he hallucinating? Suddenly, an answer came to him. The vampire was playing tricks on his senses. Psychic intervention. That's what it was called. He'd heard of it back at the Motherhospice. St. Laurue was trying to psych him into first killing Ashley, then himself.

"No!" He screamed at the walls. "I'm not going to kill her!"

Ashley whimpered and dropped to her knees in front of the door. "Raffy, you're scaring me."

A hot wave of shame coursed through his body. "I'm so sorry, my love," he said with deep contrition, realizing she'd been jittery all night. And here he was making the situation worse by behaving like a total freak. He ran to her, knelt down, and they embraced.

She stroked his forehead, "Are you all right?"

"I'm fine," he said, feeling his heartbeat slowly returning to normal. "It's just that I keep seeing the most horrendous images."

Ashley's eyes flared in anger. "See. I knew it," she said. "St. Laurue is trying to get at me through you. But don't worry. Concentrate. You can block him out. Here, this will help." She kissed the palm of his hand. Raphael lifted her adorable face and kissed her on the lips.

The passionate kiss instantly engaged happy emotional memories. So sweet were his thoughts that he didn't much mind when he felt her tongue elongate and force itself deep into his throat, blocking his air passage. He was vaguely aware that his life was somehow in danger, but as soon as the unsettling thought came, it was white-washed over by another anesthetizing lighthearted memory.

Had anyone seen them– sitting on the floor in the front hall of their SoHo apartment, passionately kissing, arms entwined around each another– they would have found it quite an artful picture; Raphael's strong muscle-toned back almost eclipsing his bride-to-be. No doubt, to any inadvertent bystander, the young couple would have appeared to be terribly in love.

Yet, what would have shocked and possibly sickened the more attentive observer was the abrupt appearance of the tip of a long tongue which made a dull cracking sound as it burst forth from Raphael's lower backbone. The leathery organ was slathered red with blood collected while drilling down the agent's throat and rooting through his interstices.

It wagged about playfully, happily splattering blood about the front hall.

CHAPTER 18

Saturday, 3:47 A.M.
Rocky's place

After having had his fun with Ashley and Raphael, St. Laurue's next stop was an issue of pride as well as a promise kept.

The moment he mentally tuned in to locate the lad, St. Laurue sensed his minion was being abused. Thoroughly outraged, he followed the scent of Fury's humiliation and found himself in Rocky Vanos' torrid third floor apartment on the lower east side of the Village. Unseen, he watched from the bedroom door.

Vanos was coming on to the handsome lad.

Fury had already taken off his pants and boxer shorts in the steamy bedroom. Modestly, he had left on his tight white tee-shirt, which barely covered his boyhood as he tried to outmaneuver the lecherous mortal.

"Just leave me alone," Fury said, pushing the older man away. "I'm not interested."

"You looked pretty damned interested back at the club when I saved your ass from the law," Vanos smirked, and crudely slapped the boy's butt.

"Cut it out," the boy yelled. "Just let me crash on the floor."

St. Laurue was beyond outrage. An insult to his minion was an insult to himself. He could have instantly swept in and killed Vanos, but held back and drank in the unfolding drama. The more scurrilous the doorman was with Fury, he thought, the sweeter his retribution would be.

Rocky stripped. The ape had hair all over, except on top of his head. He lunged for Fury. The teen turned and ran, but Vanos nabbed him by the neck of his tee-shirt. As Fury strained to get away, the degenerate yanked hard and ripped the shirt off his back.

"You're not leaving, kid," Rocky said, catching Fury by the door. "Not until I teach you what that tight little ass of yours is good for."

He shoved the boy belly first onto the bed, pinning him down with his weight. The man's stench filled the hot bedroom, as he thrust against the struggling boy's bottom like a rutting pig.

When Fury yelped in pain, St. Laurue flew into action.

Faster than the human eye could see, he tore Vanos off the boy and pierced the mortal's heart with an elongated fingernail. Rocky huffed and collapsed to the floor. St. Laurue sliced the outer layer of flesh off of the man's horror-stricken face, then carried the corpse to an open window and tossed it across St. Mark's Place into a deserted trash strewn alley.

Fury's mouth was agape, but his eyes hero-worshipped the vampire. And why not? St. Laurue thought. He'd just saved the kid. It was obvious that the boy trusted him. All well and good. But could he trust the boy?

He gave Fury a powerful hypnotic command. "You will sleep, until I return." The teen rolled over on his back and nodded off. He covered the lad's nakedness with a thin white bed sheet and once again found himself spellbound by the boy's beauty. He wanted to take the teen then and there, but held back. He was determined to savor the turning of his Fury.

Still, he thought, the initial infestation must be accomplished tonight. About to draw his own blood, he halted and sniffed the air. Instant hunger coursed through him when he saw the tiny red drop forming just above the scratch on Fury's arm, where Vanos had clawed the boy.

He ran his finger across the wound, brought the blood up to his lips and greedily sucked. His eyes flashed yellow-violet as Fury's blood rushed into his undead body.

It was a thick elixir both bitter and sweet. Immediately, he experienced the boy's loneliness, his vulnerability, his need for power. But then, he felt the ebullience of budding virility, a joyously wicked sense of adventure, and a lust to learn.

As St. Laurue gazed at Fury, he saw a vision.

The lad's skin took on the pale of a blue-veined white marble tombstone.

Vampiric eyes floated on top of the boy's closed eyelids. They were icy blue, yet overheated with an intense hunger for life that only a thing undead could muster. It was a good sign.

"Voilà," he happily whispered.

It was fate.

Assured now that the teen was meant to be his, St. Laurue bit his own finger and let a drop of blood trickle onto Fury's lips.

The sleeping boy's cherry red tongue lazily lapped up the ancient one's blood.

"*Oui,*" St. Laurue murmured softly, as if in prayer. "Let this one be turned slowly, sensuously." Besides, he thought, the dawn was only a few hours away. After the next sun, he would return and take greater pleasure in completing the ancient ritual. Fury had to imbibe his blood twice more– a second time for mental keenness, and a third for preternatural power.

While taking leave of the apartment, he cast his vampiric shade over the doorframe with the wave of a hand. Now, no being, whether living or undead, would dare to trespass without first being warned against such an ill-advised act by the *nosferatu's* lingering scent of death.

Rushing to beat the discomforts of dawn, St. Laurue flew to his lair, relishing Fury's blood flowing within him, just as his flowed through the boy. And for the present, it was enough.

The dark bond had begun.

BOOK TWO

"Hell and Heaven are near man, yes, in him–"

Emanuel Swedenborg, *Heaven and Hell*

CHAPTER 19

Saturday, 9:23 A.M.
Preston's home, New Jersey

The den was Preston's private domain. His wife, the girls, and even the cats, Ben Franklin and Betsy Ross, were regularly shooed out.

This was his thinking space.

The solid oak shelves on the walls were lined with his own personal library.

His desk was uncluttered and well organized and the plush couch invited opportunities to grab short naps, whenever needed.

Generally, the cozy knotty pine paneled room nurtured him... but not this morning.

Even perusing the Book Review section in his Saturday New York Times– usually the high point of his week– didn't help.

Marge and the girls were off grocery shopping for the family picnic that afternoon.

The house felt empty and quiet.

Up until two days ago, this would have been a good thing. But most recently, silence unnerved him terribly... and the daily countdown to sunset scared him half to death.

He restlessly moped over to the desk and was surprised to find a manilla folder marked, *The St. Laurue Chronicles.*

Where the hell did this come from?

He opened the folder cautiously, as if it were a jack-in-the-box.

New chapters!

The realization hit him like an unexpected phone call from the coroner.

The blood demon had been in his home.

This was his worse nightmare.

Stupid ass, he lambasted himself. Somehow he had held on to the outside chance that the vampire would be business-like, that the monster would respect his privacy.

That notion now seemed as absurd as expecting the dead to rise up out of their graves.

Press let out a stream of nervous laughter.

His body shook all over as he flopped down on the couch, new chapters in hand.

As he thumbed through the pages, all he could think was, that damned night spider had invaded the sanctuary of his home and he could do absolutely nothing about it.

His last bastion of safety was no longer safe and, realistically speaking, had never been.

He felt checkmated.

The vampire had won the game. Now, he had no choice but to do whatever St. Laurue demanded.

Press clenched his fist and began to read the new chapters.

Exhaustion overtook him and twenty minutes into the read, he drifted off and had a nightmare.

Marge and the kids were being stalked and slaughtered one by one. He escaped, like a coward, and hid in a dark cellar. The door flung open. St. Laurue's silhouette shook with laughter at the top of the stairs.

Footsteps sounded their descent.

Press sprinted through the cobwebbed cellar, unable to catch his breath, yet too terrified to rest, until he was forced to stop at a dead end. A rush of cold air made him turn around.

St. Laurue stood before him. His face was twisted into a victorious leer. His breath reeked of rotten flesh. His glinting blood teeth lengthened.

Rivulets of sweat streamed down Preston's forehead, stinging his eyes.

In a whoosh, lethal fangs clamped down on his neck, like two steel picks stabbing at a melting block of ice.

Press woke up in a cold sweat, gasping for breath as he caught sight of the den's wall clock.

A few hours had passed.

"Calm down," he said to himself. It was just a dream. After taking a couple of deep breaths, he sat up on the couch.

Still feeling dizzy, he tried to center himself by bending forward with his head in between his knees.

A long, cord-like orange streak was peeking out from underneath the far end of the couch.

He instantly recognized it and, as was usually the case when he felt disoriented, the familiar thing made him feel better.

He smiled. "Come out from under there, you little rascal, you."

The tabby's tail remained still.

Press reached over and gently tugged Betsy Ross out from under the couch.

"You know you shouldn't be in here," he said,

then let out a gasp.

"Oh, Jesus."

The cat was cold, stiff, and had been dead for some time. Her twisted neck hung limp to one side, frozen in position. Her eyes bulged out and her tiny tongue jutted forward.

There were two puncture wounds on her neck.

It was only then that he realized, Betsy's body had been completely drained of blood.

CHAPTER 20

Saturday, 10:24 A.M.
Ashley's apartment

Solomon looked around. He saw violence and death all around him.

The apartment– particularly the bathroom down the hallway– was pungent with the coppery smell of blood.

The girl was dead.

She was found slumped in the bathtub. Her chest had a gaping hole through it and an index finger had been hacked off.

As for Raphael, his naked body was found by the front door. His front teeth had been knocked down his throat, which was widened, as if it had been plunged by the broad end of a baseball bat. A huge hole at his lower back looked as if something inside of his body had suddenly lunged out.

Solomon bent over and picked up a long strand of auburn hair on the bathroom floor and examined it carefully.

Sgt. Barrows handed him a small plastic bag.

"Need this?"

"Thanks," Solomon said, taking the plastic bag. "How's the kid at St. Vincent's?"

"Jamie?"

"Yeah."

"…drifts in and out of consciousness."

"Can you get him to talk?"

"Have a little compassion, will you?"

"No time for compassion," Wiese said, placing the hair in the plastic bag. "We need to find the perpetrator or else there'll be other 'Jamies.' Did he give you a name?"

Barrows stiffened up. "No yet."

Wiese knew what was bugging John. He gave him a comforting pat.

"Okay John, I understand. Just look after that kid. I've got a strange feeling the killer's not done with him. If the assailant is who I think, the real question is, why is Jamie still alive?"

"Because God is good?" Barrows said.

"Hey," Wiese answered with a scowl, "we should only *be* so lucky."

CHAPTER 21

Saturday, 4:37 P.M.
Tatem Park, New Jersey

The fun family picnic at Tatem Park had been a great success… so far.

Press was both relieved and nervous when his old college buddy, Kyle Riordan, had driven up to join them. Press was relieved because St. Laurue had told him to get Kyle to ghost the book. But he was also jittery because he wasn't sure how to tell the free lance writer.

At least everyone enjoyed the food, Press thought. The picnic lunch had been a sumptuous feast: grilled hot dogs with plenty of mustard, giant juicy hamburgers, smothered with onions and catsup, and his wife's special German style potato salad, prepared just the way he liked it.

Although his appetite wasn't very good and he was still feeling a bit rundown, Press pretended to be enjoying himself. The late afternoon heat was his only comfort. The sun was still shining. His family was safe.

Marge, Kyle and Press languidly chatted on the picnic blanket under the cooling shade of a sturdy oak, while the girls, Trisha, Lori, and Judy, were off playing on the monkey bars in the nearby recreational playground by the edge of the woods.

Marge nudged Press. "Honey, it's almost five. We should get going." She glanced toward the playground. "Where's Trisha?"

Press sat up and looked around. Lori and Judy were still playing on the monkey bars, but Trisha, their youngest, was nowhere in sight.

Kyle lifted his fisherman's cap from over his eyes and sat up. "Saw her on the swings a couple of minutes ago."

"You guys clear up the picnic stuff," Marge said, with a worried look. "I'll go look for Trisha."

"Okay," Press said, knowing this was the chance for which he'd been waiting. He got up from the blanket.

The time of reckoning had arrived. He had to tell Kyle *why* he had invited him to the family picnic. He had to tell Kyle about the vampire. The two men started packing up the picnic gear.

"Trisha's probably just off exploring," Kyle said. "She's at that age. Everything's new. Don't you miss that, when life was brimming with daily discoveries and surprise?"

"No," he said, emphatically. "Too many surprises can be…"

"Old stick-in-the-mud Press," Kyle teased. "Remember? We called you that at Princeton, back when we were young and immortal. So, what's this job you couldn't tell me about over the phone?"

"Well," Press started, feeling like his heart was doing ninety miles-per-hour in first gear. "I have a new author."

"And?"

"And I want you to ghost his book."

"*That* you couldn't tell me over the phone? Is it fiction, non-fiction?"

"It's non-fiction, but reads like fiction."

"Oh. One of those stranger than life tales."

"That's hitting the ole rusty nail on the head," Press said with a nervous laugh and shook off the picnic blanket.

Suddenly, he was glad this little chat with Kyle had been sanctioned by St. Laurue. This talk was a badly needed release. Holding too many secrets could torment a man's soul.

But what if Kyle didn't believe him? The blood drained out of his face. Not an option, he thought determinedly. He had to *make* Kyle believe.

"You all right?" Riordan said. "You look like death warmed over."

The off-hand remark reduced him into a convulsion of giggles. With tears flowing down his cheeks, he spoke in between his desperate laughter, "Kyle, to tell you the truth, I have never been closer to death."

"Oh. We're talking in silly little riddles now, are we?" Kyle said, picking up some plastic utensils. "Or have we finally decided to drop all pretenses, let people think what they may, and finally let out Mr. Hyde?"

"There *is* that distinct possibility," Press said, recollecting how Kyle had always been the adventurous poet-philosopher back in college. Always searching for the perfect beauty, which was his excuse to this day for never having gotten married. He had been a student of lofty ideals. The one who had begun and actually continued to practice eastern meditation. But more importantly,

Kyle was the one who had introduced him to Marge and had encouraged them to get married. Kyle had always expanded his horizons.

But this time, Press thought nervously, it was his turn to expand Kyle's.

"Calling Dr. Jekyll," Riordan said, interrupting Preston's thoughts, "have we gone mad or not? Inquiring minds need to know."

"Not yet. At least I hope not. It's just that I don't know how to come right out and tell you what's been going on in my life without getting the reaction I just got, which was exactly what I was trying to avoid, only now it's too late and you think I'm nuts, which I'm not, like I said, I hope."

"That's quite a run-on sentence, pal. I'm starting to worry about you. Are we having a mid-life crises?"

"Who me? Naw. It's just that life passes by so fast. Years come and go. It's all one big blur. And you can't stop it, you know? So you keep on doing what you do, or what you *think* you should be doing until something stops the rush and you have to take a good hard look at yourself."

"Something?"

"And that something can be financial ruin, or a divorce, or very bad news from the doctor, or…"

"Or what?"

"…or something so incredibly extraordinary, so unimaginable that when you hit up against it you have no choice but to rearrange your whole god damned life because time stands still and there you are, ready or not."

"Yeah... so what are you trying to say?"

"I'm saying my new author, St. Laurue, is not just a man."

"Okay..."

"He *was* a man. But he's not the man he once was. And do you want to know why?"

"Why do I have the strangest feeling I should say 'no' right here."

"Because he's a *vampire!*"

Kyle dropped the picnic basket he had just repacked. There was an eerie silence between the two men.

Press peered uneasily at the writer and continued, "The vampire has to tell his life story." The eerie thick silence got even eerier. "He needs... a... ghost," he said, emphasizing each word, as one unaccustomed to speaking with a lip reader might.

"And that's supposed to be where I come in," Riordan said flatly.

"In a word, yes."

"Here." The writer tapped his left leg. "Pull the other one."

"Look," Press said, growing more upset. "See this cut on my neck?"

"Let me guess. St. Laurue?"

"Sliced it with his tongue. Kyle. He knows where I live. Last night he killed Betsy Ross."

"Not especially patriotic, is he?"

"Not funny. Come on, man. You know me. I'm not making this up."

"Well," Kyle said, rolling his eyes, "attacking one of your cats makes sense anyway."

"Why is that?"

"Folklore has it that cats, out of fear, will sometimes attack the dead. Naturally a vampire would, in self defense mind you–"

"The point is that St. Laurue needs a ghostwriter. I mentioned your name and he lit up. He *wants* you."

Kyle's face grew serious. His eyes held a look of pity. "Does Marge know about all this, pal?"

"I was warned to keep my mouth shut. Besides, it'd only worry her."

"So I'm the only one you've told about this?"

"No, I told a priest, who's now dead. Only he wasn't a real priest, he was the vampire in disguise, which I didn't know until after I–"

"Press! Help me!" Marge shouted from the edge of the woods. She raced toward them, carrying a limp child in her arms and calling for Lori and Judy to come down from the monkey bars.

"Oh my God, what happened?" Press said, rushing over and taking Trisha from his wife.

"Must have fainted from the heat," Marge said.

Kyle grabbed some napkins and made an ice compact. "This'll help."

Press indicated the cleared picnic blanket. "I'll put her on her back."

"She was in the woods like this," Marge said.

Kyle applied the cold compact to the four-year-old's forehead.

No, Press thought clenching his fists, not again. He looked at Trisha, and remembered Troy, dying of leukemia. Marge had just stepped out of the hospital room. The four-year-old boy squeezed his hand and then, was gone. His life was a question unanswered, a promise unfulfilled. And what was left? Weekly visits to a lonely cemetery, where wilted flowers waited to be replaced.

Trisha groaned and started to come around.

"Mommy."

The little girl reached out for Marge.

"It's all right, Trisha. I'm here."

"The man, mommy."

"What man, honey?" Press said anxiously.

"The scary one with the two funny looking long teeth."

"Oh Lord," Marge whispered. "She's delirious."

"Did the man hurt you, baby?" Press said.

"No. He just watched me for a while, then I got dizzy. He said Betsy Ross died and went to Heaven to be with Troy."

Marge gave Preston an angry look and whispered between her teeth, "I thought we agreed not to tell her about the cat just yet."

"I didn't... I mean, yes, we did agree..."

Press turned Trisha's head to one side and examined her neck. He glanced up. Kyle returned his curious stare with one of his own.

Ten minutes later, Marge and the girls were in the car, ready to drive to the emergency room. She honked the horn for Press to hurry.

He turned to Kyle. "You've got to do this job."

"And you've got to talk with a shrink about this vampire thing."

"Are you nuts? This was St. Laurue's warning

not to talk to anyone. I'm telling you the truth or did you think I was checking Trisha's neck for mosquito bites before?"

"Look. I believe that you believe this new author of yours is a–"

"You're scared because he wants you. Go on, admit it."

"Press, get a grip."

"Don't you see? You know about him now, and St. Laurue *knows* that you know. You're a marked man. He *wants* you."

"Do you have to keep saying that?"

"I've got to go," Press said. "Here's part of his first draft." He gave Riordan a copy of the vampire's manuscript to date. Marge leaned on the horn again and he turned to leave.

Kyle called out to him, "Well, thanks again for the nifty picnic, *and* for passing my name on to an undead, bloodsucking vampire."

Shaking his head slowly, Press turned back to Kyle. "You still don't believe me, do you?"

"I don't know what to believe."

"Believe this," Press said, in all seriousness, "the vampire will want to meet with you. Expect him." The car horn honked, insistently. " But do look on the bright side, life still holds a few surprises after all. I guarantee, you'll find him a fascinating creature."

"And why is that?"

"Because," Press said, choosing his words with a great deal of care, "...he's so terribly human."

CHAPTER 22

Saturday, 9:46 P.M.
Preston's home, New Jersey

After the emergency room, Press felt feverish and was barely able to drive his family home. The vampire's clear warning had been a rude awakening.

Fortunately, the ER physician on duty had pronounced Trisha physically fine, but went on to say that she appeared mentally agitated.

Later that evening, Marge had to crawl into bed with the four-year-old and make a promise to stay the whole night before Trisha would even attempt sleep. The child kept insisting the bogeyman was after her.

With everyone tucked in for the night, Press tried to settle down, but ended up pacing from room to room. His family was in jeopardy, but what could he do about it? He stood deep in thought in the middle of the kitchen and ran a hand over his hot forehead. Maybe a drink of cold water would cool him down. He opened the refrigerator door and felt the cool air waft against his moist brow. Then, the sight of food nearly got him sick.

He listlessly closed the refrigerator door and felt something brush up against his legs. He bolted upright with fright.

"Jesus," he said, exhaling in relief as he saw Ben Franklin at his feet, begging for food.

"Okay, little fella." He got a large bag of cat chow and filled Ben's bowl. "At least *you've* got a healthy appetite."

As Press watched the cat contentedly munch at his bowl of food, he wondered if Ben missed Betsy Ross. Obviously not, by the way he was eating so robustly.

Preston envied the cat. No guilt. No repressed emotions. No hidden motivations. Just pure animal instinct, sans psychological hang ups. If only he could be like that. But no, he wasn't that lucky. On the contrary, he was barely treading water in a cesspool of unanswered questions: How did he draw this horror into his life? Could he keep the vampire from hurting his family? How had he allowed himself to become a Judas by involving Kyle? And what wouldn't he give if only he could wake up and have everything the way it was just forty-eight short hours ago?

Exhausted from over thinking, he trudged off to his den, turned on the TV, and dozed off just before the ten o'clock news.

A loud tap on the windowpane shocked him into wakefulness.

He got up and turned off the TV. There was another harsh rap on the window. Was it St. Laurue? No, he thought. Tapping on den windows was not the vampire's style. Was it a neighborhood kid playing a prank?

Press raised the blinds and leaned out the window. No one was there, but it was dark and he couldn't be sure.

He decided his feverish mind was playing tricks on him and started sleepily for the bedroom.

Ben Franklin was curled up in a ball at the end of his bed. Strange, he thought. The cat never slept on his bed. Poor little guy probably missed Betsy after all. He reached over to gently pet Ben, but was stopped short by another knock, this time on his bedroom window.

Ben awakened, looked toward the window and arched his back in fear. Press was frightened, too. His bedroom was on the second story.

This time he figured it *had* to be St. Laurue. He raised up the blinds, looked out, but saw nothing, except for the lonely lit streetlight on the corner. Suddenly, Ben hissed and shot out of the bedroom. Press wondered what had gotten into the cat. But there was no use kidding himself. Both he and Ben felt the air thickening, closing in on them.

Could use some fresh air, he thought, and raised the window sash. He leaned out and took a couple of deep breaths. There. That was much better. Suddenly, a big black bird with yellow eyes hovered before him. Shocked, he fell backwards onto the bedroom floor, where he stayed, trying to make sense out of what he'd seen. Dorothy Parker's words came to mind. 'What fresh hell is this?'

An extraordinarily attractive, middle-aged woman was standing in back of him. Smiling, she held out her hand. "Let me help you." Her voice was confident and poised. "Come, take my hand."

"Ah, no thank you. I can handle it," Press said, as he picked himself off the floor and wondered why St. Laurue had chosen to visit him in this particular disguise. "You caught me off guard for a second."

"I can understand why he found you most suitable," the lady said.

"He who? What are you talking about? And what's with the woman's disguise?"

"Should I not be in disguise?"

"You're the boss."

"Who do you think I am, Press?"

A moment ago, Preston thought St. Laurue was up to his old tricks, impersonating someone– as he had impersonated Father Monahan at St. Michael's– but now, he wasn't sure if this was St. Laurue or somebody else. He tried to keep his composure, for appearance sake.

"You possess the three necessary attributes a mortal must have to be indentured to a *nosferatu*," the woman said. "First, you can look collected when upset. Secondly, you're devoted to your family. And thirdly, you refuse to face the seamier side of life. In short, you're a perfect candidate for conscription into his dark service."

Press stood up, alarmed. She knows about St. Laurue. No, he corrected himself. Assume nothing.

The woman sat down at Marge's vanity.

Press sat on the bed, jockeying into various positions while questioning her. "Who are you?"

"Don't worry," she said, looking amused. "I'm not a vampire."

"Who said you were?" he said, feeling like a kid caught with his hands in the cookie jar.

"You're trying to see if my image reflects in the vanity mirror."

His face flushed, then he tried to recover. "I

was not."

"I can't blame you. I'd do the same if I were in your position."

"My position?"

"Let's drop the pretenses. I only hope I'm not too late to help you."

As she spoke, the tone of her voice changed from exotic and sultry to open and frank, but even more remarkably, her accent shifted from New York to London. Meanwhile, Press had seen what he'd been so desperately looking for– her reflection in the mirror.

Great, he thought, she wasn't a vampire, but could he trust her? He tried to play along to see if he could find out more.

"Of course you're not a vampire. Who believes in vampires?"

"You do," she said calmly.

"And you?" His voice quivered a little.

"Yes, they exist."

"You said something about… helping me?"

"Now I will let you see me as I have appeared to you previously."

The auburn haired lady shimmered like a plate of water placed on a running motor. Press thought he was hallucinating. First, she turned into a black bird with yellow eyes, then, she became a person he recognized from the police station– the portly bag lady, complete with canvas sack.

"Franny?"

Her cockney accent rang out. "In the flesh, big as you please, sir."

"Which one are you? The beautiful one or…?"

The quick shift back was no less elegant a performance. Franny was again her true self– petite and perfectly shaped.

"My name is Francine Styles. Call me Slim. I was born with the gift of shape-shifting. Thanks to the Daemonion Council, I've been able to use my talents for the good of mankind. That's why I'm here. We need each other's help. Do you understand what I'm saying?"

Preston's mind raced. He was wary. It would be tantamount to an admission, but he took a deep breath and uttered the name. "St. Laurue–"

"Yes?"

Slim's voice answered too fast for Preston's comfort. He slid back on the bed in terror. He shook with fright. It *was* St. Laurue, he thought. The woman's reflection in the mirror had been a trick to gain his confidence. It had all been another test of secrecy and he had failed again.

She smiled. "Yes? Go on. It's good you've said his name. Now we can get down to business. I know St. Laurue's indentured you. Even as we speak, I'm mentally blocking him from sensing we're together. I've been watching over you since your meeting with him at St. Michael's."

Press wiped the perspiration off his brow and began to settle down. Still, he was a bit leery. "How do I know you're telling the truth?"

"After St. Laurue disappeared in the church, you heard footsteps but saw no one, remember? That was me. I was cloaked. Invisible."

"Phew. Then I'm not going completely crazy. I did hear footsteps?"

"You did. Take heart, dear Press. I know the vampire's preternatural feats seem astounding, but although he is immortal, he's not indestructible. Regardless of what he says, he's not the God he would have you believe."

Press let out a sigh of relief. Her "invisible footsteps" confession had convinced him that she was telling the truth. He decided to do likewise, and said, "I'm worried about my family... and my friend, Kyle. I'm dragging the people I love into this mess. Everyone I know is at risk."

"Kyle's not in jeopardy. The rule of thumb is– if you're an asset to the *nosferatu,* you're safe. It's when you become a liability that you're as good as dead. If nothing else, vampires are efficient creatures, experts at eliminating potential threats. But before I go on, I need to know. Do you want my help?"

"Yes! I'm at my wit's end."

"Fine. Then let me briefly fill you in. The Daemonion Council was established during the Dark Ages. Our main function is to preserve the true meaning of esoteric scriptures."

"What has that got to do with St. Laurue?"

"We also study different varieties of creatures such as the undead, ghosts, ghouls, werewolves, mummies, etc. But more importantly, as in this case, we intervene when we see the plague being spread from one species to another– for an example, between vampires and mortals."

"The plague! Are you implying that St. Laurue is sick?"

"He's spreading a highly contagious strain of HIV. That's why you must get tested immediately. That throat wound."

"What?" Press unconsciously touched the cut on his throat. "Has he infected me?"

Slim gently touched the man's shoulder. "I'm afraid so."

His jaw tightened. His head pounded. The room began to spin. It all made sense now— why he'd been feeling so run down.

Slim reached out and touched his forehead.

His world came back into focus. "What are my choices? Turn into a vampire or die?" He laughed at his own question. "I guess being a vampire and being dead are pretty much the same thing."

"No, there's a big difference. The undead are *not* resting in peace. What St. Laurue plans for you is just about anyone's guess. He may kill you, let you die of AIDS, turn you completely, or even make you his *incubus*."

"What the hell is an *incubus*?"

"A being with supernatural powers who must drink blood once a month on the full moon."

"That's it," Press decided on the spot. "I've heard enough. I'll do whatever you want. Just help me and my family."

"Very well. I'll need you to string along with the vampire. Don't let him know we've been in contact. Keep him from probing your mind."

"And how am I supposed to do that?"

"Envision large black, red splattered rats. He can't tolerate them. His psychic connection will be broken. Now. I have an urgent request."

"Anything."

"Tomorrow around noon, Wiese and his wife are leaving for Washington, D.C. and I want the vampire to follow them."

"Why?"

"Trust me. There is method to my madness."

"Fine. So how do I get St. Laurue to follow the Wieses?"

"Tell him that Detective Wiese is on his way to Washington D.C. and plans to expose him. But you must tell him this only *after* Solomon and Rita leave town."

"What if he doesn't follow them?"

"He will. He can't afford to risk exposure. Please remember, if your thoughts do turn toward me or the Council as you speak to him–"

"Black rats with red spots," Press said.

"Quite right. I must go now. Please open the window wide."

Press did so, but when he turned back to Slim with another question, she had already transformed into a beautiful, white dove.

"Please!" Press pleaded. "Don't let him harm my family."

The dove cooed softly and floated through the bedroom window.

Press collapsed onto the large double bed and fell into a deep but fitful sleep.

Saturday, 11:28 P.M.
a Manhattan mid-town hotel

Slim walked into her palatial suite back at the midtown hotel where she'd been staying between street appearances as Franny. A wave of fear ran through her. Someone other than the maid had been there. She sighed with relief when she spotted the telegram on the desk. The intruder had only been a Council courier. The communication read,

"Dear Slim, New operative has not reported in for the last two days. Find the seeker. Contact Mother for his location. TDC"

Slim put the telegram down and pursed her lips. So Jared Shannon, her replacement, was missing in action. She had suspected all along that she'd have to finish up this business with St. Laurue on her own.

Wasting no time, she picked up the phone and dialed Wiese's home phone number. His answering machine greeted her.

She left this message:

"You will be followed to Washington D.C. by St. Laurue. He *is* what you think. Protect yourself with consecrated silver bullets and crucifixes. Still, know that only your *faith* can save you. The Daemonion Council."

CHAPTER 23

Saturday, 11:47 P.M.
Manhattan city streets

Dt. Wiese drove through the dark city streets.

Before his shift was over and his two week vacation began, he had some catch-up paperwork to get through back at the station. But right now, vacations were the last thing on his mind. He had a few spots to check out– Nocturnal Rounds, Preston's office, the alley across the street, and last but certainly not least, his favorite all night coffee and donut shop.

Wiese flipped on the radio and tuned into a late night talk show.

The subject was AIDS in the city.

He listened to caller after caller criticize the Mayor's handling of the crisis.

Heated attacks drifted into the background as he remembered what Sid Putney from pathology had reported earlier. Putney was an expert in virology and genetics and was widely known to work wonders with blood evidence. But Solomon also knew the man to be a recovering alcoholic, who fell off the wagon every now and then.

Putney's report bewildered Solomon– The blood on Preston's silk handkerchief had turned out to be Preston's own. It was HIV-positive, as was the blood from the three guys in the alley and the couple in the SoHo apartment. The viral lode of the tested blood was so high, Sid called the samples "practically pure liquid virus."

That's where Putney's report crossed the line from the very mysterious to the supernatural.

Sid described the results of a DNA test on the strand of auburn hair found in Ashley's bathroom. There were no plasmic proteins, nor any genetic information at all.

Wiese decided Sid had not only *fallen* off the wagon this time, but had probably *catapulted*. But it was this odd statement in the report which bothered him the most, 'The auburn strand of hair, when analyzed under the lab microscope, exploded in a puff of purple smoke and disappeared.'

Disappeared, Solomon thought. Disappeared just like St. Laurue, who incidentally had auburn hair and a *major* motive for killing Ashley, after the girl had singled him out at Nocturnal Rounds.

Then, there was that other disturbing report. A crew member from crime scene clean-up had been accidentally infected by the street gang's blood in the alley.

The older man was rushed to St. Vincent's, but none of the recent 'cocktail' medications had proved effective and now, less than forty-eight hours later, the fellow was fast succumbing to AIDS.

The radio again caught Solomon's attention.

"Hello," the talk show host said. "You're on the air."

"Yes," the caller answered, in a soft sweet voice. "I need to talk to you, Mr. Whaley."

"And your first name is?"

"Elka."

"You can call me Franklin. What do you want to say?"

"God gave me AIDS."

Silent air space, then...

"I'm sorry, but I don't believe God punishes people with diseases."

"Oh, no. It wasn't for punishment. It was His way of protecting me. I was being attacked by the Devil. God saved me, then I got sick."

"So, God saved you from the Devil."

"I saw Jesus the Christ," Elka said. "He gave me His blood."

"So you're telling me that the blood of Jesus is HIV-positive?"

"He's God. He can make His blood whatever He wishes."

"And now *you're* HIV-positive?"

"No. I have full-blown AIDS."

"When did all this happen?"

"Last night, by the pier."

"Uh huh, I see," Whaley said. "Friday night you were infected and tonight you have full blown AIDS. Well that seems pretty unlikely. By the way, you wouldn't be calling from Bellevue by any chance, would you?"

As Solomon turned down twenty-third street, he heard the poor girl sobbing on the radio and felt sorry for her. Couldn't that bastard, Franklin Whaley, have been a little more compassionate? The girl was sick!

Elka answered the talk show host. "I'm in the diner across the street."

"Wait just a moment, honey," Whaley said to the caller.

More silent air space…

"Hello?" the girl said, coughing. "Are you still there, Mr. Whaley?"

"Elka. Can you come up to the studio? The program manager tells me our switchboards are going crazy. We've already sent someone down to meet you. John Q. Public wants to hear the details of your story."

"I think…" More coughing. "I think I would like that very much," she said, sounding both surprised and embarrassed.

"Okay folks, after a commercial our unexpected studio guest, Elka, will tell us how God gave her AIDS. Don't go 'way. Be right back."

Solomon was more than casually interested. He leaned forward and turned the volume up on the car radio as he cruised by Nocturnal Rounds.

CHAPTER 24

Sunday, June 24th 12:03 A.M.
Moondoggies, the Jersey shore

St. Laurue leaned against the back balcony of the bright neon-lit dance club, Moondoggies. He was watching the ocean's silver crested midnight waves lazily roll onto shore. Inside the club, it had been too hot, too crowded, and too smokey. He liked the open-air balcony. He needed to calm down. To make a good first impression. It was damned exciting, the vampire thought, finally meeting his ghost, face to face.

It wasn't hard singling out Kyle Riordan, especially since the mortal wore an overly vivid Hawaiian shirt and blue stripped blowzy trousers. Of course, St. Laurue already knew what the writer looked like. He'd seen Kyle at the picnic– where he had spied from the woods– after showing the little girl his fangs. Subsequent to that, tracking Riordan to Moondoggies was like taking candy from a baby.

He mentally called to Kyle, who was on the dance floor behaving like a moose in heat with several young ladies. It was not a pretty picture. All that gratuitous bumping and grinding at his age, St. Laurue thought. Kyle was hardly a club kid. But the man had spunk.

With just a little more mental focus, Kyle got the message, stopped mid-grind and wandered over by his side on the balcony. Now, he would see if the mortal had what it took to be his ghost.

After sharing a silent moment of mutual admiration for the moon, Kyle casually said, "It's almost full."

St. Laurue nodded, cordially and said, "Only a few more days."

"You know what they say about time and tide."

"They wait for no *man?*"

Both smiled. The writer held out his hand. "Kyle Riordan."

"Roddi."

"French?"

"It's Gérard, actually. My little sister, Brigitte, dubbed me Roddi."

Hands met. He thought the mortal had a firm yet easy hand shake and instantly felt an atypical feeling of respect and admiration. Riordan struck a philosophical chord in him. He sensed a measure of wisdom and wondered if the man evoked a similar response in everyone.

"Enjoying the club?" Kyle said.

"Truthfully, I like the view much more."

"Yes. Mother Nature. What more does a man need? Of course, a young fellow such as yourself may not yet understand such sentiments."

"Don't be deceived," St. Laurue said. "I appear much younger than I am." His eyes flashed yellow-violet. "Shall we go for a walk?"

Kyle stepped back in surprise, then smiled and said, "Why not? We might catch a moon tan."

Minutes later, they were out of the club and sauntering along the boardwalk in silence. St. Laurue wanted the writer to speak, but it seemed the man knew how to play his cards close to the chest. Or perhaps, Kyle appreciated silence more than most mortals. The vampire finally initiated the exchange and said, "What do you do for a living?"

"I write. Just finishing up a novel. And you?"

"Fortunately, I don't have to work, so I'm usually out trying to scare up a little excitement."

"Ah, old money, huh? It does tend to make one bored with life."

"Life," he repeated. "Now *there's* a subject that endlessly excites me. I'm obsessed with it. Starved for it, really."

Their eyes met only for a brief moment, but something deep and significant was exchanged. In an instant, he knew Press had suggested the perfect man for the job. Kyle was eloquent, sophisticated, and would lend a certain romantic and philosophical overtone to the book.

"Shall we sit and absorb the night?" Riordan asked, pointing to a bench facing the ocean.

St. Laurue was surprised at how much the writer reminded him of himself. He took it as a good sign. They sat on the bench.

"You seem to be a rather well balanced man," St. Laurue said, hoping the writer would open up and divulge more about himself.

"Don't *you* be deceived. Things are not always what they seem."

Seagulls soared through the delicious salty sea air, while moonlight surfed the silvery waves. St. Laurue's healthy sense of distrust seemed to have melted away and he was starting to grow enormously fond of Kyle.

"You were saying, 'things are not always what they seem?' " he said. "And how is that?"

"The mind plays tricks," Kyle said. "Like now. We're not seeing each other as we really are. We only see what we *hope* and *expect.*"

"We survive on our hopes and desires, *oui?*"

Kyle stared at him. "Hopes and desires and *blood,* Mr. St. Laurue."

The vampire's body stiffened. The air took on a slight chill.

"So," he said, sitting up. "You're on to me."

"Let's say I've been *expecting* you."

"Then you know why I'm here. Forgive me for being so forthright, but I must ask. You'll ghost my book?"

"A while ago, I would've said no."

"What changed your mind?"

"For all your experience," Kyle said, "you appear to have a sense of youthful innocence that I admire a great deal."

St. Laurue looked into Riordan's eyes. "Perhaps you're being duped by a calculated trick?"

"Innocence can't be calculated," Kyle said. "I'll ghost your book."

"Merci," he said, and relaxed back on the bench. "The pleasure will be mine, I assure you. Name your price and it shall be yours."

"Nothing. It'll be a fascinating adventure."

"I think, *monsieur*, we may be two peas from the same pod. Tell me, have you ever thought about living forever?"

Kyle backed away slightly. "No, I haven't."

"Well, *do!* The centuries would be yours to record for the benefit of humanity. What insights time can teach."

"Insights arise in between the ticking of mankind's imaginary clock."

"Mull it over, my enlightened friend. Spiritual immortality may already be yours, but *physical* immortality is not a gift at which to scoff. Would it not be a grand and glorious adventure?"

"If it's God's Will, it will happen."

"Perhaps, through me," he said slyly. "God *has* willed it."

"You're a tempter, sir."

"Think of the knowledge you could garner. The wisdom you could share. You'd appear the same, but you'd have enhanced physical powers and a sharper mind."

"And sharper teeth?"

"All the better with which to drink in life, my new friend. Do not be afraid. It will be your choice. Let us call it a standing invitation. Life is a unique opportunity, *n'est-ce pas?* Far stranger destinies have come to pass under this same watchful moon."

As Kyle followed St. Laurue's glance up to the waxing moon, the vampire made an exit, quicker than the mortal's eye could see.

Sunday, 12:51 A.M.
St. Vincent's Hospital, Manhattan

St. Laurue soared high above the city streets

after coming back from his meeting with Kyle on the Jersey shore. He was happy with his ghost and would have tarried longer, but the night held unfinished business.

There was more blood to let, more life to drink, more adventure to survive. He shuddered to think that the millennium rest would soon cut short all this fun. He landed on the roof of St. Vincent's Hospital and headed directly for the recovery room on a damage control mission.

A drawn white curtain divided the recovery room in half. In the first half, he saw an old lady on her sickbed. As they eyed each other in the dimly lit room, he intuited her name. It was Rebecca.

He liked the old lady at once and held up a finger, signaling that he wanted to surprise the two men on the other side of the white curtain. She understood and nodded. On a whim, he stroked her gray hair and instantly knew that she was recovering from a post surgical infection which had developed after the removal of a cyst on her back. She would survive, he thought, if what he was about to do didn't give her heart failure. He hoped not. He wanted her to survive. Somehow, Rebecca reminded him of family.

The two men's silhouettes spilled onto the white curtain divider like shadow puppets, but St. Laurue's acute senses were not to be confounded. When he psychically tuned in, it was as if the curtain, though drawn, had suddenly lifted.

The night creature sensed that Sergeant Barrows had been at Jamie's bedside since the boy's return from surgery and that the lad was being held in the recovery room for continued close monitoring. A *safety* precaution. He almost snickered, but held his tongue for the sake of surprise.

Barrows reached over and took hold of the unconscious boy's hand. A faint whimper escaped Jamie's lips. Eyelids fluttered open.

"Where am I?" Jamie said.

"St. Vincent's," Barrows said. "Do you need anything? Water?"

"Just stay with me," the boy said, weakly.

"How do you feel?"

"Safer, with you here."

"Are you up to a few questions?" the sergeant said softly.

"If it means you'll stay, I am."

"I'll stay," Barrows said. "I want to help you through this, son."

"Why? You don't even know me."

"I feel like I do," Barrows said. "I feel like I've known you forever."

St. Laurue nearly laughed out loud– The buffoon spoke of forever, while sudden death was watching from only a few paces away, more than eager to cut him free from the torturous tick of time. What did these silly mortals know about forever? At best, it was exhaustingly brutal; at worst, incessantly boring. Forever was lonely. Forever was separative. It had little to do with promises kept and even less to do with fidelity, permanence, or God. Time was more demonic than divine. Who knew that better than he? He had long been on intimate terms with time– and for him, forever was nothing less than industrious death.

"Did the assailant give you a name?" Barrows asked Jamie from behind the white curtains.

"Not exactly, but a name did come to me just before I finally passed out. It sounded like... Saint something-or-other. Something like rude."

"St. Laurue?"

"Yes. That's it."

These few casual remarks, spoken in what was assumed to be perfect privacy, had sealed their fate. St. Laurue's face became enraged. But then again, exposure always brought out the worst in him.

He flew behind the white screen, ripped Sgt. Barrow's heart out and stuffed it down the boy's throat. Within seconds, both mortals were dead, and the sanitized white hospital curtains had been sprayed with blood.

Before exiting the recovery room, St. Laurue visited with the little old lady and patted her head. He lifted a finger again to his lips. This time he needed her assurance of silence. She understood and nodded. In spite of all the bloodshed, apparently she had decided he was a perfectly charming young man, and by all appearances that was exactly what the vampire was– instant death cloaked in the romanticized charm of forever.

He quit the hospital leaving Rebecca unharmed. The old lady epitomized a perversity he prized most highly in human nature– the penchant to pardon depravity for the price of a small personal pat.

CHAPTER 25

Sunday, 1:01 A.M.
Manhattan city streets

Wiese was still glued to the car radio as he drove through Manhattan. Something about Elka was intriguing. Maybe she was just a kook looking for attention, maybe not. Either way, he knew better than to dismiss any detail that might help him find the serial killer.

The commercial was over and the light changed to green. He stepped on the gas.

"Welcome back to *Late Night Talk It Out* with yours truly, the City Nighthawk, Franklin Whaley. We have an unexpected and very unusual quest tonight. A young lady named Elka claims God gave her AIDS last night. How am I doing so far, Elka?"

"Yes. Jesus gave me AIDS."

"Let's slip off that big old hood and get a good look at you."

"If that is your wish," Elka said, shyly, "but my face is…"

"Pardon my asking, but how long have you had those purple lesions on your face and neck?"

"Since I was trapped by the Devil down by the wharf last night."

"Can you tell us why you think the good Lord Jesus personally intervened?"

"Because I'm a virgin."

"Forgive me for being so skeptical, but have you ever had any blood transfusions? You're not a hemophiliac by any chance?"

"No, sir."

"Have you used any unclean needles recently? Done any drugs?"

"No, never. This, I think, is another reason why Jesus saved me."

"But He made you sick," Whaley said. "How is that being saved?"

"I was saved for what He would have me become. For my destiny."

"And what is your destiny?"

"I will become a vampire."

Dead air space.

"...a *vampire?*" Whaley repeated.

"It's His will. Last night, after I was saved, I couldn't sleep. I was weak and restless. This morning, I couldn't face the sunlight. I pulled the shades and slept most of the day. When I awoke, I was ill and disfigured with spots. My eyeteeth were sharp and extended. What was happening, I didn't understand... until the incident late this afternoon."

"What happened then?"

"I had such a gnawing in my stomach. My body weakened. My mind became very alert. All of my senses, but especially my hearing, intensified. Rustlings from the laundry room down in the basement flew up to me on the third story. I heard rats in the cellar, crawling through the halls, in the walls. I wanted to drink their blood. The thought repulsed me, but I knew I had to drink from them or die. I dragged myself to the basement and called them. One by one, they crept out of their hiding places. I lunged forward, caught several, bit off their heads and drank."

"You drank rat's blood?"

"Yes. They tasted like life. They had the flavor of regret."

"Regret? In what way?"

"I came back to my apartment, not completely satisfied, but feeling stronger. I was in my living room, trying to imagine what was becoming of me. Then, I smelled her warm blood in the kitchen, like turkey wafting in on Thanksgiving Day morning. The hunger came again. I willed her to come to me. When she came into the room, I seized Gretel, squeezed her head off and drank. She was such a trusting cat."

"Good God."

"But Gretel's blood tasted much more refined than the rats."

"You killed your pet?"

"With regret, as I've mentioned. Now, I've an uncontrollable urge to taste new blood from richer sources. I need more. I'm a vampire."

"And God has saved you for this?"

"God works in mysterious ways."

"Well, people out there in radio land, you heard it here. But Elka, what happened last night? How did Jesus come to your rescue?"

"He appeared out of thin air, raised me up and held me close to His body. I was filled with His blood, His spirit. It was holy communion. Jesus saved me. Jesus humbled me. Even now, Jesus is healing me."

"Well I'll be a sonafa..." Franklin said. "The lesions... they appear to be disappearing. This is amazing folks. They're fading as we speak."

"His blood is healing me," Elka said.

"Unbelievable. A very sick girl came in a few minutes ago, and now, Good God, she looks absolutely radiant. After the commercial, we'll get a full detailed description of what the Son of God looked like down by the pier last night. You gotta stay tuned folks. This is just incredible."

Solomon pulled up to his favorite coffee and donut shop and double parked. Just enough time to grab a couple of jelly donuts and a cup of java during the break, he thought.

He rushed out of the car, wondering if Elka was on the level, or strictly from nutsville. Maybe the whole thing was just a publicity stunt, a pathetic attempt to get bigger ratings.

Sunday, 1:12 A.M.
St. Vincent's Hospital rooftop

After having silenced the sergeant and Jamie in the recovery room, St. Laurue was on St. Vincent's rooftop, feeling ever so much better.

Tonight, he would complete the turning of Fury. He would drain the boy's blood and replace it with some of his own. The boy would pledge his undying loyalty and they would run forever in each other's veins. It would all go just that smoothly, like clockwork.

He started to rise off the roof, but suddenly

froze midair, just over the ledge. He descended again, teetering on the brink. Something was off kilter. He sensed danger and tilted his head with a quizzical look on his face. His eyes flashed yellow-violet as he psychically heard the radio waves.

She was exposing herself– and *him!* She was stirring up the hornet's nest of a sleepy humanity. She was telling them that the undead exist. She was publicly broadcasting the truth, which had always been considered to be harmless folklore. Elka was dispatching the myth!

The careless child, he thought. She had to be stopped immediately.

By the time he arrived at the radio station, he had transformed into an avenging Christ, about to toss the money changers out of the temple.

After efficiently breaking the necks of the station-manager and the show's director, St. Laurue spied Elka and Franklin Whaley in the glass enclosed recording area. A light over the studio flashed, "On the air."

The *nosferatu* crashed through the window. Franklin screamed. St. Laurue narrowed his eyes at the yelping mortal's face, both silencing and disarming him. A host of blinking lights on the broadcasting board caught the vampire's eye. With one swift blow, sparks flew and all broadcasting was abruptly terminated.

Turning to Elka, the vengeful Christ became benign. "You've been a naughty girl," he said, softly. "You've told the world our little secret."

She whimpered, "How else could I draw you to

me again?"

"No harm done. Most mortals are asleep, and those that did hear won't believe." He indicated Franklin. "Now, I must feed."

He buried his face into the hypnotized talk show host's neck.

Once blood glutted, St. Laurue sliced his own throat and had Elka partake in his immortal blood a second time. She gulped lustily.

He pulled her back by the hair and forced her to stop, then gathered her up into his arms and escaped the building via the roof top. They flew over Manhattan through the silvery moonlight and beyond the bounds of mortality. Within moments, they were in Elka's apartment.

"See me now as I am," the vampire-Jesus said, resuming his boyish good looks.

"In any shape or form," the girl said. "You are my Savior."

"You must again drink," he commanded, "for the third and last time."

He sliced his wrist. Elka's tongue ran across her dry lips. Her sensual nature was not lost on him. He gave her his wrist and she drank insistently. The undead one tossed her away as he began to feel faint. She crawled back on her hands and knees, demanding more.

"Enough! You are an immortal now," he proclaimed. "The earth can not hold you. The grave will spit you out."

The turning was complete. Elka had drunk three times. Once, for initial infection. Twice, for immortal mind powers. Thrice, for the full baptism of preternatural speed and great physical strength.

He gazed fondly at his new blood bride. Elka was now as he was. She strong and beautiful. A preternatural light glowed in her eyes. Suddenly, they betrayed her fright. He understood. Most newborns had the same initial reaction to their new state. After all, they were now a living soul stapled to a dead physical body. A hollow shell animated by a hungry spirit. Imagine having to suddenly live one's life in the form of one's former shadow. Condemned to exist in a dull, dark and ever dying world. Is it any wonder, he thought to himself, that we vampires suck the life out of the living?

He took her in his arms.

The light of her imprisoned soul continued to frantically flare behind her eyes– trying to escape its dead meat encasement.

He stroked her hair.

As she finally calmed, he knew she was settling into the dark agreement between the spirit and body. The contract that all the undead must accept when they discover their immortal soul lodged within and committed to sustain the form that moved them.

"Be calm, my love," he whispered.

Slowly, he would teach her the advantages of her new body. He would show her the thrill of violent love.

He would demonstrate that love is a struggle in which we feverishly try to escape our own nature. A fight to deny our lifeless isolation. A battle in which we pound each other into the very pulp we ourselves cannot bear to face.

Now, the vampiric love can begin– for the undead heal swiftly.

St. Laurue fell upon her and soon they were lost in the midst of an eternal rub.

He bit her neck, then energetically nibbled all the way down to her stomach. Each lusty bite brought drops of blood, which he sucked up and savored. She looked at him in amazement. He tore off her left nipple with his sharp teeth and swilled up the flowing blood.

She thrashed and moaned as his elongated tongue pierced her abdomen and toyed inside her womb. Sudden inspiration illuminated her eyes. She writhed with pleasure and ripped at his thick head of hair.

He snorted. As fast as it came out, his hair restored itself.

She shrieked with joy. He mounted her. She clawed at his back. Her hands ran up and down his buttocks and pressed perfect roundedness into pancakes, flattening him deeper on and into her. He grunted like a beast in heat. Her outstretched tongue rolled clear across his back, then round again, making its way into his mouth. Exquisite jubilation rushed them quickly toward a juiceless climax– a climax which life had little to do with.

During *le petit morte,* they were entwined, but separate. Each was in the unity of isolated silence only the undead and a handful of mortal saints can know. Time ceased to exist– and to the time-driven undead, this brief respite was nirvana.

Returning to awareness, St. Laurue rolled off his new bride. Too soon, time's eternal pendulum swung once more and he had to be on the move.

He nuzzled against Elsa.

"You've much to learn of your new life. I will teach you."

She stretched out luxuriously beside him. Her searching eyes met his. "This is what I've wanted," she passionately whispered.

St. Laurue smiled at her and tried to mentally read her mind, but was no longer able. Being his vampiric daughter, he now had to communicate verbally. Perhaps, in the future, they would learn to trust one another so completely, they would be of one mind, as was he and his sister Brigitte. But for now, they were forced to play out the intricacies of a more demanding discovery.

He smiled and marveled at how love could so thoroughly make one blind.

"Rest now," he said. "I will return tomorrow soon after sunset, after I attend to a beautiful boy named Fury. You'll meet him. The four of us will be a family linked together for eternity."

"The *four* of us?"

"Tomorrow night, I shall introduce you both to my sister, Brigitte."

"You mean," Elka whined, "I can't have you all to myself?"

He choose to ignore her question, knowing Elka's nature was fearless and independent at its core. Most probably, she would quickly pass through this overly possessive fledgling phase.

He smiled at her and said, "If I'm delayed on the morrow, you must feed on your own after you awaken from your first vampiric sleep. You must do this to survive, do you understand?"

"Yes, Lord," she said, sounding a bit distant and vaguely morose.

After one last luscious kiss, he headed off to his lair, where he had arranged a pre-dawn meeting with another alluring, but much more ancient vampiress– his sister, Brigitte.

CHAPTER 26

Sunday, 1:17 A.M.
Twenty-third Precinct

The sound of glass shattering interrupted the radio talk show, just as Solomon Wiese turned the corner for the precinct. It was followed by an ear-piercing scream. Then, there was nothing but the sinister static of dead air. As he pulled up to the station and parked the car, he gobbled down his last jelly donut and wondered if it was Franklin Whaley who had screamed.

Solomon turned off the car radio, grabbed his coffee, and hurried into his office, where he found the red-inked note from the captain glaring at him from his desk.

"Solly, Have a good time in D.C. I mean it! If I see your sorry ass around here Sunday, I'll put you on suspension, without pay. See you in two weeks, buddy. Give Rita my love. Trevor Eckles"

Wiese grimaced and switched on the desk radio.

He spotted his heart medication, took a pill and washed it down with the last of his coffee, while listening to hear if the talk show had worked out their technical difficulties.

No. Still static. Very strange, he thought.

Wondering if there could be any truth to Elka's crazy story, he caught sight of the Daemonion Council's last cryptic note and reread it out loud, " '...to catch him, you must think beyond yourself, beyond rational truth.' "

He tried to fit together the many clues floating around in the sea of his mind. Franny had said, "They only come out at night." Press had said, St. Laurue only comes out at night. Jamie had a neck wound. Press had a neck wound. Ashley insisted that St. Laurue was a vampire.

Solomon's eyes suddenly widened. His heart pounded. His stomach plummeted. He sat down at his desk feeling unusually alone and vulnerable, having finally acknowledged the possibility that he might be dealing with something preternatural– something beyond rational truth.

He called his wife, knowing she was probably asleep. He got the answering machine.

"Ritzy, it's me. Listen, maybe we shouldn't leave tomorrow for D.C. I think I figured out who, or maybe I should say *what* the killer is. I'm not saying anything yet, but–"

Wiese shook his head at the receiver and cursed under his breath at mankind's modern technology. The damned answering machine had cut him off.

CHAPTER 27

Sunday, an hour before dawn
a Chinatown apartment

Slim started her day well before sunrise, after only a few hours of much needed rest. The Daemonion Council operative found her way to the Chinatown tenement, where Mother had told her she was to check on Jared Shannon, who hadn't been reporting in.

She hated being replaced by Jared, regardless of the fact that it was due to a lift in status from senior field agent to board member. A Council Board Member, she thought as she clambered up the front steps of the tenement. It was a lifelong dream come true. She should be ecstatic. But since the deaths of Ashley and Raphael, she'd been struggling between two strong desires– the need for the peaceful Scottish hills of Mother and the need to finish her job, no matter what it took. As usual, her obsession for closure won out and induced a mission myopia that made her feel ashamed even to be thinking of rest and relaxation. Onward and upwards, she told herself. Possibly she'd be able to finish up the mission after all, or at least be of service in its success. She was sure that, if given the chance, she could lure St. Laurue to Scotland as originally instructed.

The agent climbed up the rickety old stairs to the second floor of the rundown building and paused in front of apartment number sixteen. She checked the written information Mother had given her. Right. This was where Shannon was supposed to have set home base.

The door was ajar. Something fishy about that, Slim thought. She centered herself, took a deep breath and proceeded with due caution.

The apartment was dark, intolerably stuffy, and extremely hot.

She switched to night vision– an occult trick she had learned back at Mother– and checked for exits. Standard procedure, just in case she needed a quick getaway. There was only one, the entrance to the apartment. She checked behind the drawn shades in the living room and discovered the windows had all been nailed shut. No wonder the place was an inferno, she thought. It was then she noticed the sound of breathing. She followed it to a back bedroom and peeked through the doorway.

She saw the woman asleep on the bed.

Slim was positively stunned by the woman's beauty. She had smooth creamy white skin, set against luxurious, full-bodied light brown hair. She also had the vibrant glow of a woman who had just made love– a look that Slim hadn't personally experienced for quite some time.

Still, all was not a bed of roses here. The room itself had a whisper of something unhealthy in the air, the sour wisp of ancient death.

Slim tip-toed into the bedroom. The woman's eyes flung open. They were quite beautiful, but frightened, which took away some of their glamour.

"Sorry to disturb you," Slim said. "I was given

this address. Looking for a man named Shannon. Would you happen to know his whereabouts?"

The woman's voice was soft, but demanding. "Who wants to know?"

Slim found her tone odd, not proper somehow. And her smile seemed insincere, almost a smirk.

"This may sound a bit wacky," Slim said, "but Mother asked me to contact you." She scrutinized the woman for a reaction.

After what seemed a moment's consideration, the woman said, "Tell Mother I'm as fit as a fiddle, just a bit confused."

"You're Jared Shannon?"

The beauty on the bed shape-shifted into a gorgeous young man. His half naked body was handsomely built. But the single feature which captivated Slim's attention was Jared's hair, so full and golden, even the sun would be envious. When Shannon switched on a lamp by the side of the bed, Slim noticed his eyes were golden brown, similar to her own.

"And you must be Slim," he said, then yawned and stretched.

"That's right. Mother wants to know why you haven't been reporting in?"

"Been too busy," Jared said, casually. "I'm on to our man, or rather, our vampire. St. Laurue's a tricky one. Been putting me through my paces."

"I know exactly what you mean," Slim said. "He's very active."

"And behaving rather strangely." Jared sat up on the bed. "My guess is that he doesn't realize he's spreading a virus."

"Well, it's no longer my business," Slim said, trying hard to cover her resentment. "I'm tired of living in his shadowy world in any case," she continued, as if trying to convince herself. "First thing I'm going to do when I get back to Scotland is sunbathe on a grassy hillside." She stepped into the bedroom. "Just out of curiosity, how *will* you entice St. Laurue back to headquarters?"

"He's infatuated with a boy named Fury. If I kidnap the teenager, he's sure to follow."

"Actually, the same notion crossed my mind," Slim confessed. "May I assist you in any way before I jet back?"

"I think not. Just get home safely," Shannon said, smiling warmly.

Slim felt attracted to Jared. It was clear that he understood the need to protect people from monsters like St. Laurue. It was also clear that he was quite a beautiful looking young man. Jared was only twenty, but there were times when a young lover was just the ticket. Suddenly, she wasn't at all sure that she should leave. They could benefit the Council so much more if paired as a team.

With these thoughts meandering through her mind, Slim walked to the bedroom window and absentmindedly pulled up the shade.

As the warm dawn shafted into the room, Jared was instantly blown off the bed and bounced against the far wall of the room. He backed into a dark corner, trying to escape the sunlight. His skin discharged steam where the searing dawn's early light had touched him. The bedroom smelled of burnt flesh. Shannon hissed like a cornered animal and distorted his face. Eyeteeth lengthened and gleamed. Fear traced his drooling lips to a bitter conclusion. He was a grotesque vision of terror, the visual embodiment of viciousness. Slim knew this to be a standard vampiric trick, very often used to ward off the enemy. She watched as Jared crouched in the corner.

"St. Laurue's gotten to you I see," she said, trying to stay calm. But it was no use, her breathing was heavy and her mind raced, wondering if she'd be able to escape the bloodsucker. She made an effort to curb her thoughts, hoping to hide her fear from the vampire.

"You will come to me now," Shannon said. His mesmerizing voice was imperious.

The room began to close in on Slim. She felt as though she'd been caught in a tractor beam and started moving toward Jared. Only with great effort was she able to shake herself free of his will.

She thought to try and appeal to the former agent's loyalty.

"Jared, don't do this. Come back with me to Mother. They'll know how to cure you."

"There's no cure for vampirism, you foolish twit," he said, hiding from the dawn in the corner. "Now, be a sport and pull down the shade so we might consider other possibilities."

Slim stood her ground solidly. "What other possibilities do you mean?"

"You could be a heroine to Mother."

"How?" Slim said.

"I could help you get Fury off to Scotland. I can provide you with priceless information about our kind. Mother would love that."

"Does St. Laurue have the foggiest idea you're a Council operative?"

"Was a Council operative," Jared said bitterly.

"He doesn't even know you're a man, does he?"

"Such a clever girl, Francine."

"How did you block his intuition?"

"You mean, did I think about black red speckled rats?"

"Did you?"

"It was all in the image, ducky," he said. "It was *all* in the image."

"You mean to say you actually *became* the image of Elka? You lost your own identity, your essence, once shifted? How did you dare?"

"It was nothing really."

"But that's exceedingly dangerous. You could have lost yourself and become–"

"Elka? That's right. I actually *was* stuck for a while. I became Elka. But St. Laurue took the bait and turned me and, as you can see, I'm back to my old self again."

"Are you insane? You're not Jared Shannon. You're *nosferatu.*"

"And *you're* jealous."

"I don't envy the undead. And I'll not betray the Council for the sake of personal glory."

"Oh, please. You're much too old to play Pollyanna, dear."

"Let me help you, Jared."

"Fine." The creature held out its hand. "Come away from the light and help me. Yes, Slim. Come over here to the dark side."

"When St. Laurue finds out, he'll destroy you."

"But he won't find out," Jared snarled, as he bared his fangs. "Since he sired me, he can't read my mind… and *my* lips are sealed." Shannon snapped his sharp teeth together.

"He *will* find out, if I have to tell him myself."

"Then, at all costs," Jared said, "you mustn't leave this room alive."

The air started to swirl. On second notice, Slim realized the vortex was funneling out from Jared. He was changing.

Shannon transformed again into the beautiful Elka. "Don't you just love Elka, darling? She's a carbon copy of one of St. Laurue's past lovers. See, I've done my homework. Oh, and there's no use in trying to escape. I nailed the windows shut. Just for you. I wonder if you realize what a clever little boy I've been?"

"You're just full of tricks," Slim said.

"Aren't I though."

"Of course, you've gone mad to dream you can outwit St. Laurue."

"But I already have, ducky. I already have. And now, for my next trick, let's try going from Slim to none."

"Daylight prevails," Slim said in a firm directive voice. *"You are weak. I will escape."*

"You're going to have to do better than that,"

Shannon said. "Your hypnotic suggestions really don't appeal to my personal agenda."

Jared sped out of the sunlit bedroom and into the shaded apartment.

Slim knew that her only path of escape was through the front door. That meant, she had to confront the blood demon. She tried to quiet her fears by remembering Jared was only a fledgling and not a practiced vampire.

Still, he seemed proficient in occult trickery and that made him even more of a danger than most newborns. She crept out of the bedroom, down the dark hall and into the living room.

The vampire was waiting and the battle began.

Jared morphed into a large owl with sharp talons. Slim turned into an eagle. She knew better than to charge. Instead, she focused on averting attack. One exchange of blood might jeopardize her life. Her opponent was nothing less than a virulent, mutating virus.

His owl lunged. Her eagle skirted to one side. The wall received the smack of owl against it. As feathers flew, Jared changed into a giant king cobra and struck out at Slim's eagle, who hurriedly transformed into a fly. Jared again hit the wall.

He morphed into a huge green frog, whose tongue darted expertly throughout the room trying to catch Slim's fly, which immediately became a large kangaroo, kicking the shit out of the frog.

He turned into a nimble cat, she into a dog. He into a tiger, she into a lion. Jared altered into a rhino and charged. Slim turned into a canary.

Again, the wall took the brunt of a head on collision, but as fortune would have it, he had crashed into a window. A shade shot up and flooded the room with sunlight. The rhinoceros shrieked in pain. Slim seized the opportunity and changed back into herself, shot out of the apartment, and raced down the stairs toward the entrance of the building.

She managed to reach the front door at the bottom of the stairs, but it was too late. Jared was on the top stair, willing the door to remain shut. A dreadful feeling filled the pit of her stomach. She huddled in the corner of the vestibule and slowly looked up.

Shannon was already midway down the stairs.

"Leaving the party so soon, ducky?" he hissed, as he slithered down the last few stairs, holding her gaze with his red eyes. "We really should drink a toast to the success of our mission before you go. There's no champagne, so I'm afraid we'll just have to make do with blood. Don't worry. You're my first kill and I promise *not* to be gentle."

Five inch claws popped out at the end of his fingers, one at a time. By the time he reached the landing and was slowly floating toward her, his eyes were raw hatred.

Slim had almost given up, when suddenly, the front door flew open and morning light– like acid flung from a bucket– doused Shannon.

In a large puff of gray smoke, the *nosferatu* quickly retreated.

Rebecca, recently discharged from St. Vincent's Hospital, hobbled into the building and spied Slim in the corner.

The little old lady fanned in annoyance at the smoke filled foyer.

"No smoking in the hall, young lady. Don't make me tell you again."

Speechless and terribly shaken, Slim huddled in the vestibule corner, half hidden by the open front door. She watched the old lady search for a key in her purse, then, open the door to apartment number one and vanish within.

The agent pulled herself together and stood up, all the while eyeing the top of the stairs to be sure nothing was watching her back.

The coast seemed clear.

Slim swung around and out the front door, pulling it closed behind her. It was almost shut, when an ugly clawed hand lurched out and caught hold of her by the back of her blouse.

Sunlight seared the hand. The vampire howled from behind the door. Its preternatural roar vibrated in the pit of her bowels. Slim twisted her body and broke free from the beast, but the burning hand snatched her front belt buckle.

Summoning up all of her might, Slim closed the door on the demon's appendage with enough force to sever it from the wrist.

The fist fell and writhed at her feet. Its fingers snapped at her ankles.

Then, the claw slackened in an uprising surge of steam and sizzled into the sun-struck front steps.

CHAPTER 28

Sunday, an hour before dawn
Preston's home, New Jersey

Press awakened, drenched from night sweats.

After a night of fitful sleep, he was still dead tired and knew it would be futile to try and go back to bed.

He made a monumental effort and got up, took his morning shower, then tip-toed down the hall and looked into Trisha's bedroom. Marge and Trish were snuggled together, sound asleep. Tears welled up in his eyes. He surprised himself. Moments he'd taken for granted a few days ago now produced heartfelt emotional aftereffects. The ordinary had suddenly become extraordinary.

He burst out laughing. It was one of the greatest ironies of life, he thought. The present was never more appreciated than when the future seemed so forlorn.

Dragging himself downstairs to the kitchen, he poured himself a cup of coffee and was savoring the steamy morning comfort, when his stomach lurched and a wave of extreme nausea sent him rocketing to the bathroom.

By the time he was finally well enough to get to his den, he wasn't too surprised to find a brand new folder with more chapters waiting for him on the desk. Another night delivery, he thought. Another sneak attack. Another trespassing.

He grabbed the new chapters and crawled to the

couch, where he laid flat on his back, knees up, and tried to read through drooping eyelids.

Fifteen minutes later, Press was in an uneasy sleep on the couch. His body twitched. He was covered with a thin sheen of perspiration. The loose pages of the vampire's manuscript had fallen on the floor beside the couch.

Ben Franklin meowed at the den door, then cautiously wandered in, testing the waters. With no reproach forthcoming, the cat lightly hopped on Preston's chest. Press didn't awaken.

Being curious about his owner's infected neck wound, Ben sniffed at it. His fur stood on end. He arched his back, then leapt straight into the air.

The old cat hissed loudly and raced out of the den– as if his master had already joined the ranks of the undead.

CHAPTER 29

Sunday, an hour before dawn
St. Laurue's lair

St. Laurue made his way to his downtown lair knowing time was against him.

This struck him as not only unfair, but ironic.

A vampire usually had an abundance of time, but this Wednesday, the full moon would force him under the rejuvenating earth for a year and a half.

At least the most important matter had been resolved, he thought, as he arrived in front of his condo. His resting place had been chosen.

By tradition, some vampires choose to rest in mountain caves. Some gravitate toward coves by the ocean, while others find obscure forest areas. Many are intrigued with sacred grounds and protected national parks. For example, beneath places of worship or national monuments.

But thanks to his meeting with Kyle Riordan on the Jersey shore, St. Laurue had been able to secure the perfect sight for his temporary grave.

Even as the immaculately uniformed doorman let him into his pricey high-rise, he was able to identify his sister's ancient presence.

By the time the elevator delivered him up and onto the thirty-first floor, her delicate, yet potent scent permeated his being with pure joy.

He hurried to his lair door and entered.

Its interior was predominantly stark white, except where splashed with pools of bright red–

There were cranberry-velvet chairs, rouge red drapes, and ruby toned Persian rugs spilling along the cherry wood floors. Strawberry colored tapestries splattered the walls. Fiery sunset hued love seats with holly berry hassocks speckled the residence, on which, crimson quilts were sprinkled about. Round blush dot doilies puddled the backs of the plush cinnabar couches.

In short, the spot was unmistakably decorated for the purpose of eclipsing spilt blood.

He happily called out. "Brigitte!"

"In here," the tiny voice answered.

He ran into the bedroom and saw her, sprawled across his bed.

Her long soft auburn hair covered his lavender pillow slip like ripples on a lake at twilight.

Her form, though quite petite, was animal sleek and powerful. Her eyes were cat-like, piercing, and ever watchful.

"Ma chérie," he said, softly.

"Are we alone?" she asked, her French accent laced with concern.

He smiled at her misgivings. Unlike himself, his sister was cautious. Unlike himself, his sister was austere. But most particularly unlike himself, Brigitte was a confirmed recluse. His eyes drank in her delightful fourteen-year-old body. She was the quintessential schoolgirl. Yet, in stark contrast, her sophisticated style was steeped with ancient agility.

"Oui, my love, my sister, my daughter. We are quite alone."

The vampiress turned her head toward him and

moaned seductively.

"Do you mind my visit, Roddi?"

"You know I always encourage your worldly ventures when it suits you, sweets. It's those damned *cloistered* nuns who raised you at the Abbey. They're to blame for your reclusive nature." He walked across the plush maroon bedroom carpeting and gave her a tender kiss on each cheek. "As always, my best advice for you is to get out and live a little." He reclined on the bed beside her.

"It's all a game to you, isn't it?" Brigitte said. "Well, I'm not so easily amused. Give me one good reason why I should suffer this savage world more than is necessary?"

"For fun, darling. Something you need more of in your everlasting unlife." He gently stroked her hair. "You look anemic, sweets. When's the last time you fed?"

She got up from the bed, turned her back on him, and methodically began to inspect the room. "I'm here to speak seriously with you."

"That's my girl. Always the practical one. What's worrying you? Is it father again? Have you seen him?"

"No. Nor do I care to."

"Look on the bright side," he said. "The Marquis only *separates* you from your consorts. Mine, he *slaughters.*"

"Not that you have ever really missed any of your lovers."

"Let's just say, I haven't yet met my Bastien. You still love him?"

"It's unfortunate, but I don't possess the *virtue* of moving on so ruthlessly. Someday Bastien and I will be reunited, whether father likes it or not."

"Let him go, Brigitte. Have you forgotten the consequences the last time Bastien and father pitched battle– the great fires that spread and the terror it launched throughout London?"

Brigitte shot him a piercing glance. "You mean the plague with the blood speckled black rats?"

"Let's not get vicious." He sat up on the bed and refused to think of the ghastly rats his sister had mentally projected into his mind.

"Times change," Brigitte said, "but things often come full circle."

"Not those horrid rats again?"

She faced him fully.

"You have the new plague."

"Ridiculous," he said. "We ancients are strong and can't get sick."

"You know what AIDS does to our newborns. They go mad and kill their own kind."

"I'm hardly a fledgling," he reminded her.

"For we ancients, this deadly virus produces *different* symptoms."

"But I don't feel ill, Brigitte. Tell me. How am I different?"

"Your feeding habits have become rabid."

"What nonsense. I've always been a big eater, a great hunter."

"You've become unkempt and indiscreet. You don't clean-up after yourself."

"The devil you say. I'll have you know my

table manners are as impeccable as they've always been. Unkempt, indeed!"

He took out his silk handkerchief and pulled it through his fingers, just for the sensuous feel of it.

Seeing this, Brigitte sighed heavily and took an agitated swipe at a nearby expensive lamp, nearly knocking it over.

"You call undue attention to yourself," she said. "The ancients have asked me to intervene before it's too late. I don't have to tell you that we can't risk exposure. The hunters would then become the hunted."

He got off the bed and readjusted the tilted lamp shade back to its proper position and said, "Unlike you, I didn't have to spend several dull centuries meditating in an Himalayan ashram to know that."

Brigitte went over to the bedroom window.

"Even if it did separate me from Bastien," she said while looking out at the industrious nighttime city below, "I'm glad that father forced me to the ashram. Silence can be restorative. It is a wonder. You should try it."

"Why? The blasted millennium rest will quiet the commotion of both our lives soon enough. For me, silence is death."

"Funny," she quipped. "I find it to be golden and quite enjoy it."

"Well *I* don't. I need more life."

"But life is the one thing you can never have, my darling brother," she said, turning again toward him. "Why chase after the impossible?"

"Don't be despairing, sweets," he said. "One

has to try."

"Then try caution. The city police are catching on to you."

"What do I care about mankind's fickle moral judicial systems, run by bootleg lobbyists and stoked by the fads of popular opinion?"

She held her hands out in a worried gesture. "The ancients are going to act, unless I can talk some sense into you."

He maneuvered behind her and encircled her slender form.

"Good," he whispered, "if my boldness keeps you active, let the ancients' unwanted attention come. It will be worth it."

He inhaled the fresh scent of mountain pine needles in her long shimmering hair, then continued with his reasoning.

"Without me to rescue every now and then, you'd waste away on some ungodly Himalayan mountaintop, practicing one of your silent blood celibate hunger strikes."

"It's called meditation."

"It's internal whistling, to keep from facing life's fears."

"There *are* benefits."

He folded his arms sternly across his chest. "Are you referring to your boon from the Hindu god, Lord Agni– the fire ball trick?"

She flushed in anger and crossed over to a well stocked bookshelf on the wall and played with the edges of his esoteric texts.

"It's not like father's cheap tricks. It's known

as a *siddhi,* a power."

"*Oui.* A power which you taught your lover, Bastien, during the London Plague. And one which you still refuse to teach me."

He instantly appeared behind her and hugged her again.

"Father forbade me to teach you," she reminded him. "He doesn't approve of Lord Agni."

"Our father would have no Gods before me, but himself. He's jealous."

"In any case, I *attempted* to teach Bastien, and as you've said, the consequences were calamitous."

"Teach me the fire trick, Brigitte."

"No. I vowed never to use it again. I won't put your life in danger. But then again, I don't have to. You do that well enough on your own."

She turned away from his many volumes and wandered over to examine a gold encased pendulum clock on the wall.

He threw his hands in the air.

"Life is always a risk."

"You risk far too much. You risk yourself and others. The Ancients know of this exposé you're in the process of writing."

"You know about my book?"

"Many have heard. Do you suppose the Old Ones will stand by and not…"

Brigitte reached out and clutched the clock's swinging pendulum, as if stopping time itself.

"Oh, bosh," he interrupted. "What do I care about the ancients?"

He sent his sister a series of mental pictures.

Brigitte ignored the images of the young lady and the handsome boy.

She scowled and shook him by the arms.

"Stop it. Your cavalier attitude is the blood sickness speaking. Know this! You are in danger by your own actions."

He continued to mentally send her images.

"Do you see them? My Elka and Fury. They will ensure my survival. No. They will ensure *our* survival. I'm doing this for both of us, sweets."

He flopped on the tapestry-like snow white embroidered bedspread and playfully tossed his red silk handkerchief up and down in the air, while sending her a third image of his minion Press.

Receiving Roddi's elaborate mental images of all three of his new minions, Brigitte turned and faced her brother.

She spat out, "You're not ensuring *anybody's* survival. Least of all your own! What you're doing is getting overly infatuated with humans again."

"But these three are like family. Not family like you, sweets, but–"

"Damned right, not like me. I'm here for you *always*. Eternally!"

"Don't be jealous, love. They are meant to be our protectors."

"Let your minions be minions. Let them serve. You involve yourself too much. You trust too much. Be wary of mortals. They're so... mortal. So short lived." Brigitte walked over to the bed and snatched her brother's red silk handkerchief in midair. "If you really care for these minions, then have pity on them. You're spreading a blood poison. You're sick."

"I'm fine, I tell you. Never felt better. Now don't be a worry wart." He playfully brushed her leg. "My little bird, if it'll appease you, I promise to be more careful. Fair enough?"

Brigitte seemed to soften a little. She shrugged her shoulders as if to say she'd heard it all before.

He gave her his most charming smile.

It was clear from the look on his sister's face that she knew he was after something. She always did know him better than he knew himself.

"What is it this time?" she said.

"Nothing really, love. Just one tiny favor."

He gently stroked her soft skin. She tossed his hand away.

"I'm listening," she said with a slight, but not unbecoming grimace.

St. Laurue began to send her more mental pictures, which filled her in on the background details as he spoke.

"This evening, I must complete Fury's turning and Elka must feed on her own for the first time. Will you supervise Elka while I see to the boy?"

After a long moment of silence, Brigitte said, "If I must, I will."

She turned her head and struck the lavender satin pillow on the bed.

"To be quite candid with you, I already dislike this Elka intensely."

"You must learn not to be so jealous, *mon amour.* Elka's undead. She's no longer one of those savage humans you so love to hate."

"I don't hate humanity, it's just that there's so little in it. They're a constant worry to be around. So uncouth and frightfully short-sighted."

"Some are quite surprising. You really must meet my new friend, Kyle Riordan. Quite a refined and philosophic fellow. He'll remind you of your Himalayan guru– mortal, yet wise."

"I don't want to meet people. I don't want to get involved in their little lives. I'm involved with *you,* and sometimes wonder if I can handle that."

Brigitte restlessly got up from the bed, walked over to the window again, and wearily gazed out onto the threat of another oncoming dawn.

"My isolated little bird," he said, "you miss your Bastien. You need to fall in love again. Don't be afraid of love. Love is what makes us–"

"Human?" She placed her open palm on the cool window pane as she spoke. "That's the difference between you and me. You look at mortals and still see a measure of yourself. When I look, I feel so irrevocably alienated, so unrelated. To you, mortals are more than feed. To me, they're a bitter pill to swallow. Yet, you love them. What do you love? Their stupidity?"

"Their passion," he answered swiftly.

"Sometimes, I think you're not a blood drinker at all."

Instantly, he was behind her.

"Oh, but I am. Have I not sired you?"

"That's just my point," she said, facing him. "Look at me. You made me and I'm not truly a vampire either. I hate killing for food."

"But you must. That is our lot in life," he said, pulling his silk red handkerchief from in between his sister's fingers slowly. "Our father has created us so. Our lot in life is to take life."

Brigitte cast her eyes downward.

He placed a finger under her chin and lifted it. They searched each other's eyes.

"I sense father's about, again," Brigitte said in a fragile voice.

"Me too."

"Oh Roddi, take care. I fear it's the Marquis' plan to 'take you down a notch or two,' as he would say."

He placed his index finger vertically across her lips. "Don't speak of DeMalberet. We're together now. That's all that matters."

She tossed his finger aside.

"What matters most is that you've become irresponsible," she said. "Look at yourself! See what you've become. This blood disease has made your hunger increase. You kill indiscriminately. You leave trails. Again I tell you. Your actions are thoughtless and dangerous."

"Look at *your*self! You are only four years younger than I, almost one thousand years old, and you've never understood the thrill of the hunt, the glory of a blood kill. You even deny our natural hunger for blood."

"But you are not feeding in a natural way and the ancients will–"

"Life is an all night party, my dear sister. Why

lie comatose in some dull corner?"

"There's much to be found in stillness."

"I'd rather be an adventurous hero in hell, than an invisible nobody in heaven."

"But it's only for your own sake that I…"

"Shush. My darling. Must we quarrel? The dawn is almost upon us. We must rest. Come. Lie down, while I draw the curtains."

She slowly shook her head in frustration and silently did as her brother asked.

He unfastened the two heavy red velvet drapes on each side of the window and drew them in front of the pane, then went to her.

"Think of nothing but me," he said. "Together, we immortals will dream as we have always done since time began. Leave the sermons for God."

Brigitte protested softly, "God is all silence."

He lovingly whispered in her ear, *"Oui, ma chérie,* it may be so… but while we are here and just for now– be with *me."*

CHAPTER 30

Sunday, 8:36 A.M.
a Manhattan mid-town hotel

Slim was back in her hotel room, still a bit shaky from her encounter earlier that morning with the fledgling vampire. With Shannon's defection from the Daemonion Council, it was now her job to complete the mission. Time was of the essence, she thought. She had to find and kidnap Fury; not only to lure St. Laurue to the Motherhospice in Nairn, Scotland, but also to save the boy from Jared Shannon's fate.

She picked up the hotel telephone and dialed.

"Yeah, hello. Who'sa this?" The Italian lady's voice sounded hurried.

"Good morning, Mrs. DeAdonis," Slim said, in her most pleasant voice. "This is Miss Francine, Fury's guidance counselor. Is he there?"

"You from the school? It's Sunday morning."

"We have an emergency here. I wonder if you could put Fury on the phone. Thank you."

"All right, you wait. I go see."

Slim held on. Her heart was pounding. Her mind swam with several potential problems. What if Fury can't be located? What if the boy had already been turned? What if...?

Gina's gruff morning voice invaded the agent's racing thoughts.

"Furio's no home."

Slim involuntarily let escape a small sigh of

frustration. What now? she thought.

"Do you know where he is, Mrs. DeAdonis?"

"Eh, who knows? My son's a wild cat who sleeps in the streets. Same thing last night. Maybe I call the police. Lock him up. Then, at least I know he's safe. You call later."

"But Mrs. DeAdon–"

"I go to church now. Okay, Miss? Goodbye."

Slim heard the phone click off on the other end of the line.

She remembered she had spied Fury leaving the club with Rocky Vanos early Saturday morning and thought that he may still be with the doorman.

She looked up Nocturnal Rounds and dialed.

"Rounds." The man's voice was very gruff. He sounded annoyed.

"Good morning. Maybe you can help me. I'm looking for a boy."

"Lady, it's nine o'clock Sunday morning."

"His name is Fury DeAdonis."

"Nobody by that name works here."

"Oh, he doesn't work there. He's a friend of the doorman, Rocky."

"You know where Vanos is? He's not picking up his phone. Wait a minute. Fury. He the kid that went home with Rocky the night before last?"

"Yes. That's him."

"Haven't seen either of them since. You his mother or something?"

"No. I'm his… girlfriend. Could you give me Rocky's address? I'll pop over and surprise them."

"That'll serve the bugger right. Rocky's dump

is on St. Mark's Place. And when you see him, tell him Mario said to get his fat ass back to work. I can't manage this shit hole and man the door at the same time."

"Right." Slim diplomatically repeated Mario's message. "He's to report to work immediately."

"Okay," Mario said. "Got a pen?"

Slim took down the address Mario gave her, then hurriedly gathered her things.

Within the half-hour, she had checked out of the hotel, hopped a cab and was speeding toward Fury, hoping she wasn't too late.

Arriving at the address, she checked the mailboxes for "Vanos," then climbed the stairs to Rocky's third floor apartment.

Slim sensed St. Laurue's potent vampiric shade lingering around the doorframe and recognized it as a warning signal to stay away.

Undeterred, she knocked. No answer. She tried the door. It was locked. She looked up and down the dirty corridor to be sure no one was watching, then quickly morphed into a gnat and crawled under the shabby wooden door.

Once inside, she winged her way into the kitchen, into the bathroom, and finally, into the bedroom. The room was splattered with blood, but the lad on the bed looked to be unharmed.

As handsome as Fury was while awake, asleep, he appeared a young god. He was naked, sprawled across the bed with only a thin sheet barely covering his morning erection. His cheeks were flush. His body was boyish, yet well toned. His shoulders were broad, yet somehow soft.

Slim reluctantly tore her gnat-eyes away from him and rechecked the entire apartment. No one else was there. Still, something was wrong. She again sensed a strong vampiric presence.

Was it still St. Laurue's warning scent or was it the boy? The agent realized she couldn't take any chances. She had to find out if Fury had already been turned. Two vampiric assaults in one morning would be two too much.

She transformed into her own petite mortal frame and eased up the window shade. Slowly, sunlight spilled into the room. The boy slept on– a good sign. She went over and sat next to him.

"Fury, wake up, dear one."

No reaction.

The boy looked as though he had been asleep for a long while, Slim thought. He looked so beautiful, yet so vulnerable. She gently stroked his cheek. "Fury DeAdonis, awaken and arise."

Slim had used this strong hypnotic command many times and it never failed to awaken anyone. She was sure the magical phrase would even wake the dead, if need be. But Fury only nuzzled toward her caressing hand and sighed faintly.

Slim began to worry.

"Awaken," she commanded briskly. "You will slumber no longer. Return to consciousness. Now!" She clapped her hands together, loudly.

It worked. Fury stretched awake, very slowly and sensuously.

Slim blushed when the flimsy sheet covering

the boy's full manhood slid below his thighs.

When she reached across and caught the sheet, to pull it back over his midsection, the boy grabbed her wrist.

"Who are you?" he said sharply, shielding his eyes from the direct sunlight with his other hand.

Slim was so startled that she could barely whisper, "A friend."

The boy relaxed his grip. Slim breathed a sigh of relief. Their eyes met and a flash of white light filled the room for a second. Slim took note, but didn't stop to comment on the unusual occurrence.

"I need you to come with me to Europe," she said, gently.

"What?" The boy let go of her hand and shifted his body on the bed out of the sun's ray.

Slim asked, "Does the sunlight bother you?"

Fury looked at her, questioningly. "Yeah, it *is* pretty bright."

Slim sensed there was little time to waste. "St. Laurue asked me to take you to the British Isles."

"He did?" The boy looked excited. "That's so cool because I was just dreaming about him. I dreamt I was... like him."

"Like him?"

"Yeah, you know, really strong and all. So, you're his secretary or something like that?"

"Something like that. My name is Slim. I'm instructed to take you to Scotland. Will you come with me?"

The boy glanced around the bedroom. "Hey, where's Rocky, the guy who lives here?" His mouth dropped open. "Jeez, look at all this blood."

"Does the sight of blood bother you?"

"Well, yeah, a little. I mean, something bad happened here. I think I saw… It's all foggy. I can't remember. I thought maybe I was just having another nightmare. I've been getting them lately. But this really happened. Look at this place. I think Rocky's dead."

"Don't worry. St. Laurue's taken care of it."

Again, a brilliant white light flashed as she touched Fury's shoulder.

His face changed from wrinkled confusion to soft surrender.

"You're very beautiful, Slim," he said with an awe struck look.

Slim blushed again, then took command.

"I need to take you to Kennedy Airport. You're to see the many wonders of the world– his world."

"*Very* cool," Fury said, and unabashedly jumped up from the bed. "When do we leave?"

Slim cast her eyes away from Fury's sprightly nakedness, astonished at how foolishly one even welcomed death, when feeling helpless and alone.

"We leave immediately. Now get dressed."

While pulling on his jeans, he said, "Don't I have to pack?"

"No," Slim said. "We'll pick up whatever you need on the way. It's imperative that we're airborne before sundown."

CHAPTER 31

Sunday, late afternoon
St. Laurue's lair

St. Laurue was careful not to awaken Brigitte, as he gently lifted her arms from around his waist and got out of bed, making an early start.

First, he had to take the final chapters of his manuscript to Preston. After that, he had to bring Fury fully across, introduce the lad to Elka, and then, introduce them both to his sister. The undead one was elated. It had been centuries since he'd had the pleasure of organizing a family gathering.

He glanced at Brigitte, still sound asleep on the bed and wished that she wouldn't worry so much for him. What had she been going on about with this blood disease business? He felt fine. He ran the back of his index finger smoothly across her cheek and whispered, *"Je t'adore, ma chérie.* May your dreams be as sweet as your soul."

Peeking through the bedroom curtain, he was delighted to see that it was a cloudy afternoon. No direct sunlight, he thought. Excellent.

His powers would be weakened, but he *could* fly. Then, he looked at his sleeping sister and remembered his promise to be more careful. Taking to the sky in the late afternoon was too risky. Instead, he would hop a train to Preston's home in New Jersey.

Once on board and settled by a window, he adjusted his dark glasses and observed the passing countryside. A summer storm was fast brewing, threatening to dwindle away the day's remaining dull light.

He looked around at his fellow train passengers. They all seemed so stiff, so hemmed in, so censored by daylight. He felt sorry for them. They behaved so differently by day, he thought. After the sun went down, they tended to drop shallow appearances and were more true to their natures. More passionate. More adventurous. And even though he knew that many mortals were terrified of their own shadows at night, he also realized that they, not unlike himself, came most alive in the dark.

By the time he arrived at Preston's front door, it was notably dark for quarter-past-seven on a summer evening. He knocked and waited.

The door opened. An unnecessary invitation greeted him.

"St. Laurue," Press stammered. "I didn't expect you. Uh… come in."

"I do hope that I'm not inconveniencing you."

"Inconveniencing me? Not at all," Press said. "I was just beginning to wonder if you were still *making* personal appearances."

Press stepped aside and the vampire walked into the house.

"You've received my new chapters?"

"Yes, and what a surprise."

He handed Press a folder. "I have completed the work. Here are the final chapters."

Press took it. "It's going to be a long book."

"It's been a long life."

Press forced a smile and led St. Laurue through the hall, saying, "I'll read it tonight and post it off to Kyle tomorrow morning."

When they passed the kitchen, Ben Franklin hissed loudly and exited the room through a small swinging portal Press had built into the kitchen door for the cats. Once in the den, the publisher stretched out on the sofa and reapplied an ice pack to his feverish brow.

"I was resting."

"A necessary evil," St. Laurue said. "Where's the family?"

"Off for a month's stay at their grandma's."

"Oui," he said with a short snicker, "I know the place."

He looked at Press and grew disturbed. *What's wrong with the man?* he thought. Preston's face had lost its glow. A dull gray color had begun to creep forward into it. The mortal was sick. Why? In no time at all, he was probing Preston's mind, specifically focusing on information pertaining to the publisher's health.

The vampire mentally received the words– 'infected neck wound.'

He was about to withdraw from Preston's mind, thinking he had discovered the trouble, when a more sinister and cryptic message filtered through– 'police detective, bag lady, Slim.'

He knew the detective was probably Solomon Wiese, but needed to know more about this 'bag lady.' He refocused and began to sift through

Preston's mind for specifics, but was interrupted.

"By the way," Press said casually, "did you have to frighten Trisha like that? And did you have to kill her favorite cat? Just asking."

St. Laurue sat on the edge of the desk. "I was delighted to have met your youngest daughter. Forgive me Press. Sometimes I have an odd effect on mortals. I meant no harm. But as for the little beast, it attacked me right here in the den. What was her name? Betsy Ross? Unusually rich blood for a cat. Whatever did you feed her?"

Press shifted nervously on the couch and remained cryptically mum.

He knew this wasn't Preston's usual demeanor. They'd established more of a comfort zone. It was clear to him that something was bothering the mortal. Psychically, a notion drifted into the vampire's awareness.

He moved over to the couch, lifted the ice pack off of Preston's forehead and looked him directly in the eyes.

"You've something to tell me. I see it in your eyes. Something about exposure. Don't be afraid. You can tell me. You *must* tell me."

Press stiffened up on the sofa. "The detective. Solomon Wiese. You met him at my office Friday night? Do you remember?"

"I remember quite well. I had the good fortune to run into our detective friend later that night at Nocturnal Rounds."

"You were at Nocturnal Rounds?" Press said, with a surprised look.

"Press. You amuse me no end. That I was at a goth dance club appears to be more shocking to you than the fact that I am what I am. Now tell me, this Solly, he's going to be a problem?"

"He's on to you. He questioned me, but I didn't say a thing. I swear."

"I know. A girl named Ashley pointed me out. I took care of it," he said, impatiently, then hovered over Press. "Now then. You say that Detective Wiese *knows* about me, but tell me truly, does he *believe?* To the detective, I am simply an eccentric young author, *oui?*"

"He knows you're a vampire and plans to expose you. He and his wife left for D.C. earlier this afternoon."

"That, I cannot tolerate," he said. "Wiese has actually told you he plans to expose me?"

"He's a NYC detective. You're his serial killer. Enough said."

"But he is also a mortal man. An unpredictable breed. You say he's left for Washington, D.C?"

"On vacation. Maybe you should get to him before he talks."

"Perhaps." His eyes narrowed as he scrutinized Press, languishing on the couch. "Now tell me. Who is this Slim?"

"What?" Press shifted uncomfortably again on the sofa.

"In your mind, I picked up a name. Slim. Also, something about a bag lady. Who are these people? Are they the same? What have they to do with Wiese? Or with me for that matter? You will tell me. Now!"

He probed the mortal's mind again. The man's mental images started to surrender information. The figure of an elegant woman floated into the vampire's mind. The form had a name, 'Slim.'

Suddenly, St. Laurue saw a legion of big black, blood speckled rats. Hundreds of thousands of them roamed amidst, and fed upon, the editor's pinkish-gray mottled brain matter. The vampire abruptly backed out of the mortal's mind. He was repelled, insulted and outraged all at once.

"Who has betrayed me?" he brayed.

"What?" Press stammered. "What are you talking about?"

He again attempted to enter the Preston's mind, and once again he encountered the repugnant vision of enormous bloodstained street rats and reeled backwards. He staggered toward, then slumped over the den desktop. His mind whirled as he clutched onto the desk for stability.

Then, like a volcano erupting from the bottom up, the bloodsucker bellowed forth, "Who has taught you this trick!"

He was absolutely furious. How could Press have discovered his one Achilles' heel? How could this mortal have *randomly* stumbled on to the one image that could cripple his iron will? Perhaps it was DeMalberet's interference? Was Press in league with his father, the Marquis? Not very likely, he thought. His father's meddlesome and powerful presence was about– of that there could be no doubt– but he did not sense it around Press.

The blood drinker was sure of one thing–Someone who knew him, and knew him *well,* had coached his minion.

Managing to compose himself a little, he turned to Press with a weak smile. "It's fortunate for you that we've grown close. Clearly, I must leave for Washington and apprehend the detective. You've done well to tell me." He patted his publisher on the arm. "You must forgive me Press, if I was, how shall we say– momentarily ruffled."

"No need for apologies," Press said. "We're... old friends now."

St. Laurue turned and started off. "I'll show myself out."

"No, let me see you to the–"

The *nosferatu* swung around and with preternatural speed, appeared by Preston's side as the man was about to rise from the couch.

He lifted the mortal up and held him close.

"Trifle with me and you court disaster. I am moody of late and my affections have been know to turn in an instant. We understand each other?"

Press was struck mute, but nodded his head up and down vigorously.

Suddenly, he licked Preston's neck precisely where he had formerly lashed out and cut the mortal. The undead one's ancient saliva moistened Preston's infected wound.

"Look at your neck," he directed.

The publisher swung around toward the wall mirror just in time to see the wound on his neck fade and disappear.

"Good God," Preston murmured. "My cut. It just vanished…"

He turned to thank St. Laurue. But the vampire, like the infected sore, had disappeared.

Sunday, 10:43 P.M.
St. Laurue's lair

The telephone awakened Brigitte in her brother's downtown lair. She was upset to find that Roddi had gone. After several rings, the vampiress decided to chance answering the phone.

The sugary voice on the other end was overly ingratiating. "My sweets," St. Laurue said. "I trust you've slept well?"

"Roddi, you do love to disappear suddenly. Where are you?"

"At a diner in New Jersey of all places. I've had an abrupt change of plans. I need another favor."

"Why use the phone? I could have mentally received your message."

"Others might have as well, my love. Father's presence is stronger."

"I'm well aware of that fact," Brigitte admitted. "What do you need?"

"I have urgent business in Washington, D.C."

"You're always spreading yourself too thin."

"Will you look in on my Fury tonight? Make sure he's still sleeping and safe. Then, go to Elka and secretly oversee her first human feed. I will *personally* introduce you to them on my return at the appropriate time, so do use your characteristic stealth, my sweet."

"I understand," she said.

"You're going to love the boy. His adoration makes me come alive."

"You do realize that you're being absolutely driven by your vanity."

"Who isn't?"

"And now, you're letting yourself be run by your passion for this Fury."

"And you're not driven," he reminded her, "by your Bastien?"

Brigitte paused for a moment, then finally sighed into the receiver, "You forget. Bastien is one of us, not a mere mortal."

"Obsession is obsession."

"It's true," Brigitte said, mournfully. "When it comes to my Bastien, I lose all reason. You'd think I'd know better after all my years of meditation, but I still desperately want him. Tell me. Why is it that *here and now* is never enough?"

"Because quite honestly, it just isn't. And besides, what fun would it be if it was? Try not to analyze things too much, sweets."

"I will, if you try and keep out of harm's way."

"Pourquoi? Why shouldn't we dance into darkness, face our demons, and see the stuff of which we're made? I know what you need, *mon amour.* You need to have a most extraordinary adventure. It'll make you come alive."

To come alive, Brigitte thought sadly, as she caressed the lavender pillow, pressing it closer to her stomach. Would her brother never see that they were made of the stuff of things undeniably deceased? She sighed into the phone and said, "You have the will of a stubborn mule. Why do I allow you to continually wheedle me into your schemes?"

"Because without my imagination, ambition and sensationalism, little bird, your life would be as dry as yesterday's burnt martyrs."

Exasperated, Brigitte hung up the receiver, still mumbling goodbye.

CHAPTER 32

Sunday, 11:02 P.M.
The Wiltshire Plaza Hotel Washington, D.C.

St. Laurue soared above the clouds from New Jersey to Washington D.C.

The storm raged below.

Exposure, he thought. The very word made his undead body quake with anger.

Each lightning bolt below him, accompanied by its heavenly thunderous afterthought, escalated his raw emotions to even greater heights. His eyes flickered yellow-violet as he erupted with a belly full of bitter indignation.

How dare this bumbling detective, this mere mortal, this feeble future food for worms assume he could outsmart him at his own game!

Once in Washington, St. Laurue's intuition led him to the Wieses.

Skillfully swooping down through the stormy night sky, he found his attention being drawn to the top row of windows on the west side of the Wiltshire Plaza Hotel.

Even as he maneuvered the southern topmost corner of the building, he could hear Solomon and his wife.

He flew to their window and peeked in.

They were getting ready for bed.

The blood demon, hung suspended in midair, watched and listened outside their window.

"Some vacation this is," Solomon complained.

"The humidity. Who can breathe in this place?"

"I just turned on the air conditioning," Rita said. "Wait a little."

"I'll discuss it with my lungs," he grumbled, while unpacking his pajamas.

"The Holocaust Museum tomorrow will give us a few leads on what happened to Maury."

"Pardon me if I don't hold my breath."

"You're such a pessimist," Rita said, grabbing her robe. "Have a little faith."

The phone rang.

"Bub!" Rita gave her husband a look. "You told the precinct where we're staying?"

"Relax. It's probably the front desk. Who else? I'll get it."

Solomon sat up on the bed and grabbed the phone. Rita threw her hands in the air and went into the bathroom.

St. Laurue's psychic perception picked up on the phone conversation.

"Hello," Solomon said.

"Solly?" Eckles said, sounding upset.

"Trevor. Something happened? Tell me."

"Barrows and that kid Jamie are dead. Found them at St. Vincent's. It was pretty gruesome."

Solomon got off the bed and began to pace the hotel room. "Oh my God!"

"You okay?" Eckles said.

"Trev, I think I know what we're up against here and you're not going to believe it. I've got to come back…"

Just outside the window, St. Laurue flared with

malice. His fingernails elongated as he quietly scratched the window pane, itching to get in and kill. Instead, he made himself hold back and listen.

"No fucking way, Solly. I don't want to hear another word about you cutting your vacation short. I just called to let you know about John."

"But I've got to attend the funeral–"

"You stay there. John would've wanted it that way. You hear me?"

Solomon fell into a chair. "I hear you, Trev."

"Now don't make me sorry that I called you in the first place."

"Yeah, sure. Stay put. I get it."

"That's it. I'm gonna hang up now. You sure you're okay?"

"I guess so," Wiese said, his shoulders sinking. "You did the right thing by calling. I appreciate it."

"Sorry, Solly. See you in a couple of weeks. My love to Rita. You two have a good time no matter what, you hear me? That's an order."

"Sure. See you." Solomon put the phone down just as Rita reentered the room.

"The bathroom's free and if that call was work, don't tell me."

"Okay," Solomon said.

"What's wrong? You look funny."

"I always look this way."

"Tell me."

"Where's the antacid?"

"In the medicine cabinet. Your stomach hurts?"

"A little. It'll be okay."

Rita felt her husband's forehead. "You're hot."

"It's my Latin blood."

"Very hysterical."

"I need some rest is all."

"That call. It upset you. Who?" Rita demanded.

"You said not to–"

She tugged at his arm. "I said tell me."

"John is dead."

Solomon disappeared into the bathroom and returned, bottle in hand. He took a swig of antacid.

"You drink that stuff like it's water," Rita said.

"A lecture I get? Now?"

She went over to him and gently touched his shoulder. "John was a good man."

"We should go back, Ritzy," he said, earnestly. "I think I know who killed John."

St. Laurue's rage increased. He was beginning to morph into a vision of terror. Still, he held back for more information and better timing.

Rita shook her finger at Solomon and walked over to the bed. "Don't start with me, Bub. We're here to find Maury, remember?"

Solomon followed, trying to explain. "But the killer's a monster–"

"Calm down, Mister," she said, and reached under the bed to unplug the phone, "or you'll get another heart attack. Listen, I'm sorry about John but what? Are you suddenly personally responsible for the whole world's chaos?"

"But you don't understand–"

"Retire," Rita insisted. "That, I'll understand."

She stretched out on the bed.

Solomon sat on the edge and held her hand.

"I can't give up, Ritzy. Not now when I *know* who the serial killer is."

"Then call Eckles and let him handle it."

"I can't."

"Why not?"

"Because he wouldn't believe me if I told him."

"And why is that?"

"Because the killer's a vampire."

Rita withdrew her hand from his.

She was quiet for a second, then said, "God above, please tell me I didn't hear what I thought I just heard my demented husband say."

"He drinks the blood of his victims."

"Why are you torturing me?" Rita got up and turned down the bed. "I'll be going to sleep now. And I just hope I don't wake up with a friggin' nightmare, thanks to you."

"Ritzy, I'm not joking. The guy's name is St. Laurue. A young man pretending to be a writer. I knew something was eccentric about that kid. Too much wisdom for his age. Turns out, he's one of the ancient undead."

"Where the hell did I put my sleeping pills?" Rita went over to the hotel bureau and searched a compartment in her overnight case.

"I know it sounds crazy. That's why I haven't said anything so far."

"My husband, the lunatic," Rita said, opening a small bottle of pills.

"I'm not crazy."

"Then what, you're trying to drive *me* nuts? Look. I can jump out of the window and save you the aggravation."

"But my job."

She dramatically moved to the window sill and looked for the latch. "Okay. Fine. Go ahead. Chase vampires. I'll meet you outside on the pavement."

St. Laurue flinched in the darkness. His eyes flashed yellow-violet.

Rita screamed.

"What?" Solomon protectively pulled his wife away from the sill.

"Somebody." She pointed to the window. "Out there in the dark."

"Out where? We're on the top floor." Solomon looked up to God. "And she thinks *I'm* crazy?"

Rita didn't laugh.

Instead, she trembled and turned to her husband.

"A vampire you say, Bub? This killer you're trailing– he's a real, live vampire?"

❈❦❈❦❈❦❈❦❈❦❈❦❈❦❈

Confident they were not planning to expose him tonight, St. Laurue abandoned their window.

There would be time to devise a plan of attack, he thought.

In the meantime, he needed a temporary lair. A brilliant idea came upon him. He'd secure a suite of rooms, just across the hallway from Solomon and Rita at the Wiltshire.

As he checked into his suite, St. Laurue could hear the Wieses across the hall, still arguing about the validity of vampires.

Being the perfect gentleman, he wouldn't dream of interrupting them on their first day of vacation— not their *first* day.

He took out his red silk handkerchief and was dabbing at his temples when, out of the corner of his eye, he caught the reflection of a tall dark man wearing a shiny black top hat in the hotel suite's full length mirror.

"Father?" he called out, then whirled around, checking the room. No one was there. He rushed over to the mirror. The Marquis DeMalberet's reflection snickered, then dissolved, leaving St. Laurue facing himself.

Why had his sister accused him of being ill? And indiscreet? How could she doubt him?

He slowly and very deliberately began to strip in front of the mirror.

He didn't understand. One look at him should have assured his sister that he was ever the young god, glorious and immortal.

There was only one thing to do.

He had to get rid of the Wieses in a way which demonstrated brilliant precautionary skills.

As he watched himself undress, the fleeting thought of how vampires were able to see their own reflections, while mortals could not, crossed his mind. He decided to follow that train of thought. Perhaps it would lead to a plan of attack. Now, he stood naked before the mirror. *Naked*, he thought. The scheme had to be naked: simple, yet revealing. It had to be thorough, yet uncomplicated, to keep the risk of exposure at a minimum.

He ran both hands through his auburn hair, as Brigitte liked to do on occasion.

He remembered her touch.

A touch that always made him feel so loved, so secure. She was the only family he'd known and could completely trust throughout the centuries.

She was his loving sister, his dark vampiric daughter, his loyal compatriot in the fight against their domineering father.

She was the missing puzzle piece which made him feel complete.

Then, in a brilliant flash, an idea materialized.

He smiled, clenched his fist in a victorious stance and whispered, *"Voilà."*

The strategy was formulated and he was eager for the execution.

Both Solomon *and* his wife would be silenced forever– tomorrow, at the Holocaust Museum.

Reflections of a Vampire

CHAPTER 33

Sunday, 11:11 P.M.
Manhattan

Brigitte was more than a little annoyed.

She had to check up on her brother's Fury. That meant she had to go out and wander amongst humans. Not her favorite pastime.

She loped across the city rooftops, galloping over the dark alleyways. Flying in the city was too dangerous. Why take needless risks? In truth, she rarely liked to take flight, unless time was of the essence or it was otherwise absolutely necessary.

Her brother had mentally projected Fury's image and location into Brigitte's mind. Fury was more attractive than expected, and though she was reluctant to admit it, Brigitte was already blood smitten by the boy.

She entered the apartment building on St. Mark's Place and found Rocky's apartment door.

Her brother's intense warning scent told her she was at the right place. About to turn the doorknob and walk in, Brigitte suddenly stopped.

There was another ancient scent in the air. Something dark and sinister. Were the ancients already tracking her brother?

She clenched her jaw in a hard line and was not afraid. Time, if nothing else, had taught her to be persistent, proficient, and if need be, severe.

Her schoolgirl appearance and reserved nature had many times been misinterpreted by her enemies as a lack of fortitude– and usually to her greater advantage. But actually, Brigitte had been undead only four short years less than St. Laurue, and her quiet command was every bit as potent as her brother's brashness.

The vampiress walked into the lodgings. There it was again. She felt the awful twang of an ancient eminent evil pervading the apartment. What was it? Why did it cling to the apartment like a tenant about to be evicted? It brought goose bumps to her undead flesh.

When she made an effort to tune in, her mind was suddenly filled with a steady stream of images, all of a petite older female with auburn hair, the same shade as her own. Feeling unsettled, she attempted to block the images, but to no avail.

"Who's there?" she whispered to the heavy cloak of nothingness that surrounded her. No answer. More images. Now, she was being shown how Fury had been abducted under false pretenses and whisked off to Kennedy Airport. She also knew that the bitch with the red hair was responsible.

Brigitte was provoked and filled with jealousy. When it came to her brother, she was always overprotective and easily became irrational. How dare this mortal interfere with her brother's minion? How dare this female mortal slug have the exact hair color as her own?

Minutes later, rage literally lifted the vampiress off the tenement roof. She flew to the airport.

Knowing time was not on her side, she took a chance and appeared virtually out of thin air, just outside the busy airport terminal.

An old man about to enter the terminal saw her materialize. They locked eyes. She sent a strong silent command, "Look away, old man, or it will mean your end. I am death."

The man stopped instantly. A look of terror spread across his face. Then, his expression went blank and he hobbled into the airport lobby.

Brigitte was in a no-nonsense mood. The very thought of a woman stealing her brother's property had driven her fighting nails to the fore. She was surprised to find herself on the hunt and loving it. Enthusiasm raced through her ancient body as she marched up the long tunnel to the boarding area and immediately spotted Slim and Fury.

They were last in a line of passengers about to board a plane. She had to act fast before she lost the mortals into the hungry mouth of the jet ramp door. Brigitte raced toward them as fast as she could under human surveillance, while listening to their conversation.

"Here's your pass," Slim said, handing Fury a ticket. "Give it to the stewardess when she asks."

"Okay," the boy said. "Slim, I'm awful tired."

"Once we're in the air you can nod off."

"It's my first jet ride. What if I'm too excited to sleep?"

"Then you'll have to stay awake and enjoy it."

They were laughing. Enjoying each other.

Brigitte was pissed.

That red haired bitch was trying to seduce her brother's minion!

The vampiress plowed past travelers and cut in front of a security check-in line of worn out looking businessmen catching the red-eye. The security guards were the last barrier between herself and her quarry.

A security man spoke to Brigitte, "Have any luggage, young lady?"

"No, sir," Brigitte said, using her best schoolgirl charm.

"May I see your boarding pass?"

"I have none, sir," she said, playing innocent.

"No one is allowed past this checkpoint without a–"

"But you see my dear mother is just right over there." Brigitte pointed to the jet boarding area, indicating a preoccupied Slim. "See? The woman with auburn hair, just like mine. I have to speak to her. I'm afraid it's rather a family emergency."

The vampiress pouted, batted her eyelashes and girlishly played with her long tresses.

"Well, it's not regulation," the guard said, "but I suppose…"

Suddenly, Brigitte was tapped on the shoulder from behind.

"Pardon me. A question please."

It was the old man who had seen her appear in front of the terminal.

"These old eyes play tricks on me sometimes. I wonder could you clear something up for me?"

Brigitte had to think fast. She faced the security officer and sent him a powerful mental suggestion to let her pass.

"All right, Miss," the security guard said. "You can go through."

As she moved toward Slim and Fury, the old man called out to her.

"Young lady? Young lady!"

"Hey, keep it down there, pop," the guard said to the old man.

"You've got to stop her," the old fellow said, becoming more and more excited. "Something's wrong. I saw her. She came out of thin air… She's not what she appears to be. She's a terrorist."

The guard radioed for back-up.

Meanwhile, Fury had just disappeared into the mouth of the jet ramp while Slim handed her ticket to a pretty stewardess.

The old man's sudden shouts made Slim and the stewardess look to see what was happening.

Brigitte realized that Slim sensed her presence.

The vampiress stood still and glared at her.

Their eyes locked.

Their minds met.

'Do not move,' Brigitte mentally commanded the Council operative.

'Who are you?' Slim psychically questioned.

'Get the boy and surrender your tickets,' the vampiress suggested.

'I will *not* surrender,' Slim mentally shot back at her.

Brigitte came toward Slim.

The vampiress looked like a fourteen-year-old school girl with her arms outstretched.

She sighed sweetly, as if longing for one last

embrace from her departing mother.

Meanwhile, beneath the surface appearances, much transpired.

'You red-haired hag,' the vampiress mentally swiped out. 'Do you know whom you offend? I am Brigitte St. Laurue-DeMalberet.'

Her powerful will dug into the agent's mind, like claws penetrating jello. Slim staggered.

That one second of weakness was more than enough for Brigitte to gather crucial information from the operative's mind: Her name was Francine. She was called Franny or Slim. She was an agent for the Daemonion Council. She was kidnapping the boy, Fury, in order to lure her brother to Nairn, Scotland. It was all a plot against her brother.

The vampiress penetrated deeper into the agent's mind and more data was revealed: Elka, Roddi's female minion, was a shape shifter and was actually a *he* named Jared Shannon, another agent sent to ensnare her brother. But Jared had abandoned the Daemonion Council and was now planning to betray Roddi as well.

Brigitte could feel Slim struggling to keep her out of her mind.

The vampiress laughed out loud. It was far too late for that. The information was already disclosed; the damage, already done.

"Ma'am," the stewardess said to Slim. "Will you board now?"

Still caught in Brigitte's hypnotic power, Slim didn't answer.

"Ma'am?" The stewardess touched Slim's arm.

"Pardon me, Ma'am?"

The Council operative returned to her senses.

"What? Oh, yes." Slim quietly answered the pretty stewardess. "Sorry. Thank you."

Just as Brigitte was within several feet of her, Slim escaped onto the jet ramp. The vampiress was beside herself with rage. The stewardess said to her, "May I have your boarding pass, young lady?"

Brigitte emitted a low guttural growl, extended her right arm and raised her lethal nails toward the flight attendant's face.

She was about to strike out at the stupid girl, but a hand touched the she-devil from behind.

Brigitte whirled around.

She was circled by several security officers.

Immediately, she resumed the demeanor of an innocent young schoolgirl.

"Excuse us, Miss," the beefy guard said. "We need to question you."

The vampiress knew they thought she was a potential terrorist. That old man had brought all this unwelcomed attention. She had to think fast.

"I was seeing mother off," she offered, in her best schoolgirl voice.

"Step this way, Miss."

The security men took her to a side room and had her sit down on a plain wooden chair.

The five security guards in the office had been busy drinking coffee and telling off-color jokes. They fell silent and perked up at the sight of a pretty young schoolgirl.

"May we see a photo ID?" the obese guard said.

"I'm afraid I don't have one, sir," Brigitte said, with all due respect.

"How did you get to the airport?"

"A cab."

"All by yourself?"

"I'm a big girl."

"How big?" one of the guards said.

The others snickered.

Brigitte caught the sexual undertone.

"Am I in trouble again?" she said seductively. "My mommy wouldn't like that. You won't tell her how bad I've been, will you?"

"Well," the fat one said. "That depends on how cooperative you are."

"Oh, I can be *very* cooperative."

Brigitte uncrossed her legs and suggestively slid down on the chair.

"Well boys, it looks like we'll have to make a body search for contraband."

"Careful," she said, opening and closing her legs. "I might explode."

Brigitte knew they could not resist. Mortals are so easily seduced by attractive images, even though long dead. She plied all of her considerable vampiric charm and exuded an undeniably potent and raw sexuality. She modestly slid her hands down in between her legs in a playful attempt to shield her schoolgirl's secret.

The guards eyed her, then eyed each other.

"Maybe I can drive you home," the fleshy one said, winking at the others.

"Hell," another chimed in, "maybe we can *all*

drive her home."

"All of you?" Brigitte said brightly. "That'd be lovely, but could I use the little girls room first?"

"You understand," another guard said with a wicked wink. "You've been a naughty girl."

"Yes sir. I need to be spanked hard."

There was a palpable rise in the temperature of the room. Brigitte felt the men grow alert in an intensely sexual way.

"Big Charlie, escort this pretty young thing to the facilities." the guard in charge said, then turned back to Brigitte. "Now you be a good little gal and hurry back to us, you hear? Don't be afraid."

"I'm not," Brigitte assured him.

Big Charlie walked Brigitte across the boarding area and waited for her outside of the ladies' room.

Needless to say, she never came out– not that Big Charlie noticed in any case.

She had preternaturally sped past him and out of the terminal. As she made her escape, Brigitte caught the scent of death reaching out from behind.

It wafted from the room where she had been questioned by the guards.

She had no time to investigate.

She was on a mission.

Her brother's Fury was escaping.

Big Charlie returned to the security office, entered, and immediately slumped against the blood stained walls, gagging.

There were body parts everywhere.

His friend's heads were piled, pyramid style, on the floor in the center of the office.

None had eyeballs. *They* were stacked in a large crystal ashtray on the desk.

With a loud snap, Big Charlie's head suddenly twisted backwards. Another half rotation pinched it off entirely. It thumped to the floor and rolled on top of the pyramid of other heads.

An invisible vice grip squeezed Big Charlie's head with such force that his eyeballs shot out, splat-stained the ceiling, then landed neatly in place, along with the other eyeballs, all neatly heaped in the crystal ashtray.

CHAPTER 34

Sunday, 11:39 P.M.
the nighttime skies

"Ladies and gentlemen, we're airborne. Please feel free to unbuckle your seat belts and move about the cabin."

The captain's announcement brought a sigh of relief to Slim, who was belted into the window seat. Fury was beside her in the aisle seat.

"You still awake?" She lightly joked, nudging the handsome lad gently.

Fury rubbed his eyes and yawned.

"Yeah, but I'm fading fast."

St. Laurue's powerful hypnotic sleep command must still have a grip on the boy, Slim thought. She hoped that sleep was the *only* spell he had cast on Fury. The lad was so guileless. It would be such a stupid waste to have this stunning teen be turned into a hellish blood demon.

Together, they looked out the window, gazing in quiet awe.

Just beyond the jet's wing, the gibbous moon seemed close enough to touch. Beneath them, there was a soft bed of marshmallow clouds; above, an ebony canopy, sprinkled with twinkling pinprick lights that stretched as far as the eye could see.

"Almost infinite, isn't it?" she said, and took off her seat belt.

"It's like, as big as God or something," Fury answered in awe.

"Yes, precisely. As big as God."

Slim noted his reference to God.

It comforted her.

She felt there was something about Fury so worth salvaging. Her mother instincts welled up. She wanted so desperately to keep the boy safe and sound and prayed that she could.

They had enjoyed several seconds in silent reverence, before they spotted the strange figure on the end of the wing, struggling in the moonlight.

"What's that, Slim?"

"I... I don't know."

The agent tried to remain calm.

"It looks a little crippled," Fury whispered. "It's limping this way."

The black and red blob slithered up the wing. It came towards them slowly, but with intermittent bursts of speed.

Five feet away from the body of the plane, it ducked down, and hid under the rim of the window.

They heard scratching sounds just below their portal. It was an eerie noise, akin to fingernails being scraped against a blackboard.

Only just realizing it, Slim said in a firm but soft whisper, "It is she."

"She who?" Fury nervously asked.

Long, bony fingers, followed by a withered palm, then, a gnarled wrist, slowly scraped up from the bottom of the portal into full view.

Fury tensed up. "Holy shit!"

The hand was instantly replaced by the face of an antediluvian harpy with rotting yellow teeth between two pearly white fangs.

Her diminutive eyes were beet red. Her hair was blue white and blowing frightfully at jet speed. The inhuman harridan hammered on the window and screamed in the wind, furiously scratching at them from the other side of the portal.

"Can it get in?" Fury said, backing away from the window.

"No," Slim said. *"Her* kind has to be invited."

Then, as if the beast had heard and was compelled to validate Slim's postulation, Brigitte let out a tempestuous howl and vanished.

Slim closed the sheath cover of the portal window and turned toward Fury.

Her mind worked overtime.

Should she disclose her ruse and tell the boy the truth? She wanted to badly. She hated duplicity, which was laughably ironic, because her job so often demanded that she cloak her true identity.

Brigitte unwittingly presented her with the opportunity to convince Fury that he was in grave danger. But the boy thinks she's working for St. Laurue. Could she tell all and risk losing the boy's confidence just now?

Slim finally decided that truth was always worth the risk.

"That was St. Laurue's little sister," she said. "And if *she* frightened you, know that St. Laurue is even uglier at heart. They're evil incarnate. You're toying with the oldest, most dangerous species of beings on earth."

The boy blinked his eyes at Slim.

"Do you understand what I'm telling you?"

He looked confused and suspicious.

"Who are you?" he said.

"What matters," Slim said, "is that I can give you protection against them. If you want it."

"You tricked me into coming with you."

"*I* tricked you? No. *They've* tricked yo*u*. *I*'m trying to save your young life. You have now seen the true face of *nosferatu*. Do you still want to be among the living dead?"

"I want…" Fury stammered, as he unbuckled his seat beat. "I gotta use the bathroom. I don't feel so good."

CHAPTER 35

Sunday, 11:48 P.M.
Jared's apartment

Jared Shannon's first vampiric sleep was rudely interrupted by the insultingly loud church bells chiming clear across Chinatown. A newborn *nosferatu* needs his beauty sleep. Especially so, when he'd been blinded by the dawn's early light and had his fist severed just before retiring.

Shannon bolted upright off the bed and covered his ears, wondering why that damned noise, those church bells, sounded so threatening? Then, he remembered what he had become. The handsome twenty-year-old blond examined his right hand. It was fully restored. He strutted over to a mirror and stared at his reflection in awe. The Council's data had been accurate, he thought. The undead *can* see their own image.

A bloodthirsty smile lifted his lips. Not only had the first dark sleep made him whole again, but now, he had an eternity for revenge.

No need to shape shift into Elka, Shannon thought. He was beyond that farce. Immortality suddenly made disguises appear a foolish trick, to be used only by weaklings. Now he could do as he pleased and live as he liked. No more rules and regulations, no more monotonous humanitarian missions, no more "rare and special beings" to investigate for Mother. *He* was special now. Let the damned Daemonion Council investigate *him.*

Jared was elated. What could bring fame more quickly than to be a notorious blood drinker? And what could be more fulfilling? After all, a man's life, his passions, his knowledge, ran in the blood. Life's mysteries would be revealed, gulp by gulp. To guzzle blood, he thought. Was there ever a more instantaneous means of gaining the wisdom of life– or one as damned devilishly exciting? He threw his arms about himself. Shannon had gotten what he wanted all along. At last, he was a vampire.

As Jared dressed, he began to feel a slight ache in his belly. He bent over to put on his shoes. The ache turned into a searing pain. He doubled over, collapsed, and writhed on the floor. His tongue darted in and out of his mouth, while his eyes rolled up into their sockets.

Then, the wave of agony abated. He was not frightened. He knew the name of the sickness was hunger and eagerly anticipated the remedy, blood.

Fortunately, there was a victim nearby– an easy first target.

Jared left his apartment and crept down the rickety stairwell toward the front door. But he didn't leave the building. In the vestibule, he turned and headed for apartment number one.

Rebecca, the old lady, would be his first feed. Had she not earned her place of honor? Had she not hurled open the front door and scalded his face with burning sunshine, allowing Slim to escape his grip? It was kismet, he mused, the little old lady would provide a wonderful inaugural beverage– a delicately aged port, spiced with a hefty helping of fear. He'd see to that.

Jared tapped on Rebecca's door.

A weak voice answered. "Who's there?"

"Your upstairs neighbor, ducky. Do we have a cup of sugar?"

"Cigars? Go away. There's no cigars here."

"You *must* open the door," he commanded her.

Shannon was amazed that he was able to read the old lady's thoughts before the door was even opened: She'd been in the hospital. Her name was Rebecca. Her doctor's name was Alan P. Kravitz.

"It's Dr. Kravitz," he said, with great authority.

"You don't sound like my Doctor K."

"But I've come to check your blood count."

A number of dead bolts started to slide open in succession and the door swung open. Rebecca stood in the doorframe, tiny as a mouse.

"All right, then, come in," she said. "But it's so awfully late."

"Yes, too late, actually. Still, I believe I will take advantage of your kind invitation," the vampire said, and stepped into the old lady's flat.

Rebecca looked afraid. "You're not my Dr. K."

Jared was excited by her fear. He'd waited a lifetime for this moment… his first human kill as a vampire. The power of the hunger transformed his immortal cells. His face and forearms lengthened, as did his hands and fingernails. His eyes glowed lime green. His skin turned pus yellow. His fangs– those grim instruments of mortal annihilation– pointed proud and profane.

Rebecca stepped backwards and fell into an

overstuffed easy chair.

Jared eerily floated forward toward her.

"You're right," he said. "I'm *not* your doctor. I lied. But let me make it up to you. Let's have some fun, shall we? Let's play hide and seek."

The vampire dissolved.

Rebecca's jaw dropped.

The already limited lamplight in the small apartment mysteriously dimmed.

Odd noises came from every corner– a creak here, a scuffle there, a scamper elsewhere. The air in the room crackled with static and looked to be thickening and taking on a shape. Then, the noises stopped and Rebecca stared into empty space– until the long shiny black thing caught her eye.

A fourteen foot python slithered up her left leg and buried its head under the folds of her pale pink nightgown. The snake slid right up to her personal place, where it butted playfully, yet persistently, like a small child annoying its mother.

Perspiration splashed off Rebecca's body. Her mouth snapped shut and her lips pressed together. She seemed unsure of what to do and so, did nothing. But when the creature commenced to nip off little chunks of raw flesh from between her legs, her eyes turned up to heaven with a desperate look that seemed to plead for God's mercy.

Rebecca's mouth again gaped as the scaly python's tail reached up and caught her in a deadly neck hold. She choked out a thin shriek.

Suddenly, as the old lady's frail cry protested his ardent penetrations, Jared sensed someone else watching. The Shannon-snake turned and saw the silhouette of a petite young girl in the doorway.

"Leave the woman be," the shadow directed.

The reptile went rigid.

Rebecca's screech abruptly halted.

Brigitte stepped into the room.

The snake hissed and slithered down Rebecca's left leg onto the rug in front of the easy chair.

"I've been watching you," Brigitte said to the snake. "I'm surprised that you didn't pick up on my presence earlier. Perhaps, fledgling, your powers of perception aren't as acute as you supposed?"

Jared was not duped by Brigitte's schoolgirl image. He knew she was as ancient and lethal as death itself.

"Ah, you must be St. Laurue's sister," the python said and coiled at the foot of the easy chair, letting its powerful tail sway wickedly in the air.

"You've betrayed the Daemonion Council and now you're about to do the same with my brother."

"Let's not be hasty, sister. You're right. I *was* a Council operative. But now I'm one of you. Like it or not, I'm in the family."

"Not in *my* family," Brigitte said.

Shannon morphed back into his handsome form. The two vampires mentally sized each other up, preparing for battle.

The hostilities had begun. The room's silence was thick with mental exchanges. Each psychically pirated private knowledge from the other, ruthlessly sucking at the other's soft spots, so as to determine attack strategies and gain unfair advantages.

Within seconds, their cerebral confrontation was finished. Now, sore wounds had to be salted, flaws had to be flayed.

"You mustn't be *jealous* of me, ducky." Jared taunted Brigitte. "We *can* be one big happy family. That's what you've always wanted, isn't it?"

"Orphan-boy," Brigitte said. "Abandon your pathetic quest for fame. You are weakness itself."

The room filled with black rats covered with bloody specks.

Rebecca lifted her feet up to the seat of her chair with a screech.

"Try again, newborn," Brigitte said to Jared. "You've misread my mind. That particular vulgar hallucination is my brother's weak spot. I don't much mind those kind of rats. It's your kind that turn my stomach."

The rats vanished. The words "forgive me" echoed in the room, as Jared transformed into an exquisite fair skinned young man with violet eyes and sensuous lips. His well defined chest muscles were exposed by an opened white shirt. His thick dark eyebrows served to accent the soft depth of his warm brown eyes. The echoing disembodied voice found his face, as he said with longing, "Forgive me, my little bird. I had to see you again."

"Bastien?" Brigitte said.

The dark haired handsome lad cast his eyes down and spoke shyly.

"Do you still want me, Brigitte? Please say that you do. I'm ready to battle your father again. Even if it means my destruction. I cannot live this eternal damnable life without you. With your help, my darling, I feel certain that we can triumph over DeMalberet's will to keep us apart."

Brigitte silently fell to her knees and sobbed.

Bastien knelt down and kissed her eyelids, as he had many times, centuries before. "Please forgive me for coming to you without warning," he said, breathily. "I was afraid that if I contacted you, the Marquis would be alerted. I had to devise a credible disguise. Are you pleased to be with me again?"

"I am," Brigitte confessed. "Together, we will battle father."

"Yes, my sweet, we will battle," Bastien said and transformed into a bellicose banshee in full rage. Its gnarled hands started their strangle hold on Brigitte's neck. "And you *will* lose," the creature said, while repeatedly bashing the back of her head against the floor. In mid-pummel, the brute morphed back into Jared, tightening his strong grip around her neck.

Brigitte's body went slack and Rebecca's hands flew up to her mouth with a gasp. Jared slapped Brigitte hard across the face, then stretched her head away from her body. Her head wobbled from side to side and looked surrealistically independent of her body, which remained idle at a distance on the other end of her overstretched, reed thin neck.

Then, the vampiress lost consciousness.

Shannon sneered and raised his hand high above his head. It mutated into a sharp, double-edged axe.

His face twisted with insolence as he began to bring his slicing hand-blade down on Brigitte's distended neck.

But the karmic hand didn't descend.

It couldn't.

Something held it above his head.

Shannon turned around to see what force could be greater than his?

"Sorry," Rebecca said in a frail voice, "but I can't allow you to hurt her."

Shannon laughed in the old lady's face.

Yet, when he tried to free his hand from her grip, he could not.

A green mist issued out from the top of Rebecca's head and enfolded him. Jared's body was paralyzed by an ancient preeminent and unstoppable power far greater than his own. He could do nothing but gawk at Rebecca in confusion. How could this frail little old lady possibly…?

The last thing Shannon saw was his own reflection in the old lady's metallic orange eyes. All of his emotions had washed away, save for one– his passion for glory. Then, even that ambition– his final shred of personal identity– atomized, as he dissolved from the inside out.

As his arrogant walls tumbled down, Jared felt unbearable pain and screamed with such horrid wretchedness that one would have thought the traditionally merciless hounds of Hell would surely take pity on his soul.

They did not.

The green mist gobbled him up.

CHAPTER 36

Brigitte regained consciousness and slowly sat upright on the worn Persian carpet by Rebecca's overstuffed chair. "What happened?"

"Land sakes," Rebecca said. "That young man wasn't very pleasant."

Young man? Brigitte thought. Then she remembered. Her brother's fledgling had attacked her. "Where is he?"

"In Hell I suppose," the old lady answered with a chuckle. "Probably for lack of good manners. Are you feeling any better now?"

Brigitte answered with a nod. She *was* feeling much better. Her vampiric recuperative powers had already fully restored her strength.

"Well, *I've* got to sit," Rebecca continued. "My doctor's orders. Just had a cyst removed from my back."

Rebecca sat in the easy chair, reached for her yarn work and started unraveling the tangles. Brigitte was wary of the little old lady. "Did Jared escape?" she said, kneeling by Rebecca's side.

"Escape? Hardly. A great green mist came out of nowhere and just swallowed him up."

Brigitte scanned her mind.

"Your name is Rebecca."

"Now I just wonder how did you guess that, young lady?"

"Who are you? No mortal could remain so nonchalant after these events. Why is your mind so empty? Are you a creature of the night?"

"Well, I guess I *am* at that. Chronic insomnia. Had it for years. As for that green mist stuff and all the violence– I see it all the time on TV. No big deal. Turn to almost any channel. No problem. If you live long enough, you can handle anything."

"If only that were true," Brigitte said, still humiliated from being tricked by Jared. "In spite of a long life, one *can* still be fooled, especially when it comes to love."

"Yes. Love is a mighty powerful illusion, my little one."

Brigitte scrutinized the old lady's wrinkled face. Something about her eyes seemed so familiar.

"You remind me of my Mamá."

Rebecca put down the ball of tangled yarn and kindheartedly reached out to the vampiress. "Is your mother dead, child?"

Brigitte allowed the old lady to take her by the hand. *"Oui,* for a very long time."

"And your father?" Rebecca asked.

"My father?" Brigitte seemed distracted for a moment, then suddenly realized. "Of course. My father! I've felt his evil presence around me these last few days. He was responsible for Shannon's death. He always disguises himself as death in the form of a green mist."

"He must be quite the powerful magician."

"And of the very *worst* sort," Brigitte said, tightening her grip on the old lady's hand and peering directly into her eyes. "You will keep no memory of what has happened from the point of Jared knocking at your door, up to and including this loving kiss on your sweet forehead. Also, your back will heal quickly and perfectly."

Brigitte kissed her on the top of the head, but when the vampiress tried to let go of her hand, the old lady gripped tighter and said, "Perhaps my little one your powers of perception aren't as acute as you supposed?"

Brigitte was stunned and pulled her hand away.

"What do you mean?"

Rebecca laughed gently at first, but as she began to shape shift, the laughter turned mannish and was tinged with sarcasm.

The vampiress was startled to recognize the face and form of her formidable father, the Marquis Antoine DeMalberet.

The tall, thin, question mark of an immortal, radiated darkness. His horse long, pocked face sported a twisted grin. DeMalberet's full throated wicked laughter cut through the air as he stood up from the chair. "And how is my daughter?" he said, bowing and tipping his black top hat. "Well, I trust?" He tried to take her by the hand again, but she backed away.

"Father! How could I have not known?"

"How? Simply because I willed that you wouldn't. I tricked you. Just as that would-be Bastien did. Tricked by a newborn. Really, Brigitte. You should be ashamed. Mark my words. One day your short lived sentimental attachments will be your eternal undoing. I worry about you, pet."

"I'm not your pet. It's Roddi you dote on."

"Jealousy is most unbecoming for a young

lady of your position."

Brigitte was perturbed by her father's condescending attitude, even though she knew he was right. She flopped in the armchair, like a sulking teenager who'd just been told 'no.' And indeed, that was the way she felt, whenever her father was present. Still, she wasn't about to let him get the best of her. "Stop keeping eternal tabs on Roddi and me," she demanded. "That's not love. That's possessiveness."

"Moi, possessive?" DeMalberet said, as he picked the knitting needles up off the floor. "I give my children free range."

"Free range? Hah! Then permit my Bastien to return to me. Or would it kill you to see me enjoy my long life again?"

"Really. You must learn to stand on your own two feet, child."

"How can Roddi and I, when you use us like puppets for your entertainment?"

"Your naughty brother shouldn't have brought you over."

"I'm glad he did. I *wanted* him to do it."

DeMalberet toyed with the needles. "I know. Willful thing that you are. You were determined to immortalize Bastien and be young and in love forever. When will you children learn? Love is a passing fancy."

Brigitte grabbed the needles from her father and pointed them at him. "For Roddi and I it is. Only because *you* rip our companions away. Why won't you let us be!"

The Marquis laughed. "But you constantly get yourselves in trouble. What's a father to do? For instance, should I have let you die tonight?"

"Everyone has to die," she said threateningly. "Don't interfere."

With the wave of his hand, the knitting needles flew out of Brigitte's hand and buried themselves deep into a needlepoint, hanging on the wall.

It read, 'There's no place like home.'

"I never interfere with you and your brother's lives. I *enrich* them. I give aid when and where I can. Who do you suppose sent you informative mental messages at that appalling apartment in Chinatown, allowing you to see where Fury and Slim had gone? Who do you think killed the five security guards at the airport, after they dared to insult one of my children?"

Brigitte finally understood whose ancient evil presence she had felt back in Rocky's apartment.

"Manipulator," she spat out.

"Granted, I do tend to spice up your little games a bit. For instance, if I hadn't blocked Roddi from sensing Fury was escaping, I wouldn't have had the fun of seeing you fall on your face trying to rescue the boy."

"So glad you were amused at my expense."

"One question though– why didn't you board the plane, destroy Slim, and set Fury free?"

"You're right," Brigitte said, as she seated herself again. "I could have willed someone to invite me on board, but then what? Kill Slim in front of all the passengers? If they saw me, I'd have to crash the plane and destroy everyone."

"Such things have been known to happen," DeMalberet said, moving his little finger and making the yarn raise up off the floor and float across the room into his hands.

"I couldn't do that."

"Then why follow the plane at all?"

"That arrogant red-headed piglet. I wanted to watch her face dissolve in terror at the sight of me on the jet wing."

"Oh, I see. In other words, you were in one of your jealous snits and weren't thinking."

"I was protecting my brother's interests."

"And you failed miserably," the Marquis said, while making a cat's cradle out of a piece of yarn. "And why? Because you've never had the nerve to see things through."

Brigitte felt defensive. "What do you mean by that? I see things through."

"But do you see through things, my dear?" He reconfigured the cat's cradle into another pattern, strung tightly between his hands. "I shipped you off to that mountaintop ashram in India, not just to separate you from Bastien, but to add some depth to your life."

"Depth? I think you mean to talk to Roddi. *I'm* not the one who's superficial."

"Are you not?"

He again reconfigured the cat's cradle and eyed her intently. "Look how pretty you are, my little pet. Death's best disguise is a pretty face. But death, my dear, doesn't come alive until it kills."

"I've killed before," Brigitte said, unable to resist pulling the strings of the cat's cradle in her father's hands. She took on the stringed puzzle and held it between her hands now.

Her father smiled. "And I can't tell you how proud I am when I see you play the game, instinctually act from your depths, and come alive! My darling, when you choose to, you *do* show true genius in the art of death. But you have to learn how to *enjoy* it."

"You mean the way you enjoy things? It appears that all I have to do is fall on my face or succeed in slaughter and you're happy. What do you want from Roddi and me... besides total control?"

The Marquis took back the cat's cradle and reconfigured it between his hands. "What do I want? What an absurd question. I want nothing. I'm simply here to watch over and protect you. You're my children, my very life. I'm so misunderstood."

Brigitte had had enough. She walked over to the door and made what she thought would be the quintessential exit line.

"I understand you well enough to know you're an exploitative devil. You always *have* been, and you always *will* be." She was about to turn and leave the apartment, when DeMalberet's charismatic voice drew her back.

"Ah, but without *me*," he said, "how would things get done?"

Brigitte walked over to the Marquis DeMalberet and snatched the cat's cradle out of his hands. "You mean *undone*." She tossed the tangled yarn to the floor, then saw the truth in her father's eyes. "You helped that woman with the auburn hair escape me at the airport, didn't you?"

"Now would I do something as horrid as that?"

"Oui."

DeMalberet morphed into the old man who saw her materialize out of thin air outside the Kennedy terminal, ruining her effort to rescue Fury and take revenge on Slim. He cackled, then returned to his usual form.

"You conniving bastard," Brigitte said. "Why did you do it?"

"To make you stronger, *and* take you down a notch or two. All in good fun, naturally. You've got to learn to think on your feet."

Brigitte was foot stomping mad. "Endlessly, you insult my intelligence."

"You're so like your mother," DeMalberet said. "Much too touchy."

"I'm not like my mother. Simone was your *succubus*. Your slave."

"As have been all of my lovely little wives."

"How convenient for you, you *slave keeper!*"

"What nonsense," he chortled. "My wives all enjoyed wealth and power. The life of a *succubus* is not without its merits."

"Oh, but it's so very short lived. Just one puny mortal life span. Then poof, they're dead. And then you're on to a new plaything. Well, I've got news for you, father. I'm a vampire. An immortal. You are *not* going to get rid of me as simply as you did my mother. I don't go away and die that easily."

"I don't want to be rid of you, Brigitte. Oh, this is all my fault. I've spoiled my children. In time, you'll think better of me. I'm a *good* father."

"You're no father," she said, kicking the yarn and turning her back on him. "You're a malicious force of nature to be reckoned with!"

DeMalberet wiggled his finger. The yarn lifted off the Persian rug, untangled, balled itself, and settled on the seat of the overstuffed easy chair.

"Have it your way, Brigitte," he said softly. "You always do."

Once again, her father's spellbinding voice pushed her buttons. She turned on him in a rage. "I hate you."

"Then strike me. Go ahead. Strike me now."

Brigitte seized the knitting needles buried in the wall hanging and raised an arm in anger... then watched as it dropped back down, needles falling to the carpet.

"You stopped me," she accused.

"I did nothing of the kind," DeMalberet said. "You stopped yourself."

She wept. "I wish I *could* kill you."

"That's the spirit," he said, as he spruced up the lapels of his light summer jacket and donned his top hat. "Good to see you again, child. Far be it from me to boil the blood and run, but I really must fly. I have an urgent task to complete before the night is over."

She peered into his hypnotic, metallic orange tinged eyes and was very mistrustful. "What sport are you up to now?"

With a wink and a slight shimmer, DeMalberet vanished in a green flash.

Brigitte kicked the easy chair and it slammed against the apartment wall, bringing down the wall hanging that reminded her, 'there's no place like home.' *Home,* she thought, as she slumped against the wall. She only truly felt at home when she was with Roddi.

Confronting her merciless father was anything *but* the comforting sense of being at home.

Generally, the Marquis left her feeling empty and vulnerable. But not this time.

This time, she was filled with a sense of failure, laced with anger, anxiety and guilt.

This time she felt *accountable.*

She had let Fury escape and now had to face the unpleasant task of telling her beloved Roddi.

CHAPTER 37

Monday, June 25th 3:04 A.M.
The Wiltshire Plaza Hotel Washington, D.C.

St. Laurue felt far too energetic to night nap. It was only three in the morning and for the undead, that was the middle of the day. And though he needed to conserve his strength for tomorrow's crucial daytime encounter at the Holocaust Museum with the Wieses, the blood drinker was impatient, restless, irritable, and above all– hungry!

The vampire left his suite and wandered the hotel hallways. Several rooms disclosed whispered conversations, moans, and the most intimate of rustlings as he passed. Blood spore saturated the halls, the elevator, and the empty dimly lit lobby.

His hunger increased.

As he passed by the front desk and started down a service hallway, he heard voices coming from the employee's room by the back kitchen at the end of the corridor. He stealthily crept closer, peeked in, and listened by the open doorway. Two handsome young bellboys were having a serious discussion about job ethics.

"Fucking woman in room four twenty-one," Mackenzie said. "Can you believe it? She phones for a midnight snack. I bring her the order, put it on her bed, which she's in, naked, and you know what happens- the bitch stiffs me."

"No tip?" Leon said. "Did you hold out your hand, boner breath?"

"I did, butt lick, and the fucking lady says, 'Take it out in trade.' "

"And so? Since when do you run away from a good fuck, Mac?"

"Right, but this fucking woman made ugly look hot."

Both boys laughed and gave each other a 'high five' until Leon caught a glimpse of somebody standing by the doorway.

"Hey. What was that?"

"What?" Mackenzie said, still laughing.

"Someone was by the door."

"Let's check it out."

Meanwhile, St. Laurue had discovered a meat storage room nearby, just off the kitchen. Apparently, the hotel prided itself on serving only the freshest meat and had its own facilities.

The vampire was delighted with the medium sized room. It was lit by a naked hanging light bulb and was saturated with the sweet smell of blood from the recently butchered animals.

Large hunks of bovine body parts hung off cold stainless steel wall hooks. Floor troughs ran red along the walls toward a corner drain with the beasts' freshly dripping fluids.

He was intoxicated by the aroma of fresh blood. He strolled into the meat storage room, left the door ajar and mentally bade the boys to follow.

"Look," Mackenzie said. "The meat cooler."

"Yeah. The door's open." Leon moved forward. "Come on. We gotta check it out."

"I don't like this. Let's just forget it."

"Too bad, ass lick, somebody heard us," Leon said by the cooler door. "We've got to know who. I can't afford to lose this lame job."

Mackenzie backed away. "What if it's some freakazoid with a knife or a gun? What if it's like Jack the fucking Ripper?"

Leon grabbed Mac's arm. "What a slacker. Ya know? You got some fucked up imagination."

"I'm just saying it could be anyone."

"Duh? Now cut the shit. We're going in."

St. Laurue stood nonchalantly in the back of the shadowy room. He felt his desire for the bellboys increase. They were splendidly handsome in a street-wise way. Their young blood ran hotter than average, he thought. It pulsated loudly in his ears. He probed the lads' memories. They were full of deliciously dark passions. He started to blood frenzy, but knew he'd do better to stay in the corner and bide his time, like a black widow spider waiting for the fly-boys to enter his web.

Mackenzie and Leon cautiously walked into the cold meat room and saw the vampire pretending to shiver in the corner.

"Whassup, homeboy?" Mackenzie said. "You crazy or something?"

St. Laurue looked boyish and vulnerable. He licked his lips.

"Yeah, bitch?" Leon barked. "You want us?"

"I crave only a few minutes of your precious time," St. Laurue said.

"This is too freaky for me," Mackenzie said, and began to leave.

"Chill out." Leon told Mackenzie.

Meanwhile, the vampire's great hunger had spontaneously turned him into a blood guzzling, befanged beast. His breath was heavy. Clouds of glacial vapor puffed out of his nostrils. His eyes were a glaring yellow-violet. His hands had become lethal talons, clicking in the air.

"Don't worry, Leon," St. Laurue said, with a throaty preternatural bass voice. "Our little friend's not leaving– and neither are you."

Both boys visibly shook as they noticed the metamorphosis and heard the blood demon's words.

St. Laurue commanded Mackenzie.

"You will come to me now!"

Mackenzie about faced, levitated off the floor, and drifted in the air toward the vampire. Leon anxiously eyed the door, but before he could take flight, St. Laurue had cast his paralyzing glance at both of them.

"Be still," the *nosferatu* hoarsely whispered.

The two boys were instantly immobilized– Mackenzie, in midair, and Leon, his feet planted firmly on the cold cement floor.

"You will do as I say," St. Laurue instructed.

His green crusty tongue poked out of his blood red lips, elongated and slapped the bellboys' paralyzed bodies. Then, like a famished child might slurp up a spaghetti strand, the tongue zipped back into his mouth.

"You boys enjoy each other, no?" he said, with a sly smile. "You are close?"

"Let us go, you freakmiester," Leon said, his

face twisted with fright.

"Perhaps, perhaps not," St. Laurue said.

"If we do what you want, you won't hurt us, will you?" Mackenzie's pleading only whetted St. Laurue's raging hunger.

"You have my word as a gentleman," St. Laurue agreed. "You will feel no discomfort by my hand." Their faces momentarily calmed, while the vampire lifted his index finger and motioned Mackenzie back down to the floor. "But you must understand, I've lived a very long time and, over the centuries, have developed some rather idiosyncratic passions. I like to watch young people enjoying each other."

"What," Mackenzie muttered. "You want us to get each other off?"

"Nothing as sexual as that," St. Laurue said.

"Then what?" Leon asked.

St. Laurue smiled. "I would enjoy seeing you eat each other."

Mackenzie whined. "You said nothing sexual."

"Cannibalism can hardly be called sexual," the vampire said dryly.

The bellboys stared at the vampire in shock.

"But you promised you weren't going to hurt us," Mackenzie whimpered.

"And my promise shall be kept. You will feel no pain by *my* hand. Now please pluck out Leon's right eyeball and put it in your mouth."

Before the boys had the chance to protest, St. Laurue commanded them to be silent. Then, with only the slightest exertion of his ancient will, the *nosferatu* released the boys' fixed bodies just enough to carry out his commands.

Mackenzie quickly disengorged Leon's right eye and placed it on his tongue.

"Now, chew your food," St. Laurue cautioned. "Like a good boy."

Both boys had sweat-sheened faces. A trickle of blood spilled down from the empty socket of Leon's eye.

Mackenzie chewed.

The fluid filled eyeball popped in his mouth.

The boy swallowed.

"Now Leon, please bite off and swallow your colleague's tongue."

Both boys slowly bent forward and opened their mouths, as if about to kiss. When they parted, Leon held Mackenzie's tongue firmly between his teeth. In one swift movement, he jerked his head and yanked the tongue out entirely. It hung flaccid from his mouth, like a ragged edged piece of bloody raw steak. Then, Leon chewed, swallowed, and very nearly choked on a mouthful of his friend's tongue.

St. Laurue took great delight in watching the mortals ambitiously devour one another for awhile, then became blasé.

Nothing to get overly excited about, he decided, people cannibalize each other every day.

The undead one played with the boys until they were unrecognizable meat packages.

With half eaten fingers, toes, nipples, noses, tongues, ears, eyes and lips, it became difficult to tell one boy from the other.

Of course, he understood the lads had to be finished off. If he let them survive, even in this deplorable state, they'd become habitual cannibals.

Human flesh, once tasted, was far too sweet an addiction to desert.

By this time, both boys had blacked out and were about to expire. He could do as he pleased with them and still keep his gentleman's word—being unconscious, they wouldn't knowingly suffer by his hand.

He reached into their chests with both hands and simultaneously tore out both boys' hearts.

With an upturned face, he raised the dripping organs over his greedy mouth and squeezed. Blood squirted out like juice from a couple of ripe grapefruits. Then, the blood glutton rapaciously sucked his fill from their necks, much like a naughty little lad tearing into a couple of presents on Christmas morning.

After his able fangs had finished mining his evening fare, St. Laurue disentangled the boys and hung each of their blood drained packages on a cold, stainless steel meat hook. And there they hung, like mistletoe, beside the other butchered beef.

He was amused to think that the hotel's head chef might unknowingly serve a rare and rather exotic meat dish tomorrow night for the Wiltshire clientele, when a gut wrenching pain flared through his undead body.

His stomach grossly distended, making him look like a huge blood bloated tick.

He let out a thick stream of devitalized blood,

shellacking the boys' corpses, instantly redecorating them with the unmistakable blush of blood vomit.

St. Laurue spat the remaining blood out on the floor, then scrupulously wiped his mouth with his red silk handkerchief, but once again a river of rocketing crimson juice jettisoned up from his belly and graffitied the meat locker walls.

Having imbibed the eviscerated boys' blood essences and regurgitated the rest, the vampire quit the dead cattle coffin and returned to his top floor hotel accommodations, temporarily satisfied.

He'd had an adventure.

He'd fully fed.

And now, being less anxious, he could attempt a few hours of profound vampiric sleep.

St. Laurue fell across the bed. Soon, the after-kill visions of release came– and he was redeemed.

CHAPTER 38

Monday, just before dawn
the nighttime skies

Several hours into the transatlantic flight, the
callow co-pilot peered out of the cockpit window,
while his captain took a ten minute nap before their
landing at Edinburgh International Airport.

The radar was engaged and both the young man
and the plane were on automatic pilot, when a loud
thump disrupted his daydream. He decided not to
awaken his captain, whose nap, oddly enough,
hadn't been disturbed by the jarring noise.

He checked the instruments. Nothing seemed
out of the ordinary, so he settled back in his seat
and had already retreated into his secret thoughts
again, when he heard a mysterious scraping sound
slowly creeping across the cockpit windshield and
looked out and saw the vaporous sphere of multicolored lights materialize just ahead of the jet.

Two lights in the night sky took the shape of
large metallic orange eyes, focused on him.

The two eyes merged into one. In its pupil, he
could see another shape forming– a naked woman,
covered only by a sheer white veil. Not a word was
exchanged, but he knew what the siren wanted. His
arm shot up and hand signaled the temptress aboard.

The single eye cracked like an egg and the
beautiful nymph oozed through the cockpit window
and materialized behind him. He turned and fully
expected to see the bewitching woman. Instead, he

thought he caught the figure of a little old lady exiting the cockpit into the passenger area.

He scratched the top of his head and wondered if he was more tired than he suspected. Maybe he had jet lag? Too much coffee?

The captain was still peacefully snoring in the seat beside him and within a few seconds, the young pilot was again staring out of the cockpit window and into the pre-dawn sky– just an ordinary mortal preoccupied with his own private thoughts, and decidedly, none the wiser.

❀❀❀❀❀❀❀❀❀❀❀

Fury awakened in his plane seat next to Slim, who was still dozing. The agent instinctively stirred the instant Fury got up from his aisle seat.

"Where to?" Slim asked, still a bit sleepy.

"The bathroom," Fury said. "My stomach feels funny again."

The boy had calmed down and was starting to warm up to her, but Slim continued to worry. She sensed the teen was still fascinated by the vampire. That much, she could handle. But had St. Laurue compromised Fury's health? Had he infected the lad with HIV, vampirism, or both?

Slim watched Fury hurry up the aisle to the restroom, adjacent to the cockpit. It was occupied. Suddenly, the cockpit door flung open and a little old lady rushed out, nearly knocking the boy over.

The oldster barreled down the center aisle and sat in an unoccupied seat directly across the aisle from her.

Something seemed familiar about the old lady, Slim thought, but she was too concerned with Fury to think about it. She glanced ahead and saw the boy go into the restroom. Should she go see if he needed help? Was it just a jittery stomach? Was he dying of AIDS? Was the lad looking into the mirror right now, watching himself turn into a vampire?

"Pardon me, young woman." the elderly lady across the aisle interrupted her thoughts. "Would you please pass me that magazine in the seat pocket in front of you?"

Slim, still preoccupied with worries about Fury, turned and faced the woman. "Oh. It's you," Slim said, startled by the sudden recognition. "You saved my life."

"I saved your life?" The elderly lady seemed genuinely surprised and pleased.

"Yes. I was in the foyer of your apartment building in Chinatown. You opened the door and, see, I was being chased by this, ah, monster–"

"New York isn't what it used to be."

"I do feel safer now that we're off to Europe."

"How nice for you and the boy. Your son?"

"Fury? No. He's... he's my nephew."

"Nice boy. I'd be proud to have him in my own family, I dare say."

"I don't remember seeing you in the boarding area at the airport," Slim said. "If I had. I would've recognized you earlier."

"That nice young pilot invited me aboard to see the cockpit. Truth be known, I practically invited myself. Gave that young man the eye and worked my feminine wiles, don't you know. I have my ways, even at my age."

"Oh," Slim said, distantly, not completely convinced by the old lady's story. The agent felt she had better probe a little further. "So. You have relatives living in Scotland?"

"Living?" The old lady smiled sweetly. "No. I'm just visiting a few old friends from the year one, so to speak. How about that magazine?"

"Oh, sorry. Here you go."

When Slim handed her the publication, their eyes met.

Slim felt funny. She couldn't stop looking into the old lady's lambent, captivating metallic orange tinged eyes. They were drawing her out.

Her mind suddenly went blank. Her sense of identity collapsed into nothingness.

When Slim returned to her senses, she realized that she'd had a momentary lapse of consciousness.

Undoubtedly, she had just handed this little old lady a magazine, but something else had happened. Didn't it? She wasn't certain. "Sorry," she said, uncomfortably. "I never got your name."

"Rebecca, dear," the old lady said. "You may call me Rebecca."

The captain's metallic voice came over the cabin speakers.

"Ladies and gentlemen, we are approaching Edinburgh International Airport. Please fasten your seat belts."

CHAPTER 39

Monday, 9:42 A.M.
The Wiltshire Plaza Hotel Washington, D.C.

"You okay?" Rita said with a look of concern as she touched up her face at the vanity in the hotel room. She stole a glance at Solomon in the mirror and worried that he looked so tired.

He yawned and picked a shirt. "I didn't sleep so good. You?"

"Who can sleep in a strange bed?"

"Listen… about last night," he said, as he put on a shirt.

Rita purposefully interrupted him. "There's a gorgeous restaurant in the lobby. I checked. They serve brunch till noon."

Having completed her make up, she turned to Solomon and gave him one of her famous 'don't worry, things will be all right' smiles, which was immediately followed by her more typical 'no nonsense' look. "Now hurry up," she complained. "I'm practically starving."

Solomon tucked the pinstriped shirt into his navy blue slacks, then turned and rummaged through the luggage. He looked worried.

"What?" Rita said, grabbing her pocketbook.

"Wait a minute, will you?" The detective rifled through the inside pockets of yet another larger suitcase. He tossed the clothes haphazardly onto the bed. "Here we are."

He picked up a couple of shinning objects.

"Come on," she said, pulling his sleeve. "My stomach's growling."

"One for you and one for me." He gave her a silver chained crucifix and put the other around his neck, tucking it under his shirt.

She stood still, unsettled by the relic in her hand. "You're expecting me to wear this?"

"It keeps vampires at a distance."

"So now this vampire is on *my* ass too?"

"It could happen. Your cute little ass is not so unattractive as you might think."

"In case you never noticed, I'm a person of the Jewish persuasion."

Rita tossed the silver crucifix on the bed. As it landed, it glimmered for a second. She was surprised at first, then assumed the cross had caught the sunlight just right.

"What's wrong?" he said.

"Nothing. Let's go. My stomach's acting up."

"Put on the crucifix."

"No. And stop annoying me about it already."

"All right." He threw his hands in the air. "I don't feel like arguing."

"Who's arguing?" She smiled and patted his shoulder. "We're just having a small discussion."

He tried again. "But this could save your–"

"And the discussion is *over*. Look, your shoelace is untied."

Solomon looked. They were tied.

"Got ya." she announced, fully enjoying her husband's sentimental smile.

"You and Maury," he said. "You guys could

always make me fall for that one." He strapped on his shoulder holster and began to search in one of the suitcases again.

"Oh God," she grumbled. "What now? You brought a couple of Rosary beads too?"

"No, a silencer and the blessed silver bullets."

"You've *got* to be kidding."

"What? I always wear a gun."

"Not on vacation, and not with *blessed* silver bullets. I swear if you bothered Rabbi Lavinsky with all this baloney, I'll–"

"Don't worry. I found a priest."

"First vampires, now *priests?* Enough. Right now, it's brunch, then the Holocaust Museum. We're here about your brother, Maury. Remember?"

"I remember. I remember."

"And why the gun? You're expecting maybe to shoot a few Nazi ghosts?" She frowned as he loaded the pistol, attached the silencer to the front barrel and tucked it into his holster. "And furthermore, Mr. Big Shot," she said, dryly. "You can't kill monsters who are already dead."

"I know," he said quietly. "Believe me. That much, I already know."

She noticed what looked like a rush of futility and utter vulnerability in her husband's eyes as he adjusted the strap on his shoulder holster.

"Come on, Dr. Van Helsing. Let's do brunch and see how the other half lives."

He threw on his sports jacket and grabbed the hotel key-card. "Got everything?" he said. "Cause we're not coming back."

"Look who's talking, Mr. forget-your-head-if-it-wasn't-attached."

"Ritzy, before we go. The crucifix... Please."

Rita looked at the relic on the bed. The silver crucifix lit up again. With a sudden intake of breath, she took his arm and hurried him out of the room. Then, when they had almost reached the elevator, she turned to her husband. "Wait a minute, Bub. I have to go to the bathroom."

"So hold until the restaurant downstairs."

"You hold– the elevator door. I'm going back to the room. Give me the key-card."

He made a noise and gave her the card.

"And by the way, Mr. Smarty-pants," she mentioned, "do you have any idea what a person could catch sitting on a public toilet seat?"

"A little relief?"

She huffed, then rushed back to the room.

When she got there, the silver crucifix was on the bed, just where she had tossed it. She began to question herself out loud as she picked up the religious token by its silver chain.

"A Jew with a cross... what next, mink coats in Hell?"

The crucifix scintillated again. This time she didn't flinch. Instead, she put it around her neck, being careful to discreetly hide it beneath her blouse. The silver cross felt surprisingly warm against her flesh.

As she hurried back down the hall to the elevator and her husband, Rita felt an unexpected and overwhelming sense of protection.

CHAPTER 40

Monday, 11:20 A.M.
the Holocaust Museum

St. Laurue reached the Holocaust Museum just before sunrise.

He immediately felt at home. After finding the entrances, exits, and several hiding places where he might blend in well with the exhibits of other things long dead, he waited for the Wieses.

A few hours later, he sensed they were in the elevator and were about to unknowingly join him on the fourth floor.

St. Laurue's face lit up in fond remembrance when the elevator doors parted and the public filed out. Ah, he thought, like Jews from a cattle car.

The vampire eavesdropped on the Wieses'.

"So many floors this place has," Rita said. "Who knew?"

"How about we split up?" Solomon said. "We can meet in three hours on the bottom floor in the Hall of Remembrance."

"Are you nuts?"

"That way, between the two of us, we won't miss anything."

"What's wrong with you?" Rita gave him a look. "All of a sudden you're trying to ditch me?"

"No. I was just thinking, we could save some time if…"

"Well stop with the thinking," she said and gave him a slight poke in the ribs. "We look for

Maury together, like always."

Solomon unbuttoned his sports jacket and loosened his shirt collar. "You're right," he said. "What was I thinking?"

As the Wieses moved along with the crowd from exhibit to exhibit, St. Laurue couldn't help but notice the museum had the solemn hush of a holy place. Yet, its quiet ambiance was subtly alive with the all too mortal reaction of horror and reverence at the sight of so much violence. People spoke in whispers. Gentle weeping and wide-eyed wonder impregnated the halls. He wondered why the living wasted so much time honoring the dead?

Who cares? he finally decided, and accepted humanity's hypnotic romance with death as his own personal good fortune.

Some visitors were joining a short line about to file into a side door off the main hall, where a war documentary would begin in five minutes.

"Here's the film I read about," St. Laurue overheard Solomon say to Rita. "The one about the camps. It starts again in a couple of minutes. This, we have to see. Maybe we'll get lucky and catch a glimpse of Maury."

The Wieses patiently stood in line for the twenty-minute documentary.

St. Laurue snuck over to another corner of the hall. Rita was facing away from the *nosferatu* and chatting up a storm. Solomon listened while idly gazing in St. Laurue's general direction.

"I don't know if I can take this," Rita said. "I don't mind the photos so much, or even the relics, but the films on the camps– they're *too* real."

"We'll see it first thing and get it over with. We've got to investigate every possibility. Leave one stone unturned and it's likely to be the one that gives us some informa–"

St. Laurue, willing the detective to see him, wiggled his index finger and mouthed the name, "Sergeant John Barrows."

Solomon's jaw dropped.

"What is it?" Rita said. "You okay?"

"I... I thought I saw... I recognized... over there in the corner."

She turned around and looked toward the corner, but St. Laurue had already hid himself in the crowd.

"Saw what?" Rita said.

"My God," he said, his face blanching white.

"What is it?"

"Nothing."

"Did you take your heart medication this morning like I reminded you?"

"I took it. I took it."

The line moved forward. St. Laurue followed the Wieses into the screening area.

Almost seventy people sat in the dimly lit room on uncomfortable wooden benches. The Wieses sat on a back bench. St. Laurue stood close by. He knew he had to bide his time, but his hunger was heightening. He wondered why. He had just fed on the blood of two bellboys. Actually, he had overfed. It must be the museum, he concluded. The place affected him like a potent aphrodisiac.

Lights faded. The film began.

Rita cringed at the shocking images on the screen. Solomon held her hand. With his growing concern for Rita *and* trying to pay attention to the documentary, Solomon hadn't noticed St. Laurue sitting down beside him on the bench.

"Look, that small grouping of men," Solomon nudged Rita. "There. Look. The young boy on the end. It's Maury?"

"Where? The last one?" Rita said. "That's not your brother."

"Yes. Look again. That one. With the cap."

"No, Bub. That's not him I told you…"

"Sssh." St. Laurue whispered to them.

Solomon ignored the stranger sitting on his left and continued to talk to his wife.

"You okay, Ritzy?"

"I'll close my eyes if it gets to be too much."

"It's awful hot in here, no?" Solomon shifted uncomfortably. "Suddenly, I'm sweating all over."

He wiped his brow with the back of his hand.

The vampire offered the detective a red silk handkerchief.

Solomon was too physically discomforted to do more than gratefully accept the handkerchief from the stranger without a moment's hesitation.

He wiped his forehead dry, then turned to thank the man.

St. Laurue savored Solomon's sudden intake of breath. "You know, Solly," he said, "you and your wife really must do something about talking out of place. Silence *is* the better part of valor."

Before Solomon could speak, St. Laurue sped

out of the darkened theater and listened from across the hall.

"Rita," Wiese nudged his wife. "He was here."

"Sssh! Watch the film."

"He was just sitting next to me."

"Will you watch already?"

"But the vampire…"

"Knock it off!" Rita firmly warned him.

The exasperated husband sighed, "Okay, okay. I'll watch."

By the time Rita and Solomon exited the theater, St. Laurue could smell the fear escalating within the detective.

Solomon blotted his neck with the vampire's handkerchief.

"Where'd you get that handkerchief?" Rita said, grabbing it from him. "It's silk, for God's sake."

"He gave it to me."

"He who?"

"St. Laurue, the eccentric young writer, the vampire! He's here, I tell you. We're in danger."

"Please. This is a public place. Be sensible. Even if this writer was a serial killer, would he commit murder in a crowd like this?"

"You're right. He won't do anything now. St. Laurue's just trying to scare me."

"Will you stop already with this St. Laurue character or you'll wind up giving yourself another heart attack. Don't get crazy on me. Look at the exhibits. Try to concentrate on Maury."

St. Laurue continued to stalk them as they wandered the museum. He let Solomon get a few more strategic glimpses of him in places where Rita couldn't notice. Meanwhile, Wiese tried to persuade his wife that a vampire was stalking them, while she kept insisting that vampires do not exist.

Still, St. Laurue sensed that Rita *was* worried– but more about the living than the dead. Solomon had turned beet red and was grumbling again about being too hot.

What seemed to bother Rita more than her husband's appearance was his sudden odd behavior. He was continuously looking over his shoulder and patting his sports jacket before turning corners. The small gesture was telling for St. Laurue.

Solomon was carrying a gun.

The blood guzzler knew he had to make his move soon. Up to now he'd been reveling in the excitement of the game, but as his prey looked over the bottom floor exhibits, the manhunt had to come to its inevitable conclusion.

Solomon and Rita were in front of a crowd of people, just opposite the Wexner Learning Center, looking at a wall unit on which were hung tattered old shoes and a few yellowing photographs.

The vampire knew why the Wieses had to be up close to the pictures. They needed to examine each image and scrutinize every detail. These were desperate people, he thought. Their hopes were riding high. They were not the kind of people to let a mystery be, not the type who could keep a secret. He realized that the Wieses recklessly sought truth, and would relentlessly reveal it to an unsuspecting world. At all costs, they had to be stopped.

He took the offensive and worked his way to the front of the crowd toward Solomon and Rita. As he pushed past the people, he was a creature primed for survival.

Just as he was within striking distance, a small disturbance broke out in the crowd.

"Look! On the wall," Rita said. "The photo just below the red shoes."

"My God," the detective wheezed.

"That's him," Rita said.

"It's definite proof," Solomon announced. "My brother survived the camps."

Worried voices arose from the crowd.

A heavyset lady questioned, "What's the matter with him?"

"I think he recognized a family member," a tall man spoke up.

Another woman commented, "He don't look so good to me."

"Look at him, the guy's going to pass out," an older man called out. "Can someone get a doctor? We need a doctor down here."

"Oh my God," Rita shouted excitedly. "Solly. Please. Someone help. We need help."

Then, the unthinkable happened.

Solomon fainted– right into St. Laurue's arms.

The vampire's situation was quite impractical. He was kneeling down with the detective's head held close against his bloodthirsty heart, a strange Madonna and child.

Even worse, everyone was staring.

Rita pulled at her hair. "He's overheated, that's

all," she said. "It's not another heart attack. He fainted. That's all. Are you a doctor?"

Crouched and still cradling her husband, St. Laurue looked up and met Rita's eyes. "No, madam, I am not a doctor. My name is Gérard St. Laurue– I'm just an eccentric young writer."

Rita froze in the midst of the mayhem. A terrified expression slowly scrolled across her face. She clutched her purse closer.

A museum attendant pushed his way through the murmuring crowd. "All right. Everyone, move back," he directed. "The situation is in hand."

As the tour guide stooped down and checked Solomon's pulse, St. Laurue escaped the spotlight, humiliated and furious. He moved through the mob easily enough, but felt Rita's eyes following him. This could be trouble, he thought. Fortunately, she turned her attention back to her ill husband.

The vampire stood at a small distance from the unsettled crowd, like opportunistic death, patiently waiting to claim a couple of new victims.

Now, even more than before, he wanted the Wieses silenced forever.

CHAPTER 41

When Wiese regained awareness, the museum attendant determined– much to Rita's irritation– that he had only fainted from the heat of over excitement. But just to be on the safe side, they were escorted to an office, where Rita argued for an ambulance, while Solomon refused to hear of it.

Meantime, St. Laurue had invisibly sped into the room and lurked behind an office desk, checking out his final confrontation ground with the Wieses.

The back office had a colorful floral covered couch, a couple of business desks and a nice sized bathroom. Not exactly a battleground, he thought, but it would have to do in a pinch.

The vampire listened.

"Give me a minute, will ya?" said Solomon, reclining on a sofa. "I'll be good as new."

"Take all the time you want, Detective Wiese," the kindly museum attendant said and left the office, ignoring Rita's protests.

The Wieses were alone– or so they thought.

Rita's attention was on Solomon, who was laying on the couch with a bag of ice placed across his forehead, partially covering his eyes.

To be certain not to draw their attention, St. Laurue morphed into a subtle purple mist. And though, ever ready to pounce, he was glad to have the opportunity to listen first and possibly gain some previously unthought of advantage.

"You okay now?" Rita said.

"How many times do I have to say it? I'm

better now."

"What happened?"

"The shock," Solomon said. "All these years, wondering if Maury made it out of the camp... Then, to see that picture."

"Those horrible pictures," Rita said. "I couldn't take anymore."

"All we needed was the one. Proof positive. A picture of Maury being escorted through the gates of Auschwitz by the allies."

"And were you happy?" Rita asked. "Did you shout for joy? No. You fainted and practically gave me a breakdown. What were you thinking?"

"What *wasn't* I thinking? Where did Maury go after the war? Is he still alive after all these years? If so, can we find him? That was the real shock. I realized our search is only now just beginning."

Wiese wearily got up from the couch.

"Lay down," Rita said. "Where are you going?"

"The bathroom. I need to splash some water on my face."

"I'll guard the door."

"Fine," Solomon said with mild sarcasm. "You guard, I'll splash."

"Don't be such a smart mouth," she said, as Solomon walked into the bathroom. "It won't be so funny if you faint again and need my help."

Solomon slammed the bathroom door.

As promised, Rita stood outside, nervously glancing around the office.

St. Laurue was a subtle mist on the other side of the room, but he knew Rita sensed him.

She squinted her eyes and stared directly at him, then turned and called to Solomon, while tapping on the door. "You okay in there?"

"No," Solomon called out. "I'm drowning in the shower."

"Listen, Mr. Wise-ass, by any chance was that museum guide smoking?"

"How do I know? I fainted."

"There's a weird looking purple smokiness in here I don't feature, is all."

Rita was close to discovering him. St. Laurue had to act quickly.

He marshaled his purple mist embodiment into movement, commanding it to drift across the floor.

Rita saw the creeping mist approaching her and reacted as if it were a mouse. She jumped back too quickly and accidentally knocked her head against a wall. While she was temporarily dazed, St. Laurue slipped under the bathroom door.

He resumed his boyish appearance just behind the detective, who was bent over in front of the sink, splashing water on his face.

Solomon suddenly stopped splashing and stood up. He stared into the mirror, as if he could see the vampire's reflection. But that would not be possible, St. Laurue knew, as he watched goose bumps percolating across the mortal's forearms.

Wiese slowly turned around and faced him.

"Good afternoon, Detective Wiese." St. Laurue smiled graciously.

"Mr. St. Laurue. We meet again. I thank you for the use of your red silk handkerchief. Here, let me return it," Solomon said, and reached for his shirt pocket.

"Don't be silly," St. Laurue said, with a wave of his hand. "Keep it as a memento. I have them flown in from Italy. A gentleman must keep up his appearances, *oui?* By the way, I understand that you are planning to expose me. Many mortals have tried throughout the centuries. All quite unsuccessful. And all quite dead. Coincidence? I think not."

Solomon by-passed his pocket and reached inside his shirt, pulling out the silver crucifix. He thrust it at St. Laurue.

"Stay back," he commanded, poking it in the vampire's face.

"This isn't Hollywood, my friend." St. Laurue smirked. "Frankly, I'm rather amused that you've stooped to such empty rituals." He moved closer to Solomon. "May I borrow that for a moment?"

He snatched the crucifix and tossed it into the toilet. With only the slightest lifting and lowering of his index finger, the porcelain commode sanitized itself, gobbling down the crucified Christ, silver chain and all.

"God will punish you," Wiese said.

"God is dead, or haven't you heard?" said the vampire, and with one swift motion viciously smacked Wiese backwards.

Solomon's head thudded hard against the sink. Blood dripped from his nose into the basin.

The vampire instinctively licked his lips.

Hearing the commotion from outside, Rita flung open the bathroom door, rushed in, and saw her husband leaning against the sink in shock.

The *nosferatu* was taken by surprise and backed into the corner.

Rita stood between St. Laurue and the door.

She reached into her blouse and took out her silver crucifix.

St. Laurue swaggered forward.

"You stay back, boy," she said, thrusting the icon toward him.

"Aren't you afraid of me?"

Rita took a step toward St. Laurue.

"I said stay back, writer!"

With her words, came the strength of another force more subtle and infinitely more powerful. The ancient vampire was stunned to find himself flung back against the bathroom wall.

The woman had a strong will, he thought. That much was clear. But did she possess the other important ingredient? Did she have strong faith?

He knew, without faith, even the strongest will would prove useless.

"Do you realize, madam, what I am?"

"You're that serial killer," Rita said.

"But you called me 'writer.' "

He stepped forward.

Rita's will was again strong enough to propel the undead one backwards.

Very impressive, he thought, but he was not worried. To Rita, he was a writer, yes; a murderer, possibly; but categorically *not* a vampire.

Rita would not acknowledge his existence, and such childish denials leave one defenseless.

"*Voilà,*" he thought. The war was won before the battle had begun.

St. Laurue's body stretched out and distorted. His eyeballs swelled, as if they were balloons filling with air. They protruded, then popped out and rolled over toward Rita's feet. Steadfastly holding the crucifix in one hand while her other flew up to her mouth in horror, Rita frantically kicked at the disembodied eyes.

In the meantime, the vampire's flattened image spread out against the bathroom's back wall. An enormous purple mouth lurched forward and snapped at Rita by fits and starts, auguring attack.

Suddenly, the bathroom smelled like an ancient charnel house, filled with the decaying flesh of a battalion of corpses. Rita gagged and a wave of partially digested food erupted half-way up from her belly, while a whoosh of warm urine and watery stool rushed down her legs.

The undead one continued to spread out apocalyptically across the bathroom's floral wallpaper, like an oil spill. Boiling up, it bubbled forth and splattered a yellow-violet surge of liquid onto Rita's trembling hand.

The silver crucifix dropped to the floor.

Knowing her weak spot, St. Laurue morphed into a broad silk screen and reflected a steady stream of nauseating images of the most violent Nazi atrocities across the wall. Rita tried to shield her eyes from the war crimes, but her arms would not raise above her shoulders. He had seen to it that she was helplessly fixated by her own fears.

Solomon regained consciousness, even as St. Laurue's voice boomed: "I am the eternal business of human bloodshed!"

Rita was startled and became dizzy. She reeled backwards against the sink.

Solomon stood protectively in front of her. He had one last card to play. He withdrew his Glock and aimed it at the moving images.

The war crimes fast-forwarded.

The hallucination was so hideously fascinating that Wiese appeared temporarily overpowered. Only with great effort, did he take control and fire his gun into the center of the hypnotic images.

Immediately, the illusions disappeared and St. Laurue materialized.

With his back against the wall, he slowly slid to the floor and leaned to one side, clutching his chest where the detective's bullet had lodged. His lips pouted. Blood spilled out of every orifice. Red tears poured out of his mournful eyes, eyes that asked the sad silent question– *how could you do this to me?* Then, St. Laurue shifted into another form.

"Oh, my God," Solomon winced. "Maury, is that you?"

"Solly," Maury's image pleaded with arms outstretched. "Help me."

Solomon started to rush toward his dying brother, but stopped. "No! You're not my brother." He repeated the mantra more loudly, struggling to thwart the vampire's powerful hypnotic suggestion.

Maury dissolved into the shape of the expiring vampire boy.

St. Laurue's former radiant frame began to disclose his everlasting interior rot. His glorious auburn hair began to fall out in clumps. His lips bubbled out a stream of green, foul-smelling sputum. His hands turned into raw meat stubs. His face blanched and withered. His empty eyes were wide open and fixed, staring at nothing.

Rita recovered from her dizziness and saw that her husband had shot the demon. St. Laurue's eyes reanimated and turned malevolently upward toward them. "Stupid, stupid mortals," he gasped, wearing a crooked smile. "Do you suppose only a single bullet can destroy one as ancient as *I?*"

Rita grabbed the gun from her husband and repeatedly fired it at the *nosferatu* until the chambers were empty. Bullets from the silencer's barrel head thudded quietly into the vampire's convulsing body.

St. Laurue's eyes again became vacant and stared straight ahead.

After a minute, Solomon finally pronounced, "It's over."

He took the gun from Rita and they stared at the motionless creature in silence. Certain now that the thing was destroyed, they reached for each other's hand and turned to leave. As they started to exit the bathroom, they heard a long, gravelly intake of air.

The Wieses froze, then slowly turned back toward the vampire.

St. Laurue's body had risen in midair and was mending. The blood that had poured out, now retreated backward into his wounds, like a film shown in reverse. His features again became youthful and radiant.

Immediately, he faded back into a broad purple silk screen and projected the glaring apparition of Adolf Hitler.

Der Führer laughed scornfully at Wiese and pointed at the offending gun. Solomon looked at the pistol in his own hand. It turned into a bloody, leech infested iron swastika. The leeches crawled off the cross and bit into the detective's hand. Solomon desperately shook off the bloodsuckers.

Rita started to swoon and Solomon caught her.

St. Laurue again transfigured back into his charming boyish appearance and taunted, "Did I hear someone say 'uncle?' "

"Do what you will with me," Wiese whispered between clenched teeth. "Just don't hurt Rita."

"You have my word," St. Laurue said. "But only on one condition."

"Why should I trust your word?"

"Come now. Even a devil can behave like a gentleman, Solly. Besides, you and I are of the same ilk, my friend. I *too* appreciate the value of family and am therefore prepared to bargain for your silence. You are interested?"

"If I say no?"

"Then, I am left with no choice but to destroy you both."

"I will listen," Solomon said. "If nothing else, I *am* a man of reason."

"And on man's arrogant reasoning, I've always

thrived. For instance, had you fired the gun only once and walked away, it would have been my end. Your repeated *attention* resuscitated me. That is the way we demons work. And now, I have something that may be of some interest to you."

St. Laurue reached into a pocket, fetched out a slip of paper and gave it to the detective.

While still supporting Rita's semi-conscious body against the sink with one arm, Solomon took and read the note, then looked up quizzically.

"Is it not natural to protect those we love?" St. Laurue said, then placed a finger over his lips and whispered, "Sssh."

As the sound echoed off the walls, the vampire sped past the Wieses, fled the Holocaust museum, and headed back to New York City.

Moments later, Rita moaned.

"I must have fainted... He's gone?"

Solomon nodded and handed her the note St. Laurue had given him.

She read it and glanced up at her husband.

He cried.

She cried.

Then, in perfect silence, they embraced.

CHAPTER 42

Monday, 11:57 P.M.
St. Laurue's lair, Manhattan

St. Laurue awoke from his bed in a bloodsweat again. "Father!" he angrily called out to an empty bedroom, "Get off my grave!"

The vampire had arrived back in Manhattan two hours earlier, both needing and dreading rest.

God help me, he thought.

Another problem– prayer.

To whom does an immortal turn to for favors? The God of these mortals? Or another God, just for immortals? After almost a millennium, it was a source of sadness and frustration that, for him, the jury on God was still out.

The undead one leapt out of bed and shook himself fully awake. He tuned into Bevan Preston, wanting to know how the book was shaping up. The mental impressions came and his eyes glowered yellow-violet at what he saw. Press was gravely ill and had been rushed to St. Vincent's Hospital from his SoHo office late that afternoon.

He quickly flew to St. Vincent's and appeared by Preston's sickbed in the private hospital room. The mortal's aura was sinister gray.

"What am I to do with you, Press? I leave you alone for one night and you fall apart."

Press stared at him. "You gave me AIDS."

St. Laurue was taken aback. "I…?"

"You gave me death. Now give me life."

"Life is not something a vampire can give."

"Do for me what you did for Brigitte."

"That's not life. That is eternal death."

"Eternal." Press echoed the word, desirously.

St. Laurue was amazed. "After all I've written and all you've read about my kind, can you still wish to be one of the animated dead?"

Press lowered the top of his hospital gown and exposed the purple lesions covering most of his chest. "I already am," he said, and gave the vampire a pleading look. "Make it official."

Suddenly, Brigitte appeared by the hall entrance of the private room and approached them. Press quickly lowered his gown in an attempt to hide his lesion-covered body, but she had already seen and was keeping her distance from the dying mortal.

"Roddi, bad news. Father has destroyed Elka and allowed Fury to escape. I tried to intervene, but he prevented me."

St. Laurue went rigid with rage. Again, the Marquis has interfered with his plans. Again, the blood demon who had given him both mortal and immortal life, had made life impossible to live. He pulled out his red silk handkerchief and dabbed at his forehead, which had beaded up in a blood sweat. Only after some deep and ancient internal struggle had quieted down within was he able to regain his composure and turn back toward Press.

"Allow me to introduce my sister, Brigitte."

Press smiled weakly.

Brigitte gave the mortal a curt nod.

"Please pardon me, Press," St. Laurue said

formally. "My plans have been upset." He refocused his attention on his sister. "Where's father?"

"I don't know," she said.

"And Fury?"

"Headed for Scotland. A woman named Slim has kidnapped him. She is taking the boy to the headquarters of the Daemonion Council in Nairn."

"Merde!" St. Laurue's eyes flashed yellow-violet. "When did they leave?"

"Late last night."

"I will not tolerate this. The boy is mine. I must leave for Scotland immediately."

"Roddi, I've failed you," Brigitte said, looking away from him. "Is there any way I can help?"

"You have not failed me, *ma chérie*. The Marquis is to blame, not you."

St. Laurue started to go for the door.

"Roddi," Press called out. "Don't let me die."

St. Laurue turned around and angrily faced him.

"You knew about this agent named Slim. I perceived her name in your mind. She's the one who taught you how to mentally block me with bloodstained rats, *oui?"*

"I'm sorry. I was confused. I didn't know who to trust. Help me. You need me for the book."

St. Laurue decided quickly.

"Help him, my innocent little bird. The book must be published."

"Roddi!" Brigitte said. "Let the mortal *and* the book die. Allow me to truly help. His death can be accomplished without pain."

"Save his life, little bird. Do it for me?"

The vampiress arched her eyebrows. "But how? You can't mean–"

"Give him the blood."

"And become infected with the virus? Start to kill indiscriminately as you do? Don't you see what you've become?"

"If all you tell me is true, I've become what I am, what we both are– unnatural born killers. You asked if you could help. Help Press."

"I detest human entanglements. Where've they gotten you? You're *betrayed!*" Brigitte grabbed her brother by his shoulders. "Elka was a shape-shifting Daemonion Council agent! That's what you ask for by mingling with mortals. Betrayal and heartbreak."

St. Laurue's face grew hard with determination. "Do it, Brigitte. I'll repay the favor. I promise."

"Think what you ask of me," Brigitte pleaded.

He kissed his sister on both cheeks, ran a hand through one side of her long auburn hair and softly whispered in her ear, *"Mon amour,* I leave my friend's life to your guardianship. Am I wrong to do this? Will you, like our conniving father, murder my beloved children? Will you, too, betray me?"

St. Laurue exited the room, leaving a vacuum where he had stood only a millisecond before.

"No!" Brigitte screamed out after him. "Don't go! It's a trap!"

BOOK THREE

"So in one urn be now our bones enclos'd–"

Homer, *The Iliad*

CHAPTER 43

Tuesday, June 26th 12:30 A.M.
St. Vincent's Hospital

The nurse charged into the hospital room like a bull in the ring.

"What are you doing here?" she said to Brigitte.

"Visiting," Brigitte answered, demurely.

"No you're not, young lady! Not at this hour."

"But I have to–"

"Come on."

The hefty caregiver grabbed her by the arm and turned beet red trying to budge it.

Brigitte was amused by the big woman's look of confusion. It was funny, until the nurse tried to shove her across the hospital room.

The vampiress snatched her by the wrist.

The nurse yelped in pain.

Brigitte peered into her eyes and commanded, "You will go about your business and remember nothing that has transpired here."

The nurse's eyes glazed over.

She turned and left the room.

After a moment Press said, "Well, I must say, I am *very* impressed."

Brigitte was unable to make herself look at the dying mortal.

The mortal, who's eyes pleaded with her even now for an extension of life.

The mortal, who was hopelessly seduced by the imagined glamour of immortality.

She had to sermonize some sense into the fool. She had to make him see the hazards of so long a life and the perils of publishing her brother's book.

"I know you don't believe me," Press said, interrupting her thoughts, "but your brother *can* trust me. Please do as he asks. Make me like him."

"In God's name," she said. "Give me one good reason why?" Brigitte moved closer to the hospital bed as if proximity would enable her to decide what to do. She was angry, not particularly at Press, but at the situation.

He lifted his nightgown again.

Brigitte forced herself to look at his purple splotched chest. Deadly dots, she thought. Her sharp mind quickly connected the purple dots in numerous ways, but every strategy configured senseless patterns conveying the same essential meaning– death.

He touched her arm and quietly said, "Please don't make my family watch me die."

The vampiress didn't pull away. Instead, she drew closer. Family, she thought. A good reason not to die. The need to be connected with those you love. The need to care. To protect and come to the aid of your own blood. That she understood, as she tenderly touched Preston's hand.

"Your hand..." Press said. "It's so cold."

"As would be yours, were I to do what you ask of me."

"I don't mind."

"Tell me," she said. "Would it not be far better to face your mortality only once, than to face an eternity of death? Your life will depend only on what you can sap from another. Have you thought this out thoroughly?"

Preston's eyes began to tear up. "Yes. In fact, I've thought of little else." He squeezed her hand, weakly. "I want more life. Being close to death has a way of doing that."

She gave the mortal a knowing look. *"Oui..."* she murmured.

"All my life I've followed the rules, lived by other's expectations. I've never been me. For good or bad, grant me the time to *feel* my own feelings."

The dying mortal's petition resonated deep in Brigitte. She wondered if his desire to feel his life might not be a need she also had to address and fully acknowledge within herself.

"Do it," Press said.

Whether Press was interrupting or answering her thoughts, she did not know. Brigitte considered the consequences of her actions.

To help this mortal meant losing her freedom.

He would become her fledgling. She'd have to teach, and scold, and love, and share. She'd have to define herself by the *other*.

She'd have to relate to an insistent world, face it, admit its hold. But that much would merely be a nuisance. The real danger was twofold: If she did as asked, she would be considered an accomplice to her brother's book in the eyes of the ancients, *and* she would be infected with the blood disease.

She let go of Preston's hand and drifted over to the window, cursing her father under her breath.

None of this would have occurred had it not been for DeMalberet's interference. It was then, the idea came. Of course, she thought. She would follow her father's example. As poor as it was, it would do the trick. Now realizing what had to be done, she walked back over to the hospital bed and slid her hand once more into Preston's.

"Sit up. It appears I can help you after all."

"You'll risk infection?" Press said, struggling to a sitting position.

"It's not a risk. Infection is certain."

"Even if you get the virus, there is the chance that it might not affect you."

"Time will tell," she said.

The vampiress took him in her arms.

"Bless you," Press whispered, commending his body fully to her care and experience.

Brigitte's blood teeth found their way deep into Preston's pulsating neck vein and she drank freely.

His body quivered and shook violently.

The vampiress sliced the tip of her left breast and guided Press to it. He drank her immortal blood. When he had enough blood for her purpose, the vampiress pushed him away.

The familial *ancien régime* was completed.

Preston again reclined on the hospital bed and closed his eyes. Her powerful blood had done the trick. Everything about him brightened.

Within seconds, the purple spots on his chest and legs magically cleared.

Wrinkles around his eyes vanished.

His hair grew thick and luxurious.

His cheeks reddened with vigor.

Press opened his new eyes. "I can see without my contact lenses." With gratefulness and wonder, he asked, "Am I immortal now?"

"No. But you shall remain young until the day of your normally appointed death."

"But look at me. I am well again."

"Your physical symptoms have disappeared. You are young again. But who knows with what madness you may have to live out your days?"

"What do you mean?"

"Come," the vampiress said sternly. "We must go to my brother's lair before the sun rises."

Press sprang out of the hospital bed and did a few energetic arm and leg stretches. "I haven't felt this good in years. If I'm not undead, what have you done to me?"

"I have given you the tyrant of time. Nothing more, nothing less."

Brigitte suddenly bent over in great pain. Press rushed to her and held her by the shoulders.

She regained her composure and stood erect.

"My blood has infected you?"

"Not yours, but my brother's blood running in your veins."

"Will you be all right?"

"If you mean will I continue to exist? That's almost inescapable."

"But will you go on killing sprees?"

"Will *you?*" Brigitte said. "What you have become now will drive you to drink blood once a month on the full moon."

He fell back on the bed in shock. She gently pulled him up from the bed and whispered, "Let us leave this place of sickness."

Brigitte was satisfied.

She had accomplished her brother's will.

Press was alive.

Yet, she also felt relieved not to have sired another of her kind, not to have taken on the care and responsibility of another for an eternity.

She led him out of St. Vincent's hospital and they headed for lower Manhattan.

They were barely visible, almost ghostly, as they roamed the streets along with the rest of the city's invisible nighttime people: the homeless, the hustlers, the whores, and the nocturnal press.

They approached the front steps of St. Laurue's condominium. Brigitte said, "You will have to stay the night in my brother's apartment."

"Fine. Marge and the kids are at her mother's."

"Call them. Make them understand that you are in good heath, but do remain in the city. Wednesday night, the moon will be full. I'll return for you."

"Where are you going?" Press said, nervously.

"Roddi needs me right now. I must follow him to Europe."

"But you can't leave me," Press whined.

Brigitte pushed the door buzzer. Static came over the intercom and the doorman's voice asked, "Yes? Whom do you wish to visit?"

She turned to Press and said, "Command the doorman to push the entrance buzzer and let us in. Then, with your mind silently instruct him to go about his business, telling no one."

Press gave her an odd look.

"Do it now!" Brigitte said sternly.

He did as he was told. After a moment, the entrance buzzer sounded.

Press just stood there, dumbfounded.

"Well," Brigitte said. "Open the door."

"My God," Press whispered to her, as he opened it. "What have you done to me? If I'm not a vampire, what am I?"

Brigitte stopped mid-threshold and looked gravely at him. "Because you have fed only once on my blood," she explained, "you are an *incubus*. That is the male counterpart of a *succubus*, what my mother was, and her mother before her. My father worked this same dark trick on his many wives to keep them in line."

"In other words, I'm your slave."

"Certainly not, Press. I would not treat you as DeMalberet did my Mamá."

"But I'll have to drink blood?"

"*Oui*. It is true. Once a month on the full moon you must drink blood. And in that, we're all pitiable slaves, driven by our hunger."

Brigitte saw the look of sadness well up in Preston's moist eyes.

"Oh God, what's to become of me?"

"That is only for *you* to choose now. You've been given preternatural powers and time," she said softly, with a glance that subtly betrayed her misgivings. "Use both wisely."

Then, Brigitte and Press strolled through the threshold of the building, looking very much like a birthday girl after a night's celebration on the town with her dear old dad.

Heading for the empty elevator, they moved into an arguable future, even as the door behind automatically slammed shut.

CHAPTER 44

Tuesday, Scotland 4:30 P.M.
The Daemonion Council Motherhospice

After several hours of day sleep, catching up from the jet lag, Fury was out of bed and at the door, getting ready to sneak out of his room and explore the Motherhospice.

The phone next to his bed rang. If he didn't answer, whoever it was would know that he wasn't in his room. If he did, they'd probably mess up his chance to investigate the premises.

"Aw, shit," he grumbled, then walked over and picked up the phone.

"Hello?"

"Fury, you rested well?" Slim's voice sounded confident and gave the boy a sense of comfort.

"Yeah," he said, brightening up. "I slept great. How about you?"

"You bet. I love it here and hope you'll grow to love it as well."

"Yeah, it's cool. It's practically as big as my school in Brooklyn."

"I'm going to try to convince the board to train you as an operative under my tutelage. Would you like that?"

"I'd *love* it," Fury said, but wondered how his mother would handle it. She was probably missing him by now. Maybe even frantic and calling the cops and everything. Stay in Scotland? That would never happen, he thought. Gina would hate the idea.

Slim asked, "Did you drink the potion by the side of your bed?"

Fury spotted the goblet on the bed stand. "No. Was I supposed to?"

"Alec Priggins, the Grand Counselor, contacted me and insisted that I remind you to take it when you awaken."

Fury picked up the goblet and drained it. "Okay. It's done. I hope it wasn't poison."

"Don't be so dramatic," she said, laughing.

"Hey. Can I scout around the joint?"

"Generally, guests are made to stay in their room until they get the royal tour from one of the council members."

"I *was* kind of told to stay put," he admitted.

"Oh hell's bells," Slim said. "I guess I'd take the opportunity to scout around too if I were in your shoes. Go on, but don't get into any mischief. If you need me, I'll be in the library. Okay?"

"All *right!* Thanks, Slim. Later."

Fury hung up the telephone, then cautiously tiptoed out of his room, while keeping an eye out for castle ghosts and Council members who might hamper his journey.

The long hall was lined with oil portraits of men and women.

Their eyes seemed to follow him down the hall and he decided that they were real people who had been magically trapped behind big ugly frames.

He held his finger to his lips. "Sssh," he told them. Good. Now, they were his co-conspirators.

Where is everybody? he thought.

Not that he wanted to bump into anyone, but still the Motherhospice seemed awfully empty for such a huge place. And it smelled funny, too.

As soon as the thought crossed his mind, he felt a sneeze coming on. Bummer. Someone was sure to hear him from behind the closed doors lining the hall.

Unable to hold the sneeze in, he let loose and exploded.

It sounded practically like an atom bomb going off, but amazingly enough, nobody rushed out of the hall doors, as he imagined might happen.

Nobody yelled at him to get back to his room.

Nobody turned the corner at the end of the hall, making wild ghoulish noises, or possibly even blowing blue steam out of their noses as they charged, screaming weird mystical incantations and ancient ritualistic curses.

Nobody noticed.

Typical, he thought and shrugged.

Maybe no one even lived in this section of the Motherhospice… except, of course, for the people in the portraits.

Suddenly, he felt the strangest sensation from the knees down. It was as if his feet knew the lay of the land and were leading him in a determined direction. He was alarmed, yet excited to be on a real live adventure.

His feet found their way to an old staircase that looked like it hadn't been used for centuries.

He looked down and half expected to see a rabid rat staring back.

"Scat," he whispered loudly.

The stairs looked pretty bogus and he decided that maybe he wouldn't check them out right now. No sooner than he had the thought, his legs, as if independent of his mind, moved him down the dusty steps.

Probably just leads to an old dungeon anyway, he thought, trying not to freak out as he brushed past the cobwebs on his way down.

At the bottom, he found himself in an old wine cellar, lit by several sconces embedded in the walls.

There must have been four thousand barrels of wine on each side of the room, creating a pathway in the middle of the cellar.

Fury followed the path up to the far end, and thought, since he was there anyway, he might as well sample the stash.

He tried one of the spigots on a nearby barrel.

To his annoyance, it didn't produce any brew.

He tried another.

Nothing. About to call it quits on the idea, he tried a last spigot.

Instead of the sound of wine spilling out of the spigot, he heard an eerie creaking sound, like something was unwinding. His mind raced. A fight or flight reaction flowed through his young body.

Then, he saw it behind one of the barrels.

A large trapdoor on the floor of the wine cellar had opened.

He quickly backed away, not sure if someone was coming out, but pretty damned sure he wasn't going in.

Nobody ascended.

He saw a warm inviting golden incandescence emanating from the hole in the floor.

I'm not falling for that, he decided. I'm out of here. Fury started to turn away from the trapdoor.

But his legs had other plans.

As he entered the oubliette, he was so excited he felt an urgent need to pee and tried to ignore nature's call for the moment.

When he got to the bottom of the stairs of the hidden chamber, he saw a half lit candelabra in the corner of the small room.

Odd occult symbols were scrawled across the windowless brick walls. The dungeon felt eerie and abandoned. It had a straw covered dirt floor and was unfurnished, except for a small wooden crate. It smelled awful, being so musty and damp.

There was a small piece of paper on the crate. It was old and yellow. It looked like the Declaration of Independence, he thought.

The curious boy picked it up and read the words, "Welcome to the club."

Fury laughed out loud.

Cool. Someone was toying with him.

Someone had taken the trouble to entertain him on his first day here. Yep. He was definitely going to like this place. The Council members were fun.

It was then, that the half lit candelabra began to slowly extinguish itself. One by one, each of its lit candles were snuffed out by an invisible hand.

The teen involuntarily shuddered.

This was too much.

He didn't like to admit it, but he was afraid of the dark. He dreamed in the dark.

"Hey!" he spoke up. "There's such a thing as carrying a joke too far."

He dropped the parchment and was about to scram up the stairs to his room before anyone else knew he was missing, when he heard the trapdoor above him slam shut with a jolting *wham!*

Fury was alone, in a strange place, in the dark.

He heard a rattle, a rush of air, and his own inner voice telling him that he should never have left his comfortable room.

A green spark appeared in the corner of the oubliette. His eyes fixed on it.

It began to glow, swirl, and expand into form.

The boy got dizzy just looking at the massive gyration. Then, his knees gave way and he fell to the dungeon's dirt floor.

A dark man stepped out of the murky green mist and stood between him and the stairs exiting the secret chamber.

Fury was dumb struck.

The dark man had fire-glittering eyes and seemed to be perversity incarnate. He looked about forty and had a sliver of a mouth, which was curved like the line where ying meets yang. His large ears stuck out and would have made him look stupid, were it not for his keen eyes. His tall thin body looked like a question mark.

Although Fury was trembling with fright, he figured he'd try to talk his way out of trouble. "I know I wasn't supposed to leave my room."

The dark figure spoke. "You drank the potion?"

"I did… uh… Did! It tasted great. In fact, I was just going back for more."

"Come here," the dark man commanded. "Your destiny calls."

Fury began to feel a sense of helplessness.

His body lifted off the dirt floor and drifted toward the man, whose arms were open and waiting. As he floated, the teen's head bent to the right, exposing the excited throbbing vein pulsing along his neck.

He felt the dark man's embrace.

Death, even though expected, was a complete surprise. The bite was quick, efficient. The initial pinch brought no pain at all. On the contrary, the boy felt numb to the outer world.

Physically, he was being drained of blood, but mentally– *that's* where the real rape was effected.

As death sucked at his neck, he didn't struggle. It was far too late for that. His body had already surrendered. Instead, Fury willed himself to remain conscious, to hold on to his own identity.

But who was he?

Nobody, he thought. *Nothing. How can you hold on to nothing?*

Then, the memories began.

All that he'd ever heard, seen, tasted, touched, smelled and thought rushed out of him and into the fiend sucking at his neck.

Soon, he felt like an empty shell, stripped of all personal thought. But still, he was aware.

In his awareness, all that mattered to him was

the blood. The blood was his life. And as it was whooshed out of him, he realized that his life was being taken.

And he thought of Gina, his mother. And why didn't he go with her to church more? And if he died right here and now, would his mom miss him, would his soul survive, could he go to her and tell her what had become of him, could he tell her that he loved her and it wasn't her fault?

The dark man suddenly pushed him away, then sliced his own wrist and willed him to drink.

He grabbed the dark man's wrist and greedily sucked life force back into his body.

To Fury's amazement, he loved the taste. The man's blood was thick and warm and salty sweet as it sludged down his throat.

But Fury knew that more than mere blood was being exchanged. He felt more pure knowledge and power and glory than he'd ever known in his entire sixteen years.

Then, just before he lost consciousness, he heard the beast's faint introduction.

"I am the Grand Counselor."

CHAPTER 45

Tuesday, after sunset
Nairn, Scotland

The first all important stop on St. Laurue's itinerary had been to find a secure shelter and take rest during the oncoming day's light.

He had found the ruins of an old castle nearby and as distasteful as it was, he had burrowed deep into its foundation and tried to rest.

His mind ran mad with plans to recapture his minion, but rest did finally come, once he realized one distinct advantage was his. Of the teenager's whereabouts, there was absolutely no doubt– the Daemonion Council's Motherhospice.

After sunset, St. Laurue found the place.

The large mansion stood on top of a hill, like an offering lifted up to God, or so its members thought. An incontestable presence surrounded the outside grounds and served as a barrier for intruders.

St. Laurue, being no common interloper, had managed to secure a secret perch on top of a gazebo in the midst of the vast rose garden, just behind the main quarters.

On closer inspection, he saw the manor was crawling with an outer layer of protective ivy.

The Motherhospice seemed a living organism, within which, halls and secret passages served as its arteries, and Council members, its blood. At its heart was the office of Alec Priggins, the Grand Counselor. St. Laurue knew of Priggins, but had never seen him. And now, the undead one's keen intuition warned him to beware of the mortal.

St. Laurue's thoughts were interrupted by movement in the garden. It was Fury. Elation. But wait. His minion was with an elderly lady.

They were strolling along a cobblestone path surrounded by roses of various colors. The moonlight only served to enhance the elegance of the blossoms. Quaint nineteenth century lampposts spilled pools of amber light along the path, creating a string of luminous islands. Several silver coated ionic-columned archways propped up rigidly amongst the graceful flowers, while vigilant Greek statues stood guard against the deviltry of the outside world. Despite its beauty, St. Laurue knew this garden was not his Eden.

From his gazebo perch, he eavesdropped on their conversation.

"You're up awfully late for a youngster," the old lady said.

Fury tucked his hands in his jeans and kicked at a piece of gravel as he and the old lady continued down the garden path. "I like the dark."

"I'm quite a night owl myself," the old woman confessed, then breathed in deeply. "The roses are frightfully fragrant tonight. I've always fancied their real beauty lies in the power of their thorns."

Fury paused for a moment, then quietly nodded.

St. Laurue watched them stroll the dimly lit cobblestone path until they came to a circular area spotted with benches.

Something has changed in the boy, he thought.

Fury was more serious, more intent.

"It's so incredible," the old woman continued, "but under these charming old lamplights the roses almost glow in the dark."

"Just like me," Fury said.

"What?" she said.

"I glow in the dark, too."

"That's an odd thing to say, young man."

She sat down on one of the benches. Fury sat beside her. After a moment, he asked, "Did the airline find your luggage?"

"No. I'm afraid I'm still rather stranded. Alec, the Grand Counselor, has been such a peach to let me stay at the manor for the time being."

"I'm glad you stayed."

"Well, what nice manners you have. Your mother must have been…"

The old lady's voice trailed off. Even at a distance, St. Laurue knew why. She was put off by the boy's breathing, which became accelerated and heavy. She tried to back away, but Fury grabbed her by the hand.

His eyeteeth extended.

The old lady looked frightened. "Your teeth–"

"Don't be afraid," Fury said. "I need a little of your blood."

Rage and confusion rushed through St. Laurue as he observed Fury engineer the old lady into the feeding embrace. Had his ancient blood been powerful enough to turn the boy with only an initial feeding?

Lifting off from the top of the gazebo and

flying directly to their side, he interrupted the familiar ritual just as Fury's teeth were about to sink into the old lady's neck.

Fury hissed at first, then saw it was St. Laurue and cowered.

He gave the boy a sharp look, then turned back to the old lady.

He recognized her.

It was Rebecca, the sweet little old lady at St. Vincent's, where he had slaughtered Jamie and Sergeant Barrows.

Rebecca scrambled off to another bench by the edge of the garden as St. Laurue hoisted Fury up from the bench.

They were face to face.

He sniffed at Fury and detected the aroma of strange blood coursing through the lad's veins.

"Who has brought you fully across!"

Fury looked frightened and confessed, "The Grand Counselor turned me. I couldn't stop him."

Rebecca brazenly stood up and declared, "The lad's telling the truth. I turned him this afternoon."

With that, the old lady transfigured into the guise of a heavyset, but elegantly attired English country gentleman.

"I beseech you not to hold it against me," Alec Priggins said, in his clipped English accent. "The boy was taken on your father's orders."

"You know my father, the Marquis Antoine DeMalberet?"

"Of course," Alec answered. "And quite well, I might add. The Marquis is directly responsible for gifting me with my position as Grand Counselor of the Daemonion Council."

Priggins quickly plucked a rose, sniffed it, then held it out to St. Laurue and said, "Your father and I have worked hand in hand keeping tabs on the supernatural world, so to speak."

"So you are another one of my father's many puppets?" He took the rose, tore the petals off and tossed it on the cobblestone walk. "Fine. It will be an even greater pleasure to destroy you."

He flew at Priggins, but passed right through the Grand Counselor.

Alec snickered and teased, "Try it again, why don't you?"

He tried again, and then again, each time with more wrath. Still, he couldn't get hold of the shimmering image of the Grand Counselor.

"What extraordinary magic is this?" he said to the fat beast.

"Do you like it?" Alec replied. "Your father mentioned how much you appreciate tricks, and just as he cautioned you nearly a thousand years ago when you were first turned, 'no matter how great you imagine yourself to be, *I* am always greater.' "

St. Laurue's anger turned to shock. Those were his father's words to him when he had been made a creature of the night. Truth dawned on him, with the chilling impact of a winter's first frost.

"Father?" he said, in a wavering voice.

Alec's metallic orange eyes glared. "Oh my. You've found me out." As the words spilled out, Alec's corpulent body transformed into the thin snake-like appearance of the Marquis DeMalberet, impeccably dressed, complete with his shiny black top hat proudly tipped atop his head.

Priggin's English clip was replaced by the Marquis' hypnotically melodious French accent.

"Please allow me to introduce you to the Grand Counselor of the Daemonion Council."

"You're the Grand Counselor?" St. Laurue said, trying to hide his anger.

"How better to keep tabs on the ancients?"

"Why have you lured me here? Why!"

DeMalberet placed his top hat on the bench and sat beside Fury, who watched them in awe.

"Because this blood virus is making you draw undue attention to our kind. I must intervene, lest the ancients take matters into their own hands."

"Let them try."

"I assured them that you will soon take the millennium rest, which will cure this disease. But they're still concerned about the book you plan to have published. Gérard. You should know better than that."

"I'll do as I please."

"Not any longer. Fortunately, I can and will stop the book. As for the symptoms of the blood disease, the Council has developed potions to ward them off. Fury has already taken the elixir. You must as well."

"I refuse."

DeMalberet ignored him and continued.

"Then there's Brigitte and Press. They must get the medication. What a nuisance. Can you see how naughty you've been? Finally, I've taken the liberty to secure a safe burial spot for you tomorrow, here, at the Motherhospice."

"You have it all planned, don't you? Well for all I care, you, the Daemonion Council, *and* your damned potions can go straight to hell."

DeMalberet tilted his head, as if he'd heard someone coming, and instantly shifted back into the guise of Rebecca.

He chuckled and said in the little old lady's voice, "Oh Gérard, I fear I must have brought you up wrong." She indicated Fury. "Perhaps I'll do a better job with this one."

St. Laurue screeched, "Don't you touch him. Fury is mine!"

Rebecca made a grand show of hugging the boy, then smiled at St. Laurue and continued, "As I was about to say, I've decided to give up my post as the Daemonion Council's Grand Counselor. That way I can devote myself full time to my children." She looked lovingly at Fury and added, "And, naturally, my children's children." She stood up and began to hold court. "In order to keep myself up to date," she pontificated. "I'll have to appoint another vampire to oversee the important work done here. Someone I respect and trust."

"Don't you mean some weak willed lackey?" St. Laurue spat out.

"I've got just the perfect candidate in mind. Her name is Slim. Perhaps you've heard of her?"

"But Slim is not a vampire," Fury protested innocently.

Rebecca smiled, sat down by the lad's side and whispered gently, "Not yet."

As if on cue, Slim appeared and rushed over.

"So, St. Laurue, you *have* arrived," she said. "I sensed it while studying your father's diaries in the library. I know your scent all too well after tracking you back in the States."

St. Laurue turned blood red, faced Rebecca and howled, "You gave them your diaries, then caution me about my book? Hypocrite! Devil!"

Slim threw herself in between St. Laurue and the old lady. "Leave Rebecca alone," the agent said sharply. She held her arms up protectively and called behind her, "Rebecca, Fury, pay no attention. The bloody devil will try to confuse us if he can."

Rebecca went to Slim and pretended to cringe in her arms. The old lady wore a helpless look on her face, but on closer inspection, St. Laurue could see his father's derisive jeer dancing in her old eyes.

"Mortal," St. Laurue said to Slim, "Are you so certain that you are not *already* confused? Do you not know who this old lady is? Madam, you hold sudden catastrophe in your arms."

"Liar!" Slim said, holding Rebecca even closer.

It was now or never, St. Laurue decided.

He dashed over to Fury and snatched the boy off the bench to make their escape.

The Marquis– still disguised as Rebecca– cast his vampiric shade over Fury with the mere flick of his little finger.

It was done so fast that Slim hadn't noticed.

The boy was now an unmovable statue, and St.

Laurue knew the game was up.

He bellowed, "Release my Fury, you bastard!"

Rebecca had a faraway look in her eyes.

Suddenly, the air was thick with the smell of death and St. Laurue's inner alarm bells went off.

He heard the patter of tiny feet under the rose beds and his fortitude slackened.

There was a squeak.

Then another.

And another.

A rat scurried out from under a rose bush. It was big, black and speckled with blood.

St. Laurue's knees began to buckle.

"Oh dear me," Rebecca feigned fright to Slim, then secretly shot an immensely amused look at St. Laurue. "Rats!"

Rats? St. Laurue thought.

One, he could handle, but more than one would be his complete undoing.

The garden became a brawl of squeaks as an army of big black rats bespattered with unclean blood marched to the edge of the cobblestones. St. Laurue felt dizzy and fell to his knees.

The rats crept closer, as if they could smell his weakness. Behind their beady red eyes, he felt the immobilizing grip of his father's will.

"The plague," St. Laurue cried out.

As they inched toward him, he covered his face. And still, he could see the fiendish creatures in his mind's eye.

A notion came to him.

If he could count them, he could beat them.

If he named them, *knew* them, then somehow, he could control them.

As they crawled across every part of his body, he became a creature possessed and tried to identify and categorize each of the tiny vile beasts, systematizing each rat's minutiae– their smell, touch, sound, breath, and teeth marks as they tore him apart piece by piece.

Then, in a supreme effort, he managed to clear his head, open his eyes and call out for salvation.

"Help me father!"

Even as his words formed, Rebecca transfigured into the Marquis Antoine DeMalberet.

Slim stood back, her mouth agape. "It's you! The Marquis Antoine DeMalberet!"

"Smart girl," the Marquis said, wickedly. "How lovely of you to be so interested in perusing my dairies. Did you know that the Council needs a new Grand Counselor, my dear? I've chosen you."

"A new–" Slim said. "You've killed Alec!"

"I'm afraid Alec Priggins dissolved under job pressure. But one man's loss is another man's gain. You'll accept the position?"

"Find yourself another pawn," Slim said, and attempted to make an escape.

Instantly, DeMalberet was on her with blood-teeth extended.

Meanwhile, St. Laurue was about to succumb to the incessant calculations in his mind once more.

It was all too much. Too overwhelming. The rats would be his end, he thought.

He looked up, just in case there was a God and

started to verbally formulate a final prayer.

Then suddenly, standing on top of the gazebo, he saw his sister, Brigitte. Hope rose in his heart.

The Scottish hillside winds played with her long auburn hair and her bright green dress.

Brigitte looked like a flaring emerald candle.

Her voice boomed.

"Father! You! Be! Damned!"

To St. Laurue's amazement, she was actually taking their father on, single-handedly. Something she had never dared ever to do before. Then, another astonishing phenomenon took place.

A power far beyond any this world had known materialized just above Brigitte's right shoulder.

The night sky lightning-zippered open and a fire-red dwarf came out of the aperture. Lightning bolts flew out from the edges of the dwarf's bright form. Its impassioned eyes flared fiery sparks, while its hot tongue flashed fluorescent blue flames.

The dwarf was crowned with a flame that gave off an otherworldly, terrible heat.

Beneath the torrid headpiece, its copper colored hair twitched madly, as if animated with a mighty stratospheric life force all its own.

St. Laurue knew he was in the presence of the immutable Lord Agni, the ancient Hindu god of fire. Here was the passion of life.

The Hindu fire deity was flamboyant, free and flamingly independent.

St. Laurue loved him instantly and thought to himself– *perhaps there* is *a god after all.*

The middle of Brigitte's forehead lit up and a

white laser beam of spirit fire poured out from Agni, through Brigitte, and into DeMalberet.

The Marquis was caged by multicolored laser bars of light, which lifted him several feet above the ground. He appeared outraged as the soul fire spread through every part of his body, racing up and down. During his electrocution, DeMalberet looked like an x-ray illuminated by an aurora borealis of vivid rainbow colors.

While still suspended in midair, the Marquis howled in agony and began to rapidly rotate. After several futile attempts to extinguish the god fire, he seemed to will himself downward, barreling deep into the coolness of the earth. Then, the hole into which DeMalberet had burrowed closed itself up and with this, the rats vanished.

Slim, Fury, and St. Laurue were all alone now amongst the roses.

St. Laurue's body healed instantly as he kicked the rising dust where his father went under. "Good riddance, you king of liars, master of disguise!"

Brigitte instantly appeared by his side, looking a bit disoriented.

With a severe look, she silently approached Slim. "Well," she said, "what have you got to say for yourself?"

Slim was awed. She looked at the vampiress with reverence and said, "Thank you for saving me from your father."

Brigitte eyed Slim, reading her deepest desires.

"DeMalberet offered you the position of the Grand Counselor," the vampiress said sternly. "It's what you've always hoped for. What made you turn him down?"

Slim seemed hardly able to speak. Finally she managed an explanation.

"The Daemonion Council is the only family I've ever known. How could I serve them in good faith, if I first betrayed myself?"

St. Laurue expected those words to be Slim's last, given his sister's jealous and overprotective nature. But to his astonishment, Brigitte simply nodded at the mortal, then turned to him and said, "Make your escape with the boy before the other Council members stir. I'll follow shortly."

Roddi lifted up Fury, who was still thawing out of the Marquis' paralytic spell.

They flew up into the Scottish night skies.

Now, he thought, his sister would make short work of Slim. Should he look? No it would be too terrible. He liked Slim. There was something about her that he admired. Her loyalty. Her courage.

Still, he had to look. Turning back briefly, he was dumbfounded to see Brigitte embrace and kiss the Council operative.

Not more than an instant later, his sister was again by his side, and along with Fury, the three of them headed across the Atlantic Ocean and back toward Manhattan.

As they flew in silence, St. Laurue knew both he and his sister shared a feeling of long overdue satisfaction. They'd triumphed over their father. After suffering centuries of his meddling, justice had prevailed.

Flying closer beside his sister, he finally broke the silence.

"My little bird, what would I do without you?"

"I shudder to think," she laughed, the wind dancing through her hair.

He took a moment to admire her.

Something about his sister was different. He wondered what. Then he knew.

She had *enjoyed* the adventure.

She'd had *fun.*

He was overjoyed, but two things still puzzled him. Never being one to hold his tongue for long, he had to ask the questions.

"What made you fight father with Agni's fire trick? It was brilliant, but you broke your vow never to use the power again."

"I did not break my vow."

"But the god of fire came and destroyed father."

"God came?"

"Yes," he said. "Didn't you know?"

"No. I lose time. I don't remember. It must be the effects of the blood sickness."

He worried about her answer. Was it possible that she hadn't been aware of the heroic rescue she effected? He decided to think about it later and moved on to his next question.

"What made you embrace and kiss the mortal named Slim?"

Brigitte looked embarrassed as they soared through the brisk air.

"I did no such thing," she said defensively. "I only whispered a spell of forgetfulness in her ear."

"Yours, or hers?"

"I looked at her and all of a sudden, I felt…"

"Oui, exactly, you *felt,"* St. Laurue said.

"For her? Don't be foolish. She is feed to me."

"Then why didn't you kill her?"

"Because… I… I don't know why, and stop asking me!"

"If this is a result of the blood illness you say we both have, then perhaps it's not all bad."

Brigitte remained silent, ending the discussion. St. Laurue was a little disappointed, but knew there were times when words only confused what's best left unsaid.

Suddenly, Fury became animated in his arms.

"Voilà," Brigitte said. She gently touched her brother's arm and peered deliberately into his eyes. "It's true… the dead *do* come back to life."

Her words held a double meaning that was not lost to him. In her own quiet fashion, Brigitte was acknowledging the change he had felt in her.

He beamed at his sister, then looked adoringly at Fury. "Tell me, *mon amour,* do you enjoy flying about without a jet?"

"Let *me* try it," Fury demanded, struggling to get free.

Brigitte and St. Laurue laughed.

"You are far too young to fly on your own," he told his minion.

Then, surprisingly, Fury broke out of his arms and soared up ahead.

St. Laurue was amazed.

Brigitte looked worried. "The boy may fall. We

should catch up."

"Let him try," he said. "What else are we, if not fallen angels winging our way back home. The boy must learn to fend for himself."

"But he's your fledgling– your responsibility."

"Our responsibility," St. Laurue corrected her.

The lad was somersaulting through the moonlit sky, frolicking toward New York.

"But his blood is mixed with DeMalberet's."

"Who, thanks to you, my dear sister, is finally dead and buried."

"He lives on… in the boy."

"Oui. And the lad already possesses great powers because of it."

"My point is this, can I trust Fury after you go underground for the ancient rest tomorrow night?"

"You worry too much. You must learn to look on the bright side, little bird. Thanks to Kyle, I've found the perfect resting place. That above all is the key to safety. "

"Still, I worried." Brigitte said. "The boy may turn against you with father's blood in him."

St. Laurue laughed. "The boy loves me."

Then, he raced ahead, and took delight soaring through the air and tumbling in the moonlight with Fury all the way back to the States.

Still shivering from Brigitte's hug, Slim anxiously watched the vampires as they made their air born escape. Then, suddenly feeling vulnerable, she headed down the rose garden's cobblestone path to the Motherhospice, wanting to get inside to safety as fast as possible. Meanwhile, her mind worked overtime.

She wondered why Brigitte allowed her to live? The vampiress had every reason to kill her. Perhaps, Slim thought, she had underestimated St. Laurue's sister. Hadn't she seen a glimmer of tenderness in Brigitte's eyes just before the cold, but surprising compassionate embrace? Another thought. They had Fury. Well, nothing could be done about that at this point. She picked up her pace on the path. Then, she remembered the most important recent revelation. Alec Priggins, the Council's most secretive Grand Counselor, was the Marquis Antoine DeMalberet! No wonder he never appeared before the board. But what does that mean? Was DeMalberet the only vampire in the Council? Or was she even now surrounded by cloaked blood suckers? No. That would be an impossibility. She had worked too closely with many of the Council members. No vampires were they.

An inexplicable rush of chilled air surrounded her body and filled her heart with fear. She suddenly realized that she was no longer alone. Someone or some *thing* was watching her from the dark shadows just off the cobblestone path. She heard the growl of an animal close behind. Hitching up her long dress in order to take wider strides, Slim dashed out of the rose garden toward the back entrance of the Motherhospice.

She stopped short when, just ahead, a green

mist appeared before the entrance to sanctuary. She watched as the haze settled into the shape of a large black animal with glowering metallic orange eyes. A wolf, she thought. Her eyes widened, her heart raced, and her self confidence waned as the wild animal growled and advanced toward her.

Thinking quickly, Slim morphed into a beautiful white dove and took flight. But the wolf darted forward– as fleet as a frog's tongue snatching a fly– and buried its sharp fangs into the dove's right wing.

The dove and wolf tumbled to the manor grounds and rolled violently, one over the other. Then, both bird and beast morphed into other shapes. Slim resumed her human form, while the beast, now more man than wolf, drank deeply from her neck.

CHAPTER 46

Wednesday 7:45 P.M.
Washington Square Park, Manhattan

After returning from Europe, the vampires had rested at St. Laurue's Manhattan lair.

On awakening, Fury arranged to join the others sometime before midnight in New Jersey.

In between time, the fledgling decided to drink in the new and exciting sensations of the city with his vampiric eyes… and *maybe,* go see his mother.

After drifting around the ever darkening city for awhile, he ended up in Washington Square Park.

The scent of death mixed with formaldehyde warned Fury of the older man's initial presence.

He eased back on the secluded park bench and felt the man's attention focus on him. He heard the furtive footsteps. The boiling blood. The heavy breathing. The rapid heartbeat of a hunter.

"Come on," the boy anxiously groaned in anticipation as he tightened his fists and felt his well-toned body switch on to animal alert.

From his isolated bench, Fury glanced ahead. The park was filled with tourists and town dwellers alike. A hundred yards away, there were lovers, loners, and families drifting around the park's large circular fountain. All hoping for that special kind of cooling baptism, which comes from close friends, chance strangers and chilling city crowds.

The older man was directly behind him now. A leathery hand hovered over his left shoulder, faltered like a sick butterfly, then pressed down on the cotton fabric of his tight black tee shirt. Fury's back hunched up, a nearby park lamp blew out and the man and he were instantly shrouded by a deeper shade of night.

"May I join you?" the older man whispered in his ear, sucking in an optimistic breath.

"Yes," Fury said. "I've been waiting for you."

"For me?"

The man danced around the bench and sat down.

At a distance, a frolicking child shrieked for joy as Fury innocently took the man's hand and, almost tenderly, examined its lines.

"I sensed you watching me."

The man smiled and raised an eyebrow.

"Did you?"

Fury closed his eyes, inhaled, then looked at the man with a surprised but knowing look.

"You paint the dead."

"What!" the startled man said, withdrawing his hand quickly.

For a moment, Fury saw regret in the man's eyes and tried to sound less accusative this time.

"I mean… You make the dead look alive again. Am I right?"

The man's eyes widened. "Do I know you?" he stammered. "How could you know that?"

Fury shrugged. "It's a gift."

"Well," the man said, "I guess that makes you both good-looking *and* talented."

The teen grinned.

"I work in a Manhattan mortuary," the man

admitted, "preparing the departed for viewing."

Fury was attacked by the pungent odors emanating from the man's body now, as if the funereal chemicals knew– once the truth was out, the devil be damned.

A young boy suddenly whizzed by on a brightly colored skateboard. He glanced briefly at Fury and the older man, frowned, then pushed on.

After what seemed like an eternal moment to Fury, the older man sighed, wiped small beads of perspiration off his furrowed brow and asked, "Does my job bother you?"

The question went unanswered.

Fury was fascinated by a small child splashing about in the park's great coin shaped fountain. The tot pranced in the water. Its proud parents watched.

The teen's eyes misted over.

"Are you all right?" the man said.

Fury's mind jerked back into the present.

"I have to go."

"It's my profession," the man said. "It bothers you, doesn't it?"

"No. No. It's just…" Fury felt sorry for the unattractive older man. "I have to go see my mom."

Fury got up from the bench.

The man grabbed him by the hand.

"Hold up a minute."

"Better not," Fury said, "for your own sake."

"For my sake?" the man cooed. "For my sake, please stay. Death doesn't rub off, you know. It's not as if *I'm* dead."

Fury stared at the man and didn't know whether

to be ashamed, debate the statement, or be insulted.

The man clutched the boy's hand harder. His eyebrows knitted as he gave the lad a puzzled look.

"You're like ice."

Fury felt uncomfortable and tried to gently pull away, but the man held tighter and kept on.

"I've felt warmer hands in the morgue. Look at you. You're so pale. Haven't you been eating?"

An unexpected breeze rushed through the leaves overhead and suddenly the prattle of other people in the park switched off. The teen studied the desperate man and instead of pity, he felt a pang of hunger.

"You're right. I *should* eat first. Then my mom won't…"

The boy's voice trailed off.

The man finished the sentence.

"…worry if you're getting fed?"

"Yeah," Fury said.

"Right." The man squeezed the teen's hand and winked at him. "You're *good*," he admitted as he dropped Fury's hand. "That's some line. 'I have to visit my mom.' "

The man's face grew serious. "What do you say we cut to the chase?" He got up from the bench and patted Fury's bottom. "Let's head back to my place and slap some color into those cheeks. And don't worry. I'll pay. I've got plenty of money."

Fury didn't care about the harmless pat. He understood the man wanted to move matters along and that was okay by him. What should he do now? he asked himself as he stood there staring into the man's eyes, feeling like a dumbass kid.

A cold shiver worked it's way up his spine.

The man glanced around– just to be sure no one was watching– then leaned forward and kissed the teen hard on the lips.

Fury was relieved to find the dark instincts immediately take over. The heat of the kiss teased his newborn fangs out from under sensitive gums. Not yet accustomed to the pain of transformation accompanying the feeding ritual, Fury tightly embraced the man and panted.

The man said, "I've got what you need, kid."

"I know," came Fury's muffled answer as he buried his fangs against the older man's neck. Clumsily, the boy's virgin razor-sharp teeth pierced the man's hot beckoning jugular.

The first trace of blood tasted salty and sweet. It was a delicious promise of more to come.

"Like to play rough, huh?" the man slurred.

To which, amidst the rising hunger, Fury managed a quick and breathy, "Yeah," then drew the first mouthful of blood.

Still unaware of danger, the excited man held the teen in a vice grip. But suddenly, the man's body stiffened with alarm, then he fought to get away. The struggle was short lived as his strength drained away into complete surrender.

At first, Fury found the man's passivity distracting. This wasn't much fun, the boy thought. Where was the passion? The active offering? The resistance? Where was the man?

Fury continued to mouth vacuum the blood-filled, but vacuous body sack, even though it felt like revving up a car in neutral. Then, just when boredom threatened to set in, the blood frenzy began and wild euphoria nullified his reason.

His lips became an automatic motorized suction pump. His throat constricted and swallowed large gulps of vital fluid. His vampiric body spiked with rising waves of intense thirst simultaneously being fully quenched. He was that thirst, satisfied. That need, fulfilled. He was in the hellish bliss of the damned, where nothing was minded, and everything just happened. And oh, the colors. Colors not only seen, but felt: the inaugural panic of sacred purple, the crush of society blue, the grip of greedy hunter green; all flourished forward against a background of riotous red.

Then, Fury was surrounded by a clear white light; a light where time did not exist, where space was a stillborn child, where the "I" of "me" was nothing but silence.

And it was from within that perfect silence, Fury was harkened back to life by the faint thump of the man's last lonely heartbeat.

The blood intoxicated teen instinctively backed away, feeling bloated. He rubbed his distended belly with glee, and only then lazily noticed that the old man had fallen against the park bench and was in a dead sprawl on the grass.

Fury heard no heart beat. He kneeled down and quickly riffled through the dead man's pockets.

Cool, he whispered out loud. *A hundred and forty-eight bucks!*

CHAPTER 47

Wednesday, June 27th   8:04 P.M.
Trevose, Pennsylvania

Rita was skittish and skeptical at the retirement home. She blamed it on the full moon, excused herself from Solomon and the older gentleman, and walked out of the claustrophobic room.

I'll let Bub handle it, she thought. He'll know what's true or not.

But she couldn't excuse herself from a skeptical mind. She didn't know who or what to believe.

It had taken a day for the Wieses to travel from Washington D.C. to Trevose, Pennsylvania, where they had checked into an adequate, but not well kept– Rita's assessment– motel room.

After gathering up all his nerve, Solomon had finally made the necessary telephone call, and they visited the Sunnygrove Retirement home.

Now, Rita was pacing the visitor's lounge, waiting for her husband's verdict. She still held the crumpled slip of paper the vampire had given him at the Holocaust Museum.

It read, "Maury Wiese is alive and has taken the name Harry Eisen. He resides at the Sunnygrove Retirement Home, Trevose, Pa. I trust a mystery revealed will keep a mystery concealed. It is a fair trade, *oui?* Gérard Arnaud St. Laurue."

Rita was sure this so-called 'vampire' was mistaken. The old man in that awful room wasn't Maury. Sure, he looked like he *might* be Solomon's brother, but proof was needed. There had to be some link to the past. Some name recalled, some incident remembered. Something meaningful and distinctive.

Something only Maury Wiese would know.

The private room reeked of strong disinfectant. The old man reclined in an easy chair, paying more attention to a small portable TV than to Solomon.

"Look," the old cuss said, all the while eyeing the baseball game, "I don't remember."

"Take your time," Solomon said.

"I don't remember." He pointed to his arm with the tattooed numbers. "This is all I have to prove that I was even in those god damned Nazi camps."

Like the camp numbers branded on the old man's arm, Solomon's hopes were slowly fading. Was it right to force this fellow to remember such a past– one which was so savagely inked into his skin, yet mercifully erased from his memory? Wiese felt guilty, but needy. For what? Truth? And at what price? He pulled out a few old snapshots and moved closer to the man's chair. "Look." He pointed to the image of a boy holding a red toy boat. "It's you." He pointed to the smaller boy holding the first one's hand. "This is me. And these people here. This is your family."

"Sonofabitch!" the old man suddenly yelled at the TV. "You see that? The sonofabitch struck out. Trade him. Trade the no good bastard."

"Maury," Solomon said patiently. "The photo.

Take a look." Wiese waved the picture to draw the codger's wandering attention.

The old man gave the snap shot a cursory look. "Me, this kid is not."

"Sure it is. Look closely at the eyes. There's a warmth. It's you."

"So the *boychick* looks a little like me. The others, I don't remember. *You,* I don't remember. And another thing. The toy boat in the picture?"

"What," Solomon said, hopefully.

"That, I don't remember either."

Solomon visibly slumped.

"It's not personal. I'm a blank before nineteen forty-three. *After* that, sharp as a tack. You want to know who won the pennant in fifty-seven? Just ask. But *before* forty-three, forget it. Feh. Question 'til you're blue in the face. You'll get *bubkis.* "

"Bubkis?" Solomon raised his eyebrows. "I say that all the time."

"Listen Bub, don't get excited. It's nothing."

"Bub! That's my nickname from when I was a kid. You gave it to me. Rita's the only one who calls me that now."

He placed his hand on Solomon's shoulder.

"I don't mean to cause you a small breakdown, but I call everyone Bub. Even the no good Nazi bastard attendant who comes in and wipes my ass after I make in my pants, I call Bub. So you shouldn't be overly impressed."

"Okay, you don't remember," Solomon said. "So where's the rush? These things take time. I can visit again tomorrow?"

"You want to visit? Visit. I wouldn't care if you got me chocolates either. I like chocolates."

"Maury loved chocolates."

"That's nice, but I keep telling you my name is Harry Eisen. Listen, when you visit tomorrow, you'll bring the nice variety chocolates with the cherries and assorted nuts?"

"Okay Harry. I'll bring plenty. Can I have a hug before I leave?"

"A stranger I should hug? Oh, all right. What do I care if a strange man hugs me, as long as he doesn't forget the chocolates tomorrow, right?"

"Right."

The old guy lifted a finger. "Dark."

"What?"

"Dark chocolate. Semi-sweet. Not the milk. Feh. Them, I hate."

"Dark, semi-sweet, not milk. Got it."

Solomon stood, bent over, and gave Harry an awkward hug. Weary and more than a little discouraged, the detective headed for the door.

"Hey you," the old guy called out. "Solomon. Take a look!"

Wiese turned around. The old man was excitedly pointing down at the detective's shoe.

"Your shoelace!" Harry said.

"What?" Solomon couldn't believe his ears.

"Your shoelace is untied, for God's sake!"

Wiese looked down. His laces were tied.

The old man's eyes lit up with an uncommon warmth as he said, "Got ya!"

CHAPTER 48

Wednesday 10:06 P.M.
SoHo, Manhattan

From a nearby rooftop, Brigitte watched Press leave his SoHo office building and head out into the maddening moonlight.

She was beside herself with expectation as she leapt along the city rooftops, keeping an eager eye on her newly made *incubus*. She felt giddy and couldn't decide if she was upset or excited or god awful angry. Where was the sublime silence she usually enjoyed? She had no time to think about it right now. She had to try and stay alert.

Tonight was Preston's first full moon and he would have to feed.

The vampiress wondered if a refined man such as he could handle the blood-lust.

Brigitte watched Press approach St. Michael's Church. The evening mass was just letting out and he mingled like a wolf in sheep's clothing with the newly communioned crowd.

But would he pick a target and act, or would he bungle his first dinner?

In the meantime, Gina DeAdonis and Kitty O'Flarity were enjoying a chat on the front steps of the church.

Although the church had long ago dropped the obligation, both ladies were traditionalists and insisted on covering their heads during Mass.

Like an excited bull about to charge, Brigitte's

leg scraped against the rooftop as she listened to the ladies, while her *incubus* listened amidst the parishioners in the street.

"You *got* to pray for the dead," Gina said in broken English, then kissed her rosary beads and put them away in her shiny black patent leather pocketbook. "It's good you make a novena for your husband and son."

Kitty looked disheveled and dazed, but managed to nod. Then, she started to waver on her feet. Gina held the woman upright by the arm.

When Kitty regained her balance, Gina took out a tissue and handed it to the grieving woman. "Here, you take this, Mrs. O'Flarity. Death is a terrible thing. I pray for my dead Salvatore... and for my son, Furio."

"Your son died too?" Kitty said.

"God forbid," Gina said and crossed herself quickly, then unpinned her torchon lace head scarf and stuffed it into a pocket in her dress.

"You've still got your son," Kitty said. "With Sean and Jamie gone, I'd be better off dead."

"No talk like that, Mrs. O'Flarity. God has a plan." She patted Kitty's arm. "See you tomorrow at Mass. I got to go now. Furio's gone two nights. That kid, if he's hurt I'mma gonna kill him."

"Don't worry. He'll turn up. But you never know, huh? One minute they're alive and the next..." Kitty dabbed her tear-filled eyes with the tissue, then drew an index finger across her throat. "Like Father Monahan."

"God have mercy on him." Gina's head bobbed

in agreement. "Eh, that's life. The dead are dropping like flies. You cheer up, Mrs. O'Flarity. God's just around the corner. Good night now."

The two ladies nodded goodbye to each other.

Gina headed for the subway, while Kitty drifted in the direction of Preston's office, hoping to hail a cab back to Chelsea.

From the rooftop, Brigitte watched Press trail Mrs. O'Flarity. The vampiress felt a rush of pride when she spied the rivulet of drool spilling out from the corner of his hungry mouth.

Kitty unpinned her Valenciennes silk head scarf and carried it in one hand, while wiping her hot brow with the tissue in the other. She mumbled something under her breath.

Brigitte grinned. Was it another death wish?

As Kitty passed the alley across from Preston's office, he muffled her mouth with one hand and, swift as a cheetah, dragged her down the alley to its dead end, where he transfigured into a semi-human, ferocious looking jungle cat standing upright on its hind legs.

Press growled, "Does kitty wanna play with the nasty old tom cat?"

Mrs. O'Flarity dropped her silk scarf to the pavement and couldn't speak. On seeing this from the rooftop, Brigitte involuntarily changed as well. Her eyeteeth, chin and ears elongated and came to a point. Her eyes flashed tiny red sparks. Her arms and legs lengthened. Her fingers turned into fierce talons. Her flesh turned slimy brown, bunched up, and folded over itself. She shifted her rooftop position to get a better view.

In the alley, Press let out a guttural growl. His claws extended as his mouth swung open with the weight of great hunger. Saliva spilled down his chin to the pavement.

He lunged at Kitty and latched onto her neck.

Trés bein, Brigitte thought.

Her *incubus* would survive.

By now, the smell of blood overwhelmed Brigitte. She felt a hunger beyond any she'd ever experienced. She flew into the alley, knocked Press off his feed and sank her blood teeth into Mrs. O'Flarity's neck.

Brigitte mouth-vacuumed the woman's fluids so mightily, that Kitty's body began to shrivel from the inside out. Deep wrinkles gathered around Kitty's eyes and mouth. Her cheeks webbed. The neck flesh thickened and drooped. Her skin was loose, yet leathery. Her arms and legs became little more than flimsily covered bones. Her back hunched up and her clothes suddenly seemed far too large for the haggard frame.

The flow of blood stopped. Brigitte withdrew her fangs and looked at the shriveled cadaver. With great curiosity and all the wonderment of an innocent, she lifted the woman's head again and again, only to watch it fall limp. It was then that she realized Kitty was dead.

Brigitte's undead face inflated with indignation.

"You Irish she-pig!" she screamed at the top of her lungs. "How dare you have the audacity to die before I'm fully satisfied?"

The blood-bitch flew at the wasted woman and tore one of her legs out of its hip socket, then hovered in midair, beating the corpse ferociously with the bloody stump. She bashed the body into the dead end of the alley, then stabbed the appendage through the widow's withered chest. With one last kick to her belly, Mrs. O'Flarity's body hit the brick wall, bounced off, and lay motionless in a bloody heap.

Meanwhile, Press had returned to his business-like appearance.

Breathing heavily, Brigitte turned and faced her creation. Her lips twisted into a worming leer as madness crept across her blood smeared face.

Press backed away from his mentor.

She was confused. Sensing her *incubus* was afraid, she morphed into her charming schoolgirl appearance and approached. She wondered what was wrong. They were family now. Why was he afraid of her? She lifted her hand– to tell him it was all right and that she wouldn't hurt him– but he got panicky, broke into tears, and raced out of the alley.

Press would survive, she decided, but the disease had exacerbated his inherent sadness. He had killed, but was obviously troubled by the act. He had the excruciating madness of melancholy– an idiosyncrasy with which she was well acquainted, and one she wouldn't wish on her worst enemy.

Suddenly, it dawned on her that she wasn't exactly certain where she was or what she had just done. The last thing she remembered was being on the rooftop.

She vaguely remembered being exhilarated, but didn't know why. She looked toward the end of the alley and saw the disfigured cadaver of a woman, then saw her own blood covered hands. She sighed.

Just beyond her hands, on the bloody pavement by her feet, was a soiled silk Valenciennes headscarf. It reminded her of one of her brother's red silk handkerchiefs. The vampiress was overcome with sadness. She had lost control two days in a row and had done something extreme, something *not* of her own free will. Yesterday, with Agni, and today… What had she done? She didn't have an inkling, but whatever it was, it was sufficiently harsh to frighten away Press.

This, she knew, was not good.

Her brother had asked her to bring Press to his resting place for the internment tonight, where they would meet Fury. St. Laurue had also asked her to pay Kyle a visit. There was much to do. But would she be able to do it? What if she blanked out and was again possessed? What if she wasn't herself? The thought made her tremble.

She took flight out of the dark blood splattered alley. As she soared toward the full moon, she let loose with a long tortured bawl which sounded like the ear-splitting suicidal squeals of a legion of bedeviled swine leaping over a steep cliff, plunging toward certain death.

As the squall echoed through the nighttime sky, it seemed to ask the question– Who am I now?

CHAPTER 49

Wednesday 11:11 P.M.
Brooklyn, New York

Fury had picked up his mother's scent– a not so subtle blend of cheap Italian wine and stale lilac perfume– well before he reached her apartment door on the dimly lit second floor hallway.

He tried the knob. It was locked.

The dilapidated building smelled of cigar smoke and cat piss. He didn't remember it smelling that bad before. But that was before, he thought. His senses were keener now.

He listened by the door for signs of life.

The TV in the living room was blasting her favorite sitcom. He heard her steady breathing. She was probably half asleep in her favorite chair, her feet propped up on the frayed ottoman.

He glanced into the cracked hallway mirror by the door. The mirror had been cracked since his dad died eleven years ago. Fury was only five at the time, but still remembered the two men dressed in white who had come to cart his dad's body off. They had accidentally let the gurney hit against the mirror, causing it to fall and crack. He also remembered how the cheap building superintendent– stupid assed bastard that he was– hung the cracked mirror right back up.

As Fury looked at his own reflection, his father's face appeared in its place, glaring at him. A sick feeling erupted in the pit of the boy's stomach.

The teen whimpered, "Why did you leave me?"

The image began to fade and Fury palmed the mirror, as if to try and hold his father's vanishing specter. No luck. The boy's hands dropped down to his side. No big deal, he rationalized. He was no longer his *mortal* father's son.

A sudden panic overwhelmed his undead body. *Who is my father?* His head filled with dark images from the last few days. He'd been given the dark blood by two mighty vampires: St. Laurue and the Marquis DeMalberet, St. Laurue's father. Now both the father's and the son's blood ran in his veins and the boy felt like a ghost, a drifter floating through corporeal world with no place to rest his head. To whom could he turn? Where did he belong?

The hallway seemed to close in around Fury and the lad's head started to spin. He leaned against his mother's door and tried not to think.

After a minute, he straightened up and shook his mental demons away, while taking one last look into the hall mirror, just to be sure he was... presentable. His split face in the cracked mirror stared back and Fury decided that, all things considered, he didn't look too bad. The earlier feeding in the park had flushed his cheeks nicely. He felt good and, more importantly, he looked alive. Healthy. Normal.

Of course, the teen knew he was anything but normal in the eyes of the world. To the world, he was a monstrosity. A vile creature of the night. A hungry roaming thing to be feared and shunned.

He lowered his head in shame. Being one of the

undead wasn't turning out to be all that great so far. He had assumed, once vamped out, that he'd be able to do as he pleased. He would be all powerful, in control, not so alone. What a joke, he thought. As it stood, he wasn't even sure if his own mother would invite him back into the apartment.

The boy thought hard. There had to be a way to make his new life work *for* him. After all, he *had* gained some very cool powers. That was a plus. Wasn't it? He wasn't just a little kid anymore. He was a force to reckon with. Wasn't he? And if his mom invited him in, things would be different. He would make sure of that. She could quit her job and relax. He would provide for her. He would make her proud. He'd be the man of the house.

Feeling more buoyant and confident, Fury knocked on the apartment door. He heard his mother heave a sigh and push her hefty trunk out of the overstuffed chair in the living room. Tired footsteps padded nearer. A voice erupted from behind the door.

"Who'sa there?"

What a surprise. Fury liked hearing her voice. It was the same old voice that, just a few days ago, had irritated him so. But now, it meant home.

"Ma," he called out. "It's me."

Latches slid open and after a moment the apartment door stood ajar.

The teen wore a comic grin, shyly shifted from one foot to the other and opened his arms wide.

"Look ma, I'm home."

Gina DeAdonis glared at him. Anxious words flew out of her mouth, hands all aflutter. "Some kid

I got. Like a wild cat sleeping inna the streets. What? You get hungry and come home to eat?"

"No, ma. I came to see you. Can I come in?"

Gina put one hand on an ample hip and gave her son an icy stare. "You want to see your mother? Here. Take a good look." The woman threw both arms above her head and wiggled her hands about. "How I look, eh? I look so different from a couple of days ago when you disappear anna run off?"

"Sorry, ma," Fury said. "I'll explain, but you gotta ask me in first."

Gina cocked her head to one side and looked at him strangely. "Furio, what'sa matter for you?"

"You gotta say it, ma."

"*Que Pazzo.* What I gotta say?"

"You gotta invite me in!" the boy insisted.

Gina's complexion turned marinara. "You need a personal invitation to sleep inna you own bed?"

Fury tried to step into the apartment, but it was no use. Without his mother's invitation, he was instantly heaved backwards against the hallway wall by an invisible protective force.

Gina gasped. Her hand flew over her mouth.

A deep ungodly rumble within the apartment commandeered her attention. She turned away from the door and froze when she saw the large iron crucifix on the wall– the one that had belonged to her sainted mother and had been blessed by the Holy Father in Rome– ferociously flip upside down.

"Come on, ma," Fury yelled, while getting up off the hall floor. "Invite me in. Say the words!"

Gina turned and squinted her eyes at Fury, as if

questioning if he was really her son.

"What?" he shouted. "A stupid cross slips on the wall and suddenly you don't know me?"

The teen's blood boiled. A sickly lime green glow surrounded his elongating body. Pus yellow liquid oozed from his eyes. His soft youthful skin took on the consistency of dull gray putty. At first, Fury transfigured into a wicked caricature of his boyish self, then, he further festered into a hideous "thing," altogether inhuman and filled with rage.

Gina stepped back from the door. "*O Dio*," she murmured over and over again, falling to her knees and making the sign of the cross.

The creature in the hallway glared at her. How dare she not recognize him, the thing thought. How dare she not serve and obey the magnificent dark prince he was. For this insult, the newborn vampire fumed, the old lady deserved slow death.

The demon's eyes sparkled reddish yellow as he angrily stormed the door, but was again violently repelled backwards against hallway wall.

The hall mirror fell and shattered.

The ghost of Fury's father rose out of the shattered pieces. Shards of broken glass whirled around the phantom. They tinkled and pinged as his father's deep voice boomed out, "Begone!"

Fury's mouth gaped open. Between the shock of seeing his father and the second wallop against the hallway wall, his anger had turned to grief and he morphed back into a sulking kid.

"Papa," he cried, arms reaching out. But his father's spirit vanished, and the despondent boy slowly picked himself up off the floor and looked at his mother, trembling on her knees, praying to a God he suddenly wished he knew.

His undead body shook, but his deep loneliness compelled the teen to reach out once more.

Fury dug into his pocket and pulled out some money. "Ma, look!" He tossed some bills across the threshold. They landed on the floor in front of his mother's knees.

Gina eyed the money.

Sweet, Fury thought. She was going to do it. She was going to invite him in. Everything was going to be cool again. He was home. He belonged.

His mother spat at the money like it was so much scattered filth, then prayed all the harder.

"Take it!" Fury urged. "I can get us more."

Gina prayed on.

The boy began to plead. "Come on, Momma! Invite me in! Oh God. Please let me in."

Gina suddenly stopped praying.

Fury saw the corners of her lips curl into what looked like a smile of divine forgiveness.

She stood up and came towards him.

"Yes," he encouraged her as she got nearer. "Oh God, momma, yes!"

Gina's jaw set hard with courage and resolve as she gripped the edge of the front door and slammed it in her son's face.

CHAPTER 50

Wednesday 11:41 P.M.
Kyle's home, New Jersey

Four days ago, Kyle Riordan could not have cared less if vampires existed, but after several days of being immersed in St. Laurue's world– editing and rewriting, working under a literal deadline– the ghost writer was entranced by, and even a bit envious of the lives of the undead.

The book was going to be well received, he thought. It was a blood chilling page turner that almost made you *want* to be a vampire.

He leaned back in his swivel chair and gave his eyes a chance to rest.

Glancing out of the window, he saw the moon was devilishly full. He was grateful. His creative imagination always heightened under the rays of the full moon– and right now, while tackling the final chapter, he needed that extra "umph."

Suddenly, the hairs on the back of Kyle's head stood on end.

He felt a presence enter the room and looked over his shoulder. No one was there.

"Ooo-kaay," he said, drawing out the syllables, "what the hell was that?"

He was just about to refocus on a difficult paragraph, when a jolt of energy shot up his spine.

He sat up straight.

The room had suddenly gotten several degrees cooler. Not an unwelcomed event on a muggy night in late June, he thought. But very, very weird.

The whispered voice had a trill that sometimes accompanies a child's, while also brandishing an underlying ancient authority.

"My brother insisted that we meet."

Kyle spun around from his desk and saw the young girl. His face lit up in a half-question, half-smile. "Brigitte?"

The girl said nothing, but studied his face, x-raying him with her extraordinary eyes.

"Oui. Roddi has asked for me to come to you," she finally said. He says that for a man who hasn't lived even one mortal lifespan, you are very wise."

Kyle blushed and was tongue tied.

He had imagined meeting Brigitte ever since reading St. Laurue's softhearted description of her delicate beauty, her enduring loyalty, and her sincere search for spiritual wisdom. In his imagination, the meeting had always gone sensationally.

It played like a scene out of a romance novel. Definitely love-at-first-sight stuff.

But now, face to face with her, all he could do was get up and silently hold out his hand.

Brigitte declined to take it.

"You won't like touching me," she said. "I'm a bit cold for most mortals."

Kyle didn't care.

He impulsively took her by the hand and said, "Not so cold. Rather like slightly warmed marble, kissed by the morning sun."

"Kissed by moonbeams, or not at all," she said sweetly, then discreetly withdrew her hand.

There was a slight pause, then...

"I... uh... Sorry to stare," Kyle said. "It's just that I'm so fascinated with you."

She smiled.

"We vampires are fascinating creatures."

"May I ask a question?"

"Only if I may choose to leave it unanswered."

He nodded and motioned for her to have a seat.

The vampiress settled with the quiet dignity of an early morning snowfall. She, herself, was like a snowflake. Tiny, pristine, and perfect. Undeniably cold... yet amazingly able to melt his heart.

"Now don't get me wrong," Kyle said. "I love that you're here, but I'm curious. How did you get into the house?" He sat down in his chair. "I thought that– well, that someone like you had to be personally *invited.*"

"But you *have* invited me. Many times."

Kyle had trouble forming his words.

"I... invited...?"

"You've held me in your thoughts."

"You knew?" he said, once again turning red.

"How else are the dead drawn to life?"

Her soft, yet insistent voice made him yearn for her. But she was a vampire, he told himself. A vampire, yes... *and* the woman of his dreams.

"Perhaps I should go?"

"No. Don't leave me. I need you... uh... That is to say... I need you to fill me in on a few details about your brother's life. If you don't mind."

She remained seated. "Very well."

"Yes? Okay. Good."

Kyle took out his notebook and pencil.

"Well, one questions that's crossed my mind is how did you–"

She held up her hand and whispered, "I know."

Brigitte spoke, dead-on with details, as Kyle took notes. When she finally fell silent, he reviewed his shorthand to see if any clarification was needed. No, he thought. She'd answered his every unasked question.

The writer looked up from his yellow pad and was about to thank her, but stopped short, aghast at what stared back at him.

Without the slightest sound, Brigitte had transformed into a horrid nightmare. Her face was swollen and bleeding. Her sensuous lips were torn by elongated fangs. Her eyes, only moments before irresistibly beautiful, now hemorrhaged with hatred. The surface of her putrefied body crawled with the small lives that fed off of things dead– flies, maggots, centipedes and earthworms freely roamed in and out of cavernous wounds.

The room was at an Arctic temperature and filled with the ominous sound of coarse wheezing.

She lifted up off the chair and spat a glob of viscous, green mucus on to the floor. An inflated reptilian tongue darted out from the malodorous cave of her mouth. The slimy green scaled organ outstretched in an odd surrealistic way, ferociously lashing at Kyle like a bull whip, barely missing him each time.

Then, from deep within the creature's bowels, an earsplitting bawl of perfect outrage intermingled with total despair piped across the room.

Kyle forced himself to speak to the thing. He knew it was his only hope of summoning back the real Brigitte.

"Press told me how you saved his life. Now I see at what expense."

The creature's voice was deep, gravelly and almost unintelligible.

"We do what we must to survive," it said. "We kill to live."

He stood up and faced the demon. "But must you *live* to kill? Must you follow in the footsteps of a world held hostage by its own hostilities?"

The thing paused and seemed dazed. But then, it's mouth opened so wide that Kyle realized instant decapitation was a very real possibility.

Riordan closed his eyes tight and patiently waited for death.

And what goes through a man's mind at the moment of death? In Kyle's case... nothing.

If his life flashed before him, he didn't notice.

What he did notice was the sensation of soft fluttering wings surrounding his body. He wondered if these were the proverbial wings of death. If so, then it was in the midst of mortality that his immortality blazed brightest. He felt safe. At home. Delivered from the many frailties and foibles of a world of fleeting appearances.

So filled with bliss was he, that he could even forgive her this, his own physical death. Wasn't that what true love was meant to do– make us forget our limitations and live our grandness?

And so, while waiting for the jaws of death, the writer felt the wings of his soul.

At that point, the harsh rasping stopped.

He opened his eyes and again saw his Brigitte, the beautiful young vampiress.

She behaved as if nothing had happened.

"Is that enough information for the book?"

"Brigitte!" he said, flopping back down on his chair, anticlimactic perspiration dripping off him. "You were about to kill me!"

Her hands flew over her mouth. "I did it again, didn't I? I blanked out." Her eyes darted from one side of the room to the other, then back again. "I must leave. I am a danger to you."

She went to the door.

"No," he begged her, "please stay. I don't care."

"*I* do," she said in a terrified voice. "I alter involuntarily. I lose time. The hunger seizes me. Understand, there is no controlling it."

"I know, and still, I want you to stay."

She looked at him and tilted her head.

"What manner of a mortal are you that you do not fear death?"

"Death of what? Do you mean these physical bodies? These remnants of ancient exploded suns, moons, and stars?"

"But surely even suns, moons and stars dread their demise."

"What is real can never die."

"Ah. You speak of the soul." She seemed to will herself to be calm and sat down again. "Tell me about the soul, Kyle. Please."

"Without it, we are walking ashes."

"Mine is lost."

"Not lost, just playing hide and seek."

Like a orphaned pilgrim, one tiny pink tear slowly traveled down Brigitte's right cheek. She hung her head in shame. "Sorry," she said, brushing the tear away. "I loathe the mad thing I've become."

Kyle took her hand and gently squeezed it.

He looked into her little girl eyes and wanted to comfort and protect her.

"We all live with a little madness. That may be the one ingredient which makes this little life as wonderful as it is."

"I cannot bear the brutality."

"Reserve judgment on yourself. Give it time."

"Time," she sighed. "*Oui*. I do have an eternity of that."

"In time," Kyle said, "one forgets how little one thinks of oneself."

"Alas," Brigitte said. "We vampires are cursed with keen minds. We cannot forget the long past. If only you could teach me how."

Kyle leaned forward and touched her heart. "Only love teaches that."

The vampiress kissed his hand, then smiled graciously. "I thank you for your chivalrous words, my friend."

"Who knows," Kyle said. "Maybe one day you and I will collaborate and write *your* memoirs."

He reached for her hand.

"It is possible," she laughed demurely, skirted Kyle's hand, and kissed the cheeks on each side of his face. "As you have said, 'who knows?' "

"Will I see you again?"

"There is an unfinished mausoleum not far from here where my brother has decided to take his millennium rest. He requests your presence... that is, if you'd *like* to come. Press and Fury will be there, waiting for us."

The clock on the wall struck midnight.

She held out her hand. He gladly took it.

Once out of the house, she whisked him off his feet and, together, they sailed through the magical moonlit sky to the mausoleum.

CHAPTER 51

Late Wednesday evening
The Motherhospice, Scotland

Slim sat in the lavishly decorated rooms reserved for the Grand Counselor of the Daemonion Council located in the heart of the Motherhospice.

She was safe. The apartment was purposively secured against any and all unwanted visitors.

Thoughts of St. Laurue and Brigitte and Fury came to mind. How she had tried to stop them from escaping the Motherhospice. She shook her head in amazement. What had she been thinking?

Like the Lady of the manor, she sat serenely in front of the vanity with only a solitary candle to illumine the Marquis Antoine DeMalberet's diary lying upon her lap, opened.

The story of his life was fascinating.

Ah, to have lived such a long and adventurous life such as Antoine's.

To hold the spark of life throughout the ages.

To have witnessed so much history, so much joy, so much heartbreak, so much life.

The many endings. The new beginnings. The eternal cycles of hope and despair.

She read a passage aloud.

"Life. Eternally writhing. Twisting and turning until its whirling wheel melts into a bright ball of light. And that being all there is, is Who I Am."

She let her mind gently drift for a moment.

Minutes later, she glanced back at the diary and

this time read silently.

Her very breath rose and fell to the rhythm of the great one's words. Her eyes drank in the sorrows and the glories of his wondrous life.

She was experiencing his every taste, touch, sight, smell and sound.

By his written word, she found she was able to merge with him more closely. In each passage, it felt like she had actually been there.

Helping him.

Caring for him.

Loving him.

It was as if she had never known a life that did not revolve around his indomitable will.

And so, it happened that Slim was so intrigued by DeMalberet's writings that only once or twice did she stop reading to glance up at the mirror and curiously inspect her rapidly healed right arm and admire a somewhat younger looking reflection– a reflection which, from now on, would be invisible to mere mortals.

CHAPTER 52

Wednesday evening
back in the States, the Jersey shore

Three restless spirits haunted the unfinished
two story mausoleum.

The abandoned construction site looked ghostly
in the middle of the cemetery. The full moon sent
her silvery slanted columns shafting through
apertures in the walls and its half finished roof. The
spacious circular area within was surrounded by tall
brick walls, which held coffin sized built-in sliding
compartments, designed for the remains of the dead.
And there, the non-human trio stood; in the middle
of the dirt-floored structure, in a spot meant to be
used as a viewing gallery for the dearly departed.

"The earth will overtake me here," St. Laurue
said. Suddenly, he cocked an ear and his eyes flashed
yellow-violet.

"Somebody's out in the cemetery," Fury said.

"Shall I see…?" Press started, but was cut off.

"You and Fury stay where you are," St. Laurue
said. "I will discover who dares to walk among the
tombstones tonight."

St. Laurue left the mausoleum. As he walked
through the headstones he heard a low-keyed
continuous scream coming from the oldest part of
the cemetery. The squall gave him the impression
of a legion of lamentations flung together in a
restrained riot of agony, the cacophony of the dead.

A vortex of swirling green mist appeared by an

old oak tree up on top of a nearby hill. He sped to the place.

The din increased as the mist materialized into a tall figure wearing a red hooded robe. At first, only the figure's back could be seen, but when it slowly turned toward him, he could make out a green-eyed skeleton face.

St. Laurue was not overly concerned. He'd been in many cemeteries and knew that most had a spectral sentinel protecting the grounds. Still, he didn't want this ghostly guard to be a problem for his minions while he was at rest. He decided to try and put the ruffled bone curator at ease.

"Sir," St. Laurue spoke, "Do I know you?"

"All men are, in part, familiar with me from birth," the thing said in a deep baleful voice.

"Who are you?"

"Death."

"What business do *we* have?"

"It has long been my custom to visit the sick."

"To steal away their lives?" St. Laurue asked.

Death grinned and spoke softly, "To help them rest in peace." The red robed figure elevated His arms, as if nailed to a cross, and bellowed, "Look and behold your sins."

Blood filled snapshots of the dead gang in the alley reflected, one after the other, across Death's red robes. They were grotesque, all shot from odd angles under bizarre lighting.

St. Laurue recoiled. "Why show me this?"

Death boomed out. "All left exposed!"

Next, as fast as a magician shuffling playing

cards from one hand to the other, Ashley and Raphael's bloody images flickered across the robes.

Death echoed. "All left exposed!"

Then, in a whirling collage of pictures, each one unevenly cut like puzzle pieces, the two cannibalized bellboys from the hotel cinematically cycloned onto the cloth draped arms of Death.

"All left exposed," Death repeated a third time.

Each image seared into St. Laurue's soul. He felt the suffering of each of his victims. Howling, he fell to his knees and placed his hands over his eyes, shouting, "Enough. Enough!"

But Death insisted on one last reflection.

St. Laurue's hands dropped from his eyes, as if they had a mind of their own. Then, on Death's raiment, he saw a line of patriarchal vampires appear and begin to ascend the very hill on which he stood. He knew these beings. They were the ancients. Coming for him. Seeking retribution. Fear gripped his very being. These were the Makers of Makers. Those who must be obeyed. He shuddered as one stepped forward, opening up a large book. He read the title. It was *his* book. *His* life. *His* words. The ancients scowled with contempt, then bared their blood soused fangs and hissed, "Beware!"

The word rocketed off Death's robe on a swirl of blood red mist. It bounced off the nearby gravestones, then doubled back at the red hooded figure, enshrouding it completely. In an explosion of bright colors, Death's voice rumbled out one last time, "All left exposed!"

St. Laurue was alone now on the cemetery hill top. He circled on all fours, but saw no one. Had Death gone? No. He knew that Death had simply seeped into his bones. The game was up. He stood, feeling a surge of surprising relief. A night breeze caressed his ears and moaned, "Rest." His inner rage was displaced by quiet resignation, even as he returned to the mausoleum.

Back in the viewing gallery, Fury asked him, "Was anyone there?"

St. Laurue smiled. "Just an old friend."

Press said, "Did he come to see you go under?"

"Oui. He is here even now, but not so you'll notice. *Tradition* has done me in. Let nature take her course."

Press began to weep uncontrollably.

St. Laurue gently touched his shoulder.

"Still afraid of the dark?" he said softly. "Afraid the poisonous spiders will come for you?"

Press cried, "I don't know *what* I am."

"You are mine. Fear not. Now, you *are* the spiders that come out in the dark."

"Thanks," Press said between sobs, "I think."

St. Laurue smiled at him. "You will stay with me tonight after I succumb. *Oui*? It comforts me to know that you will be my first watch."

"I'll miss you," Press said, sadly.

"Me, too," Fury chimed in, holding out his arms to his mentor.

Under a shaft of glossy moonlight, St. Laurue embraced the teen-vampire and whispered in his ear, "Even though my father completed your turning, I will always think of you as my own."

The boy melted in his arms.

Brigitte's sweet voice rang from above. "Roddi, we're here." She and Kyle floated down through the open rooftop of the modern ruin.

St. Laurue reclined in a pool of moonlight on the earthen spot he had chosen for his grave, while Fury and Press knelt by his side.

"Ah. My family is all here," he said. "And just in the nick of time for Socrates is about to drink the hemlock."

"Oh don't be so dramatic," Brigitte said, "In eighteen months, you will rise and soon after that, you'll have to watch *me* go under."

"Brigitte, dear ones, indulge me for a moment. I have a confession to make and I want you all to hear. I know now beyond a shadow of a doubt that I have been infected with this blood sickness. Death Himself has shown me. Sadly, I have become the monster humanity has always made me out to be."

Press took St. Laurue's hand. "But you saved my life."

"Oui," St. Laurue said, *"after* I carelessly infected you."

Brigitte took her brother's other hand.

"You didn't realize what you were doing. All that is over now. The earth's silence will heal you."

"And what will heal you, my little bird? Or Press? Or Fury? You'll all have to live under the effects of my venomous actions," he said, feeling his mind slowly shutting down.

"But the Council has a special potion to…"

Fury started, but St. Laurue was too mired in his own guilt to think of anything else.

He clutched his sister's hand and said, "It isn't fair. I am *not* a monster. I was trying to survive, just as anyone would."

Brigitte held her brother's hand. "Rest now, *mon amour.*"

Still, he continued to plead his case, "Everyone needs one being, whether mortal or immortal, through whose eyes they can be loved, and through whose loving attention they can survive."

Kyle said, "All mortals *will* love you, once they've read your book."

"They'll see you differently," Press added.

"True," he said with an empty smile. "Through my book, I will abide. The living will *attend* me. They will *mind* me." He lifted his arm in a half-hearted triumphant gesture and said, "Though dead, I will live on!"

The earth quaked beneath him.

"Now it begins," he announced. "Leave me."

Brigitte reluctantly dropped her brother's hand and she, Fury and Press joined Kyle at a distance.

Taking on an oily texture, now, the dirt under St. Laurue roiled.

He looked at Kyle.

"This is for you, my dear ghost writer." With a sleight stirring of his little finger, his red silk handkerchief floated toward the mortal.

"A gentleman should never be without one."

Kyle plucked it out of the air. "I accept it," the writer said, "as from one gentleman to another."

"Perhaps one day, Kyle, you will choose to be more fully with us. I stand by my offer to make you immortal on my return."

The stark moonlight appeared to pull the earth up around St. Laurue. What had started as a small boiling of soil became waves of earth, lapping at the reclining vampire. He tried to move, but could not. His legs felt like lead. As he began to very slowly sink into the ground, a terrifying feeling gripped him. "Brigitte," he called out in panic, "come with me!"

Brigitte looked shocked and turned to Kyle, then to her brother.

"No!" Kyle said hoarsely, and locked his arms around her waist.

"But I, too, am sick," she said.

"My sweet little bird!" St. Laurue called again, his eyes pleading. "Don't desert me."

Press pulled at his own hair and screamed, "Don't abandon us."

"It's not your time, Brigitte!" Kyle urgently tried to reason with her.

"I know..." she answered, her eyes anxiously watching her brother slowing sinking under the uprising earth.

St. Laurue reached out to her and whispered, "Together, my little bird? As always?"

"Stay here, Brigitte," Fury entreated. "We need you. We have no one else to turn to now."

Brigitte reached out to her brother.

"Please," Kyle said, holding her tight. "I love you." But before the words were fully out of his mouth, Brigitte had already broken away and was in her brother's arms.

The earth began to quiver and the mausoleum walls started to shake. Dust waves billowed out from the cracking cement walls, while dust devils appeared and patrolled about like whirling prison guards. The unrelenting earth rumbled and reared up in a monstrous wave, hovering above Brigitte and St. Laurue like a dark curtain about to ring down on the last act.

Press started to dash forward in a half-hearted rescue attempt, but Fury caught him and held him back, while Kyle shouted, "Brigitte!"

St. Laurue held Brigitte in his arms. His panic-stricken eyes calmed as she nestled close to his chest. Everything would be all right, he thought. The eighteen month entombment would not be so bad after all. It was just the next great adventure. He was ready, feeling simultaneously exhausted, yet thrillingly complete– his little bird was with him.

He lifted his tired eyes, longingly took one last look at his Fury and whispered, *"Au 'voir."*

⚜ ⚜ ⚜ ⚜ ⚜ ⚜

The dark curtain whooshed down over them...

Within a few seconds, it was finished and the redemptive earth had settled down and flattened out.

Everything was still– save for several tiny air bubbles, which noiselessly surfaced and disappeared where immortals had been only moments before.

CHAPTER 53

Out of the corner of his eyes, Fury thought he saw an unearthly light on top of the mausoleum wall at the moment Brigitte and St. Laurue were consumed by the hungry earth. It only flashed a second. But at that second, he began to hear the strange voice in his head.

Our time is nigh, it said.

What in hell was that? Did all vampires hear a weird inner voice? Was this normal? He glanced at Press, who was sobbing on the ground, and knew *that* wasn't normal. It was the blood disease.

Kyle tapped him on the shoulder. "It's just the three of us now."

"They'll be back in eighteen months," he said with a shrug.

Kyle nodded. "Till then, we've got each other."

Yeah right, a bunch of slackers, Fury thought gloomily, a melancholy *incubus*, a mortal writer, and one flipped out fledgling vampire, hearing voices in his head.

Suddenly, the lad was startled by another flash of light coming from the top of the wall. He must have involuntarily reacted because Kyle gave him a strange look.

Fury looked back sheepishly, but said nothing.

"Let's get Press on his feet," Kyle said.

As they gently lifted Press off the ground, the voice in Fury's head said, *let the* incubus *stay!*

Then, Preston spoke up and said, "I'll stay," and Fury wondered if Press also heard the voice.

"You sure, buddy?" Kyle asked Press.

"Yeah. I'll survive," Press said, giving Kyle a curious look. "But the real question is... will you?"

Kyle glanced at Brigitte's burial spot and said, "I don't know..."

"Come on," Fury said, tugging at Kyle's arm. "We should go."

Press continued to stare at Kyle, questioningly.

The writer suddenly widened his eyes, and Fury saw that Kyle had just caught on to the implied subtle threat carried within Preston's last casually spoken remark.

"Right," Kyle anxiously said to Fury. "Let's get out of here."

Fury smelled Kyle's fear, but said nothing as they left the mausoleum and traipsed through the tombstones. The teen was far too preoccupied with himself. He felt totally overwhelmed, but not altogether unhappy. No way was he going to end up a sad sack like Press. Or lonely like Kyle. So what if his mother kicked him out. Life– whatever that was– goes on. And from here on, he thought, nobody would tool around with him and get away with it. He was a kick-ass teenage-vampire now and the master of the freakin' universe!

Then, there it was again.

That strange flash of light. Only now, it wasn't just a flash. The greenish glowing mist hung in front of the full moon, making the silvery orb look like a giant's eye maliciously peeking over the edge of the mausoleum wall.

Take him! the inner voice commanded.

"No!" Fury shouted. "I won't!"

"Won't what?" Kyle asked, looking confused.

"I do what I want!" he yelled at the heedless moon. "I'm the one in charge. I'm in control. I'm powerful, damn it! I'm a vampire."

"Okay by me," Kyle said. "Whatever you say."

Fury turned from the moon and stared at Kyle.

He felt a terrible hunger coming from within.

It pounded insistently in his stomach, then raced to every fiber in his body, as he began to feel himself transfigure into the decayed undead.

As if from a great distance, he thought he heard Kyle say, "Hey, wait a second there, partner," but he wasn't sure. The voice was too loud.

It thundered within him,

Take the mortal!

He felt his eyeteeth push through his gums and twin-pinch his bottom lip.

Then, in a plaintive voice too deep and terrible to be his own, he heard himself say, "Sorry, Kyle."

"Stop," Kyle said, backing off between two grave markers.

"I gotta," Fury said, hoping he'd understand.

Kyle countered, "St. Laurue said that I was supposed to be given a choice."

"Yeah. I know. But... It's just... like... I'm so *incredibly* hungry right now."

The smell of Kyle's blood was driving him crazy. It was impossible to hold out any longer.

He plunged his fangs into the writer's neck, while simultaneously noticing the figure of Death on top of the mausoleum, silhouetted against a fully matured and unforgiving moon.

The Grim Reaper's green eyes glowered in the shadow under its red hooded robe as it shrieked, "Drink the blood!"

It was the same voice he'd been hearing in his head. Fury had no choice but to obey.

He greedily sucked on Kyle's throat. The blood made him swoon with pleasure. One sip, and Fury was overwhelmed by the blood induced ecstasy of omnipotence, the chosen drug of immortals.

The power, he thought, *oh, the power.*

When his eyes popped open again, they were still fixed on top of the wall.

He saw Death discard the red hooded robe and begin to dance naked in front of the full moon.

A shiny black top hat appeared out of thin air on his head.

Instant recognition.

It was the Marquis Antoine DeMalberet.

Fury released Kyle.

The semi-conscious writer fell to the earth.

The boy didn't even notice, so mesmerized was he by DeMalberet's hypnotic dance, replete with magical steps and mystical twists and turns.

Suddenly, the Marquis' hands jutted forward and swayed from side to side as if he were conducting a symphonic orchestra.

Fury's body responded like a fine bass cello perfectly attuned to the maestro's every movement.

And the teen finally understood that he was just another powerless Pinocchio stepping to the tune of DeMalberet's dynamic and demented Geppetto.

Note from the Author

Thank you for buying my novel, *Reflections of a Vampire.* I hope you had as much fun reading it and I had writing it.

Other Books by Damion Kirk

I HELD OUT MY HAND IN LOVE
ANOTHER WAY- Allowing Inner Peace

About the Author

Damion Kirk has lived an extraordinary life in which he's had one foot in this world and the other in the next.

Growing up, he could see, hear and speak with the dead. His grandmother, who also had "the gift," taught him not to fear the call from those beyond the grave.

Early on, Damion realized that dead people were not so different from the living. To him, that made the *living dead* our most seductive and altogether captivating first cousins.

Mr. Kirk was born and bred in Red Bank, New Jersey and now resides in the Boulder area of Colorado, close to the hotel which inspired Steven King's horror classic, *The Shining*.

You may reach him through his publisher by e-mailing **RahuBooks@aol.com**.

This book is available for purchase
on line at

Amazon.com